To Jackie,

EASTGATE

A ROBERT HOON THRILLER

JD KIRK

Happy retirement!
Congratulations on
surviving 18 years and an
army of gun-toting Santas!
Best wishes,
JD Kirk

EASTGATE

ISBN: 978-1-912767-68-7

Published worldwide by Zertex Media Ltd.
This edition published in 2022.

I

www.jdkirk.com
www.zertexmedia.com

BOOKS BY J.D. KIRK

A Litter of Bones

Thicker Than Water

The Killing Code

Blood & Treachery

The Last Bloody Straw

A Whisper of Sorrows

The Big Man Upstairs

A Death Most Monumental

A Snowball's Chance in Hell

Ahead of the Game

An Isolated Incident

Colder Than the Grave

Come Hell or High Water

City of Scars

Here Lie the Dead

Northwind: A Robert Hoon Thriller

Southpaw: A Robert Hoon Thriller

Westward: A Robert Hoon Thriller

For Clare McBride
(Didn't see this coming, did you?)

CHAPTER ONE

IT WAS the utter fucking contempt on her face that really brightened his day. She loathed every fibre of him. Every atom. And, she was making no attempt whatsoever to hide that fact.

From his seat in the court's gallery, he gave her a wee wave — a cheeky one at that, all wide palm and rippling fingers—and he backed it up with a wink and a grin that bordered on the mischievous.

The woman sitting down there in front of the judge wasn't best pleased about that.

Robert Hoon sat back then, fingers interlinked behind his head, that big smile still fixed on his face while he enjoyed the show.

During the investigation, her name had been revealed as Samantha Something-or-other. Hoon hadn't cared enough to bother learning it.

She'd first introduced herself to him under the name Suranne, and he was happy to stick with that. He wasn't about to give her any additional room in his head by memorising whatever the fuck her real name was. She wasn't worth the brain cells.

And, to be fair, that's what she was still referring to herself as, too. She'd denied her real name was Samantha, and refused to answer to it, for reasons Hoon neither knew nor cared to discover.

Now, Suranne sat at one of the tables down at the front, next to a lawyer far too well dressed to be one of the local guys. She'd brought him in from somewhere. Of course she had. The bastard was probably just as crooked as she was, if not even more so.

It had been a few months now since she and her squad of would-be assassins had made the mistake of coming after Hoon on his home turf.

He could've killed her then, of course, like he'd done with half of her team, but the presence of various members of the polis, including a certain lumbering Detective Chief Inspector, would've made doing so difficult to justify.

Besides, had he finished her off then, he wouldn't have had the pleasure of this moment. He wouldn't have experienced the joy of seeing that look of raw hatred in her eyes, while she listened to the judge banging on from behind her big desk.

And this was just the appetiser. Today was just a hearing to set a trial date for one of several charges Suranne was facing. The good stuff—the trial itself, where he'd get to take the stand and testify against the khaki-fingered, hatchet-faced bitch—was still to look forward to.

He was already imagining it, though. He'd hold eye contact with her the whole time. Smile, all friendly-like, as he helped condemn her to her fate.

It was going to be fucking marvellous.

"What are you grinning at?"

The question came as a whisper from his left. Hoon kept his eyes locked on Suranne, but turned his head a degree or two to acknowledge that he'd heard.

Beside him, Miles Crabtree, the MI5 man who'd either helped or hindered him during his recent misadventures in

London—Hoon still hadn't made his mind up on which it was—sat with a hand partially covering his mouth, like he was afraid the judge might catch him talking and give him detention.

"All of it," Hoon replied, just loud enough for a couple of the court officials to shoot warning looks his way. "The whole thing. It's just a fucking joy to behold."

He gave Suranne another wave, and enjoyed the way her face turned an even darker shade of beetroot.

"And to think," he said, with a contented sigh. "I was just going to shoot her through the head. This is far more fucking entertaining."

"I'm going to pretend I didn't hear that, Bob," intoned the man sitting on his right. He was built like a bear, and stuffed into a coat that seemed just barely up to the job of containing him.

DCI Jack Logan sat with his hands clasped in his lap, staring straight ahead. Unlike Hoon, Logan wore a look on his face that suggested he'd rather be anywhere else but there in that courtroom.

Then again, he pretty much looked like that regardless of where he was, so that wasn't exactly anything new.

"You go right ahead and pretend what you fucking like," Hoon told him, and this time, even the judge shot an impatient look his way. He nodded at her, mimed zipping his mouth shut, then gave her a thumbs up.

A look flitted across her face, like she was considering addressing him directly, but she had experience with Hoon from his time as a detective superintendent, and seemed to conclude that admonishing him would be more trouble than it was worth. She settled for a shake of her head and a wag of a finger, then got back down to business.

After all the boring technicalities were out of the way, and a surprise request from the well-dressed lawyer to strike the case was all but laughed out of court, a date was set for just shy of three months down the line.

Given the seriousness of the charges, there would be no bail set. Nor, however, would the accused be held in a Scottish prison. She had further charges she was facing south of the border, including the murder of a senior Met police officer.

On top of that, Suranne knew things. Or claimed to, anyway. She had information that could help bring down members of a terrorist organisation. As such, she was considered an 'at risk' prisoner, and would be handed into the custody of a specialist cross-sector security task force, who, with the support of Police Scotland and various local constabularies, would ensure she reached her next court hearing alive and in one piece.

"A 'specialist cross-sector security task force'?" Hoon muttered. "And who the fuck's that, exactly?"

There was a squeak from his left as Miles shifted in his chair. It was enough to make Hoon tear his eyes away from Suranne for almost the first time since he'd sat down.

"You?"

"Yeah," Miles confirmed with a whisper, though he looked a little embarrassed about it. "Me. They put me in charge of it. Given my firsthand experience with the Loop, and how I helped you to... You know?"

"No. I don't know," Hoon said, turning all the way to face him. "Remind me what the fuck you did, exactly?"

"What? I did loads!" Miles protested. "I helped."

"My arse, you did. You bought me a *Mr Men* T-shirt. How the fuck does that qualify you to lead a specialist cross-sector security task force?" Hoon asked. He was whispering, but each word was louder than the one before. "The fuck's a 'specialist cross-sector security task force' when it's at home, anyway?"

"It's an inter-departmental team of—"

Hoon waved both hands at him. "Jesus Christ, I'm going to stop you right there. You started boring my tits off at, 'It's.'"

A shrill, slightly nasal voice piped up from further along the row. "It's actually very interesting, actually."

Hoon leaned forward enough to glower at the man sitting on Miles' other side. He was dressed like Miles, in a white shirt and grey tie, but he was smaller, like he'd been shrunk in the wash. His hair was arranged into a fastidiously neat side-parting, and had a glossy sheen from whatever chemical compound was required to keep it plastered in place.

"Oh, it *actually* fucking *actually* is, is it?" Hoon whispered.

He glared until the younger man buckled and looked away, which took approximately three-fifths of a second, then he sat back.

"Who the fuck's that?" Hoon asked Miles. "Your long-lost bastard offspring?"

"No, he's—"

"Did they clone him from one of your less-impressive bowel movements?"

"No. He's my assistant," Miles explained before Hoon could offer any further guesses as to the man's origins. "Alright? He's just my assistant, that's all. He's not my son, he's not my..."

"Shite-clone," Hoon said.

"Yes. I mean, no. I mean, he's not any of that! He's just a graduate who works as my assistant. Alright? He's scored very highly in the testing. He's a good lad."

"Alright, keep your fucking hair on," Hoon replied.

Before he could say any more, a throat was gently but firmly cleared over on his right.

"You might want to shut your mouths, gentlemen," Logan warned.

All eyes went to the judge, who sat with her arms folded, glowering over her wire-rimmed glasses at them all.

Miles seemed to draw himself into his seat, like a tortoise retreating into its shell. Hoon, on the other hand, sat a little taller.

"Sorry about that, sweetheart," he said. "We were just all

sitting here saying what a cracking job you're doing. We're all dead impressed back here. You carry on."

"Thank you for the vote of confidence, Mr Hoon," the judge replied. She sighed, like a condemned woman accepting her fate. "But you and your chatty friend there can stay behind after court is adjourned. I think a few etiquette lessons are in order, don't you?"

"No bother, doll," Hoon told her. He linked his fingers behind his head again and relaxed. "Whatever you think yourself..."

CHAPTER TWO

TWENTY MINUTES LATER, Hoon strolled out through the doors of the court, with a sheepish, red-faced Miles scurrying along behind him.

"That was humiliating," the MI5 man muttered. "Absolutely humiliating. I mean, I get that we were out of line talking like that, but did you hear how she spoke to us? She treated us like we were children, or—"

He stopped, all of a sudden, and squinted up at the sky. Fat white flakes fluttered down, swirling on the cold December breeze.

"It's snowing!" Miles cried, holding out his hands and ejecting a giggle. "It's actually snowing. It's properly snowing!"

"Aye," Hoon confirmed. He watched in silence while Miles stuck out his tongue to try to catch a falling flake. "You should try eating the yellow stuff, if you see any. That's the best kind."

He turned to walk on, then stopped when he saw a woman steamrollering towards him. Roberta Hoon, his older sister, looked furious.

No change there, then.

"Well, thanks a fucking bunch for that!" she ejected. The

way her breath condensed in the cold air made her look like a bull on the charge. "Arse-numbingly tedious from start to fucking finish. What was the fucking point in me coming to that?"

"I thought you might enjoy it," Hoon said, rocking his weight onto his back foot as Berta *clumped* to a stop just a pace or so in front of him.

He'd got dressed up specially for the hearing—shirt, tie, suit jacket, the works. It was a big day, after all. A special event.

Now, though, with the cold air rummaging around inside the jacket and seeping through the thin nylon of his shirt, he was wishing he'd at least brought a jumper.

Of course, it was possible that the faint shiver he was developing was more to do with his sister than the weather.

"Enjoy it?! *That*?!" Berta seethed, stabbing a finger past him to where the new, swanky, and somewhat grandiosely named *Inverness Justice Centre* loomed behind him. "I'd sooner have sat at home munching my way through a jar of fucking wasps! And as for making me sit next to this half-wit...!"

She jabbed a thumb back over her shoulder to where a slight and scrawny-looking man stood watching the passing pedestrians and traffic, as if any one of them might be about to attack him.

His hands fretted away in their fingerless gloves, and his gaze darted from each imagined threat to the next like his head and neck were powered by pistons.

"I mean, look at him," Berta said. "One eye away for the shopping, the other coming back with the fucking change. And as for trying to get conversation out of him! Took me bloody ages to get him to start talking while we were waiting for you to come out, and the moment he did, I immediately wished he'd button his fucking hole again."

"He's got a glass eye," Hoon offered, although he knew that

wasn't any sort of defence for the latter part of Berta's tirade. Still, he couldn't really think of anything more convincing.

Iris was an old army mate from back in the day. He was a good guy, deep down, though he was odd. Very odd. *Spectacularly* odd, in fact.

'Iris' wasn't even his real name. It was a nickname that he'd been given early in his basic training—not because of his eyes, which were both still safely in his possession at that point, but because of his tendency to get himself into trouble.

It was an acronym—IRIS—that stood for 'I Require Intense Supervision.'

The amount of supervision he required had not lessened any in the decades since. He now lived alone in a bunker in the woods on Skye, utterly convinced that 'the man' was out to get him. Hoon couldn't imagine what the fuck 'the man' would want with someone like Iris, or what he'd do with him once he had him, but there was no dissuading him on the matter.

Despite living in Scotland for years, Iris' hermit lifestyle meant he hadn't lost so much as a hint of his thick Scouse accent, and when he spoke, he sounded like he'd just stepped off the streets of Liverpool.

It had taken a fair amount of persuasion by Hoon to get Iris to come to the court, but today had been an important baby step. Sooner or later, come the actual trial, Iris might need to stand up and give evidence. Better to get the mad bastard acquainted with the place now when he had nothing expected of him but to sit there quietly.

"Did he try to run off?" Hoon asked.

Berta scowled. "Of course he fucking tried to run off. Just like you said he would."

Hoon glanced over at Iris, who was now warily eyeing up a white van that had stopped at a set of nearby traffic lights.

"You managed to hold on to him alright, though?"

"Well, I managed to hold on to his testicles," Berta said. She made a clawing motion with her right hand, then tightened it into a fist. "The rest of him didn't have a lot of fucking choice but to stick around."

She sniffed, tucked her bright red scarf into the neck of her faded tweed coat, then fired a nod in Miles' direction.

"Who's this lanky streak of pish?" she asked.

"Hi there. I'm Miles," the MI5 man said, offering out a hand. "I'm a friend of Bob's."

"That's a fucking stretch," Hoon said, but Miles ignored him.

"You must be his sister. Roberta, isn't it? I've heard a lot about you."

"Have you fuck," Hoon countered.

Miles kept his smile fixed in place. "Well, no," he admitted. "But the few bits I *have* heard have been good."

"Have they fuck," Hoon countered again.

The battle to keep his smile going became a losing one. Miles cleared his throat gently, formed his mouth into a little circle like he was about to say something more, then thought better of it.

He kept the offered hand held out through it all. Berta considered it for several long, silent seconds, then turned her attention back to her brother.

"Christ on a bike. I bet this one's hard work, isn't he?"

"Don't even get me started," Hoon grumbled.

Miles looked down at his hand like he thought something might be wrong with it, then he let it fall back to his side. "Yes," he said, somewhat vaguely. "Well..."

He seemed visibly relieved when he heard the clattering of footsteps rushing up behind him, followed by a slightly breathless cry of, "Sir! There you are!"

The identikit assistant—Miles 2.0, or whatever he was meant to be—slowed to a jog as he approached the group, then threw out his arms and yelped in fright when he almost lost his balance on the slippery pavement.

"God, what's this now? Don't tell me there's another one of him," Berta remarked, apparently even less impressed by Miles' assistant than she was by Miles himself. She looked between them both, her nostrils flaring in a grimace of disgust. "Christ Almighty. It's like that film. What's it called? With that big muscleman and the fat dwarf?"

Her brother frowned at her, which made her tut loudly with annoyance.

"You know the one. He's weird-sounding. The big bugger, I mean. Like a fucking... I don't know. A trombone with learning difficulties."

"What the hell are you on about?" Hoon asked.

"Oh, Jesus Christ. Come on, you know! It's that film. The daft-sounding German, or Russian, or whatever he is, with the big shiny muscle tits. He's in it with that wee tubby bald lad. They're brothers. They're twins."

Hoon stared at his sister in silence for several seconds, before finally suggesting, "*Twins?*"

"Aye! That's what I just fucking said, wasn't it? They're twins." She tutted. "God. What's it called?"

Hoon rubbed his temples. The day had started so well, too, but he could now feel the first stirrings of a tension headache coming on.

"No. I mean that's the name of the film. *Twins.*"

"Oh. Right. Aye, that might be it, right enough," Berta conceded.

She sniffed loudly, as if to suggest she wasn't entirely satisfied with the answer, then turned and regarded Miles and his assistant with thinly veiled contempt.

"Mind you," she remarked. "At least in that, they managed to have one fucking good one."

The assistant's eyes darted around the group, like he had no idea how to respond to the remark and was searching for someone who did. When nobody stepped in, he settled on the only sensible course of action. He ignored the comment completely.

"Uh, prisoner is secured, and the security detail is awaiting your orders, sir."

"Fucking 'security detail,'" Hoon said. "You mean the four boys from the polis?"

"It's a mix. Some of my guys, some police," Miles said. He smiled weakly, then turned to Kevin, forcing an uncomfortable-sounding laugh. "I keep telling you, you don't have to call me 'sir,' Kevin!"

Kevin, the assistant, appeared taken aback by this news. "Oh. What? I... I don't, sir? But you've always said..."

"Haha! Oh, Kevin, you... japester! It doesn't matter what I said! I was just joking," Miles insisted, laughing a little too hard. He deliberately avoided looking at Hoon, so as not to see the derisory smirk he knew would be on the former detective super-intendent's face. "I'm telling you now, you don't have to call me 'sir,' alright?"

"What, never?"

Miles shifted on the spot and tried not to look too disap-pointed by this.

"No. Never."

"Well, OK. Right. Yes. No more, 'sir.' Will do."

Kevin nodded, tapped the clipboard he had tucked under his arm as if locking in the instruction, then pointed over his shoulder with a forefinger.

"What should I tell the security detail?"

"Tell them I'll be right with them," Miles replied.

Kevin gave a nod so big it was almost a bow, backed away a few steps, then turned and went scurrying off in the direction of the court.

"Sorry about that," Miles said. "Duty calls, and all that."

"They really gave you a fucking assistant?" Hoon asked.

Miles smiled. "They really did."

Hoon grunted, but said nothing. Heading a cross-sector task force was quite a jump up from the admin role Miles had been relegated to the last time Hoon had seen him. Still, better him than some crooked bastard. Miles might be something of a useless bugger, but at least he was on the straight and narrow.

"What's going to happen to her fucking ladyship in there?" Hoon asked.

"You know I can't tell you that, Bob," Miles said.

Hoon stared at him. It took just eight or nine seconds for the boggle-eyed glowering to take its toll.

"Jesus. Alright. Between you and me, she'll be held locally until our flight south at seven tonight, then it'll be a closed-door hearing down the road tomorrow."

"You're flying her?"

"Well, we can hardly shove her on the bus, can we?" said Miles. "And besides, we've got intel that says the Loop is going to try and get to her. Easier to keep her secure in the sky than on the ground."

Hoon's eyebrows rose halfway up his forehead at the mention of the Loop, but they didn't hang around there for long. He shouldn't be surprised. The last thing they'd want was for Suranne to start talking.

"They looking to rescue her or take her out?"

"We don't know," Miles admitted. "But they want to get their hands on her. Whether that's dead or alive...? Well, hopefully, we'll never have to find out."

Hoon looked past him to the towering pillars of the Justice Centre. It was an impressive building, he had to admit, though it had an arrogance about it that he didn't like—an audacious, cock-sure sort of air that, were it a human being, would almost certainly see it getting its teeth knocked out in a pub car park.

"So, she's more connected than we thought, then?"

Miles shrugged. "To be fair, I always thought she was very connected. It was you who thought otherwise. But... we'll keep her safe, and then, with a bit of luck, and a bit of persuasion, we'll find out what she knows."

Before Hoon could ask any more, the scowling face of his big sister leaned into view, breathing out a cloud of white vapour as her arms wrapped across her matronly bosom.

"Are you two going to kiss goodbye, or can we get a bloody move on?" she demanded. "I'm about to start shedding fucking toes out here."

Hoon and Miles both looked, just for a moment, at the thick blanket of grey-white cloud hanging high above their heads, and the falling flurry of flakes that muted the sound of the traffic crossing the Longman roundabout.

"Right. Well. Make sure you keep me posted," Hoon said, meeting the MI5 man's eye again.

They shook hands.

"You know I can't do that, Bob."

Hoon grinned, and tightened his grip just enough for the discomfort to register on Miles' face.

"Aye," he said. "I think you'll find you can."

Miles rolled his eyes, but smiled back at him. "I'll see what I can do."

They both released their grip, then Miles turned and headed back towards the court, his feet leaving dark imprints in the thin, mushy layer of snow gathering on the pavement.

"How is she?" Hoon asked. He flinched, gritted his teeth, and clenched his fists by his sides. He hadn't meant to ask the question. He'd been trying very hard not to, in fact, but it had slipped out all on its own.

Miles stopped, but only half-turned, like he didn't want to get dragged back into a conversation. Or perhaps just not this particular conversation.

"She's OK," he said. "She's, uh, she's getting there. Slowly. She's been through a lot. But, I mean, you know that."

Hoon nodded slowly. He tried to turn, but his feet remained planted on the spot.

"Does she ever talk about me?" he heard himself ask.

Miles hesitated before replying. "Would it help if I said she did? Would it help you feel better about what you did?"

Hoon gave the question some thought, then responded with a shrug. "Maybe. I don't know. Does she?"

The smile had fallen from Miles' face, but now it tried to rally. The one that curved up the corners of his mouth now, though, was a thin parody of his usual effort.

"No," he said. "I'm sorry, Bob. I wish I could tell you different." He sighed, and there was real regret in there. "But, no. She doesn't talk about you."

The bottom half of Hoon's face broke into a smile, but the top half betrayed him, pain shining from his eyes.

"Good for her. Quite bloody right," he said. He pointed to the Justice Centre. "Now, off you fuck."

"Ten-four," Miles said, tapping a finger to his forehead in salute. He started to turn, then paused again, just long enough to say, "Merry Christmas, Bob."

Hoon snorted. "Bah fucking humbug!"

He watched Miles go trudging off through the deepening snow, then jumped when Berta spoke just a few inches from his right ear.

"About fucking time, too," she hissed.

"Jesus!" Hoon ejected. "Personal fucking space, Berta. We spoke about this."

His sister tutted. "Well, clearly I wasn't listening," she said, then she grabbed for one of his nipples and twisted it sharply through his shirt, really giving it some welly.

"Ow! Fucking quit that!" he protested, slapping her hand away.

"Your wee pal over there—Charlie Cyclops, or whatever the fuck his name is—he's whinging about his train," she said. She indicated Iris with a look that lasted barely a nanosecond, yet still managed to be brimming with horror and revulsion. "I told him nobody would bat an eyelid if he just pissed off, but he was having none of it. Wanted to say goodbye."

Hoon looked past his sister to where Iris stood right by the side of the road, idly polishing his glass eye on his sleeve, and apparently blissfully unaware of all the fast-moving traffic behind him.

"I think he's got a while yet until he has to head to the station," Hoon said, checking his watch.

"I don't see how that's our problem," Berta shot back. "If a grown man hasn't got the wherewithal to kill a couple of hours on his own, we might as well throw him in *front* of the fucking train, because he's clearly neither use nor bloody ornament."

Hoon didn't even have to give this any thought. He knew full well the dangers of leaving his old army pal to his own devices. Hoon had been one of the ones to come up with the nickname for him, after all.

"Iris," Hoon called, completely ignoring Berta's rant. "You fancy a quick coffee before you shoot off?"

Iris' eyes widened in surprise. Well, one of them did, anyway. He popped the other back in its socket so it was pointing *almost* the same way as the real one.

"Eh, bit dangerous, isn't it?" he said.

"Dangerous? How the fuck is it dangerous?" Hoon asked. "Are you planning on fucking drowning in it?"

Iris rubbed his chin, deep in thought. His lips moved as he ran through a list of potential dangers in his head, but then he concluded that it was probably worth the risk, and his face lit up with a bright, beaming smile.

"Sounds great then, Boggle," he said, much to Berta's disappointment. "Count me in!"

CHAPTER THREE

AFTER MUCH DEBATE, and a tense few moments when it looked like they might all come to blows, Hoon, Berta, and Iris settled on a small, charity-run café in the Eastgate Shopping Centre, a stone's throw from the railway station where Iris would be catching his train.

Costa had been an option—it was at the side of the centre closest to the station, after all—but Hoon tried to avoid using the big chains where he could, Iris believed that any company with a loyalty scheme was trying to steal his genetic code, and Berta couldn't be arsed walking any further than she absolutely had to.

"And anyway," she'd announced, as they'd trudged through the snow. "It's going to be full of bloody yuppies and ladyboys, isn't it? They always are."

"What sort of fucking *Costa*s have you been going to?" Hoon had asked, but she'd dismissed the question with a grunt, and a middle-finger salute.

Their café of choice was tucked away on the right, just inside the southernmost entrance—or the *Boots* entrance, as the locals knew it, due to its proximity to the pharmacy chain's big split-level store.

As soon as they entered through the sliding doors, they were assaulted by movement, colour, and noise. Dozens of shoppers crowded the escalators leading to the centre's upper level, all chattering away, bags of presents and other festive goodies weighing them down.

From the centre's speaker system, *Last Christmas* by *Wham!* segued tidily into the opening bars of *Mistletoe & Wine*, the first few notes of which made Hoon hiss through the gaps in his teeth like he was in physical pain.

"Christ. Cliff Richard. What the fuck have we done to deserve that?" he muttered.

"And what's wrong with Cliff Richard?" demanded Berta, practically squaring up to her younger, slightly shorter brother.

"Everything," Hoon told her, not backing down. "He's like someone waved a magic wand and made mediocrity sentient. Or like a mannequin came to life and started having delusions of fucking grandeur. He's a sanctimonious, turkey-necked, plastic-eyed fucking harlequin, and I cannot abide the bastard."

"Well, *that's* a load of bollocks," Berta said.

"I quite like him," Iris remarked. Then, he started to whistle a tune that bore no resemblance to the one playing through the speakers.

"What's that meant to be?" Hoon asked.

Iris continued to whistle tunelessly, only stopping to throw out the words, "*Tutti Frutti.*"

"Cliff Richard didn't sing *Tutti Frutti.*"

The whistling stopped. A slow, lumbering sort of frown drew lines across Iris' forehead. "Yeah, he did."

"No, Iris. Did he fuck. That was *Little* Richard," Hoon said.

Iris continued to stare back at him with his one good eye. The glass one, on the other hand, was apparently more interested in the ceiling.

"That's what you said, wasn't it?"

"No. Was it fuck. I said Cliff Richard. Cliff."

Iris just kept right on staring, as shoppers squeezed past them on their way to the escalators. Hoon had to fight the urge to lean over and bite the other man's head off.

"What the fuck are you no' getting here?" he demanded. "Cliff. Little. They're two different words, Iris. They're two different fucking people. Cliff Richard. Little Richard."

Iris opened his mouth, but Hoon had already anticipated the question.

"And no, Little Richard's no' just a smaller version of Cliff Richard, before you fucking ask. They didn't make a wee mini clone of him in a lab somewhere. They're two different guys. One of them's decent, one of them's shite."

Iris pointed upwards, roughly in the direction his glass eye was looking. "And what one's this?"

"This is the shite one," Hoon explained.

"He's not shite!" Berta objected, but Hoon dismissed the complaint with a scowl and a wave.

"He is so. He's a fucking human cardigan with a neck like an old pair of tights. My arse carries a tune better than that bastard."

Before his sister could offer any further argument, Hoon turned sharply to his right, and started to cut through the throngs of Christmas shoppers, leading the way towards the café.

"Now come on, let's get moving. They'll be shutting us in for the night if we don't get a fucking shifty on."

When they eventually made it through the crowds and into the café, there wasn't a table to be found. Despite the cold outside, the place radiated with the warmth of all those bodies huddled over their teas, coffees, and hot chocolates laden with cream and marshmallows.

There was an aroma of gingerbread and Christmas spices in the air, and even Hoon might've experienced a flicker of festive feeling, had it not been for the complete lack of available seating.

Nobody looked like they were getting ready to leave, either.

Even if they did, there were half a dozen other people in the queue already, and a few wandering around with loaded trays, all of whom would be quick to swoop in as soon as a seat became free.

"Fuck's sake," Hoon muttered. "No point trying here. We'll have to go somewhere else."

"My arse, we will," Berta said. She had locked her sights on a man who sat alone at an empty table, frowning at his mobile phone. "You get in the queue. Tea for me. A scone, if there's one going, but none of that cherry or cheese shite. Plain or fruit. Don't fucking waste my time with anything else, because I'm not interested."

While delivering her order, she hadn't shifted her gaze from the man at the table. Before Hoon could ask where she was going, she set off, pulling the strap of her handbag higher on her shoulder as she crossed the café floor.

"What's she doing?" Iris asked, chewing on a thumbnail as he watched Berta closing in on the seated man.

"Oh, Christ knows. What are you wanting?" Hoon asked, gesturing to the menu.

Iris continued to watch Berta for a moment, then turned his attention to the list of available beverages.

"Do they do just hot water?" he wondered. "You can't be too careful with other stuff. They put chemicals in it."

Hoon thought about arguing, but instead just pinched the bridge of his nose, ran a hand down his face, and sighed.

At the far end of the café, Berta stopped with a *clop* of her sensible shoes, and indicated the table with a sweep of a hand.

"What the fuck is this?" she demanded.

The man looked up from his phone, and when he saw the stern-looking older woman looming over him, his face settled into an expression of amiable confusion. He was in his mid-thirties. Old enough, Berta thought, to know better than to leave the house with the horrible under-chin beard he had.

"I'm sorry?" he asked.

"You heard me," Berta said.

His smile widened, like this was all just a misunderstanding they'd laugh about in a minute.

"No, I'm sorry, I didn't," he said. "I was trying to get a phone signal, but there's something wrong with the network or—"

"What do I look like, son?" Berta asked, cutting him off. "Technical fucking support?" She pointed to the table, then swirled her finger around, like she was tracing the circular outline. "What do you think you're doing sitting here?"

The man followed her swirling finger for a moment, then looked back up to meet her glare. "I'm just... I'm waiting for—"

"Ah-ah-ah! Stop right there," Berta told him, raising a hand. "You're waiting?"

"My, eh, my mate's just in the queue, he's—"

Berta leaned over and placed both clenched fists on the tabletop, like a silverback gorilla asserting its authority.

"So, what you're saying is, you crept over here like a fucking nonce at a junior disco, and poached this table before you even had your order?"

The man, who presumably wasn't best pleased at having been compared to a predatory paedophile, sat up a little straighter.

"No, I'm not saying... I'm just, I'm saying my mate's in the queue."

"I don't care if he's in the fucking royal family, son," Berta hissed. She gestured behind her with a tilt of her head. "Look at these people with their trays, wandering about like gormless bastards, trying to find a seat. But they can't, can they? Because they did things properly. They lined up, got their order, *then* came looking for a seat, like decent human beings. But too fucking late, because some arsehole had already rushed over and poached the last one."

"I don't—"

"You're the arsehole in that scenario, by the way," Berta said, straightening up. "I thought I'd better clarify, because you look like you're thick as shit, and I didn't want to leave room for any confusion." She gave another tilt of her head, but this one had some force behind it. "Now, off you pop, go join your pal in the queue, and wait your fucking turn."

The man's chair gave a *creak* as he shifted his weight back on it, and for a moment, it looked like he was going to stand—or at least sit—his ground.

But then, with a sigh, a slap of the table, and some under-breath muttering, he got to his feet and stormed over to join another man who was standing three back from the front of the queue.

Berta watched while the story of what had just happened passed from the first man to the second, then she slowly lowered herself onto the recently vacated seat, and placed her handbag on the table.

She held eye contact with the man she'd chased off even when a woman with a tray came shuffling over to the table, and Berta dismissed her with a wave.

"Sorry, love," she said, and she smiled, thin-lipped at the man she'd just sent packing. "These seats are taken."

Hoon sipped his second coffee while he waited for the caffeine buzz from the first one to kick in. He'd ordered two, both black, and had necked the first in a couple of big gulps in the hope it gave him the energy he'd need to cope with Berta and Iris.

Berta hadn't yet poured her tea from the pot. She liked to leave it to stew for as long as possible, then would shove a spoon in, stir it all about, before mashing the bags against the side in order to wring every last drop of flavour from them.

It took so long that the tea was stone cold by the time she

came to pour it, and she'd then top up the cup from a separate pot of hot water, thus diluting the tea, and rendering the whole exercise completely pointless.

Then again, she usually kept her mouth shut while she waited for it to brew, and Hoon wasn't going to object to the peace and quiet.

"What time's your train, exactly?" he asked Iris, who was nursing a mug of hot water with a slice of lemon floating on top. Hoon had refused to order it for him, and had quickly walked away once he'd been handed his own order, so he could pretend they weren't together.

"Not sure," Iris admitted. "Think it's leaving here about... eh... afternoon."

Hoon brought his coffee to his lips, then moved it away again without drinking.

"What? What do you mean? Afternoon's no' a fucking time, Iris."

"Course it is. *Afternoon time,*" Iris replied. He took a big slurp of his water, licked his lips, then gave a nod as if to declare the argument had been won.

Hoon did not agree.

"Bollocks. You can't just say 'afternoon time,' and that be the fucking end of it. It's no' a time. It's a period of time," he shot back. "It's a fucking *spell* of time. It's no' an actual time."

"Well, I think it is."

"Well, you might think it is, but you're wrong. No one's ever phoned the speaking clock and heard it say, 'At the third beep, it'll be precisely the fucking afternoon.'"

"Well, no, because the speaking clock wouldn't swear," Iris reasoned.

"I bet it fucking would if you phoned it," Hoon told him.

He drained the rest of his coffee in one exasperated gulp, muttered below his breath, then leaned over onto one arse cheek and fumbled in a trouser pocket until he found his phone.

"Where is it you're going? Here to Skye?"

Iris ducked so low his chin was practically resting on the table as his one good eye scanned the café around them. All the other punters in the place were chatting away merrily—perhaps because of the oncoming festivities in just two days, or, as Hoon suspected, despite them.

"Keep your voice down, Boggle. That's top secret information," Iris whispered.

"Is it fuck. Nobody cares," Hoon informed him, without skipping a beat. He tapped the screen of his phone to wake it up. "So, Inverness to Skye, aye?"

Iris took another look around before shaking his head. "Train doesn't go as far as Skye. Stops at Kyle of Lochalsh."

Hoon peered at him, his phone still clutched in one hand. "And what, you'll get a taxi from there, or something?"

Iris sat bolt upright, squared his shoulders, and stared right through Hoon's head at something beyond the café's walls, that only he could see.

"That's classified."

"Fuck's sake. Fine," Hoon said. "Kyle of Lochalsh."

He set about tapping at his screen, while Berta lifted the lid of the teapot, looked inside, and decided the tea wasn't yet strong enough.

"Nice journey, that," she remarked. "Assuming you're not sat next to some pain in the arse, of course. Nice views out the windows."

"I don't look out the windows," Iris told her.

Hoon raised his eyes from his phone. "What do you mean?" he asked.

"Well, windows work both ways, Boggle," Iris said.

The statement sounded more insightful than the actual words suggested. Then again, that wasn't really saying much.

"Oh, what the fuck's he on about now?" Berta groaned.

"If I'm looking out," Iris said, shifting his one-eyed gaze

between each sibling in turn, "then you've got to ask yourself, who's looking in?"

"Well, considering you're going at eighty miles an hour through the arse end of fucking nowhere, I'm going to go out on a limb here and say *nobody*, Iris. No bastard's looking in."

"Yeah, well, you can never be too careful, Boggle."

"No, you can," Hoon insisted. "Sometimes, you definitely fucking can be too careful. You, especially."

Iris shook his head. "Then why's it a saying, then? Why do they say, 'You can never be too careful'? and not 'You can sometimes be too careful'?"

There wasn't enough coffee in the world for this conversation, Hoon realised, and he made the decision to end it there.

"Fair point, aye," he said, then he turned his attention back to his phone and gave a tut of annoyance. "Can't see the train times. No fucking signal in here."

Iris leaned forward in his seat. "Maybe someone's jamming it," he suggested.

"Or maybe it's just because the signal's notoriously shite in this building," Hoon countered. "It's alright under the big glass roof at the other end, but completely hopeless everywhere else."

Iris sipped thoughtfully on his now-lukewarm water. "We could go to that bit," he suggested.

"Christ, thinking outside the box there, eh?" Hoon said. He tapped Berta's teapot with a spoon, making it *ting*. "Hurry up and chew your fucking tea. We need to get moving."

Berta paid him no heed. Instead, she sat gazing out through the café window at the automatic doors they'd entered the shopping centre through.

"Oh, for the love of fuck, will you look at that lot?" she remarked, and both men sitting at the table turned to follow her gaze.

A gang—a procession, maybe—of men in jolly red suits and scraggly white beards were flooding into the centre, big brown sacks slung over their shoulders. There had to be a dozen of them, at least, though they were bunched so closely together that they looked less like a group of individuals, and more like one giant, homogenous mass—a massive, multi-limbed Santa monster with a single shared consciousness.

"He ruined Christmas, that fucker," Berta said, sniffing and turning back to her teapot.

Hoon frowned. "Santa? Santa Claus ruined Christmas? That's a fucking bold statement."

After a quick sniff of the teapot's spout, she decided the liquid inside—if, indeed, it still qualified as a liquid—had reached optimum strength. She half-filled her cup with the brooding brown tea, then set down the pot and reached for the metal jug of hot water on the table beside it.

"Remember when Christmas used to be about Jesus?" she asked.

"Oh aye, back in... what was it again? Year fucking one?" Hoon asked. He looked his sister up and down. "And since when were you religious?"

"Oh, Christ, no, I'm not. But, at least with Jesus, you can just ignore him."

She pointed with her water jug at the Santas, most of whom were now headed up the escalator, leaving only a couple in the downstairs foyer.

"Not that fucker, though. All jingling bells, and 'Ho-ho-fuck-ing-hoing' in your face, all the time." She tipped the hot water into her tea, shaking her head. "No. Not for me, that, thank you very much."

"Aye, well, I'm no' sure 'angry old spinsters' is his target audience, to be fair to him," Hoon said. He pushed back his chair, rose to his feet, then pointed to his sister's tea. "Now, get that necked, and let's go check this train."

Berta reached for her cup, but in a way that could best be described as 'leisurely.'

"Don't bother waiting for me," she said. "You go pack him off, then come back for me." She looked across the café, to where the man she'd ejected from the seat and his mate were still searching for an empty table. She smiled, showing her teeth. "I'm perfectly happy right where I am…"

CHAPTER FOUR

THE SHOPPING CENTRE, once Hoon and Iris were up a floor and into the main body of it, wasn't as jam-packed as the bottleneck at the entrance had made it appear. Yes, it was busy, but it wasn't *hoaching*.

It was still only early afternoon on a weekday, though, and the centre opened late in the run-up to Christmas. Come the back of five, when people got off work, you wouldn't be able to move.

Hoon had been forced to stop on their way through the centre, so Iris could watch the big clock next to *HMV*. It was an antiquated thing, built to resemble Noah's Ark, with wee flappy doors opening, and mechanical animals springing into life on the hour, to the tune of *The Animals Went in Two By Two*.

It was one of only a handful of such clocks remaining in the country, and had been a fixture of the centre for as long as Hoon could remember—so much so that he'd stopped even noticing it long ago.

Iris, however, stood rapt from the opening notes to the closing of the final door, transfixed like he was watching real, actual magic happening right before his eye.

"Right, come on," Hoon urged, once it had finished, and Iris trotted along behind him, grinning from ear to ear, until they reached the glass railing that looked down on the big, circular food court.

Or down on the empty space that had once been the food court, at any rate. There had been a *KFC* and one of the big pizza chains here at one point, as well as some smaller, one-off places.

They'd all cleared off for one reason or another, though, and where they'd been had been walled off with a swooping curved billboard that promised exciting things were coming soon.

A bronze sculpture of a man with a falcon stood in the centre of the circular area. Hoon wasn't sure who the man was meant to be, exactly, but whoever it was, he suspected they wouldn't have a lot in common, given that the guy was wearing a crown, and looking, quite frankly, a bit up himself.

Overhead, above it all, the enormous glass dome that covered this whole section of the centre was whited out by a layer of snow. It cast thin grey shadows across both this floor and the one below, and the electric lighting was having to work hard to push back against the gathering gloom.

"Still no signal," Hoon muttered. He gave his phone a shake, as if this might somehow clear some blockage somewhere. "Must be the snow."

"Or someone's blocking the signal," Iris said, refusing to let the idea go. His eye darted around, getting the measure of the place. "Wouldn't be hard, place like this. Few jammers scattered around behind the scenes, bish, bash, bosh. Job's a good 'un."

"Or, again, it might be the fucking blizzard going on outside," Hoon said, then he grunted when a man in a Santa costume went barging past him, clipping him with a shoulder. "Here, watch where you're fucking going!"

Father Christmas appeared to be in too much of a rush to

stop, though, and he hurried on through the crowds, visibly struggling with the weight of his sack.

Several other Santas were rushing across the upper level, their faces hidden behind their big bushy beards.

"Quite a skinny Santa, that," Iris observed.

"Aye," Hoon grunted. He eyeballed the back of the man who had collided with him for a few moments, glanced around at the other men in red suits, then shook his head. "They don't make them like they used to."

"They make a lot more of them, though," Iris said. He gestured down over the railing to the former food court below. More Santas were crisscrossing through the crowds—more, even, than the small army of the bastards they'd seen through the café window.

"Fucking hell. It's a swarm."

Before they could dwell any more on the matter, a couple of bum notes blared out from a trumpet somewhere over on their left, near the *Waterstone's* bookshop. A brass band from one of the local schools launched into a rendition of *Good King Wenceslas* that could best be described as 'enthusiastic.'

Or, some of them were enthusiastic, anyway. Around half of the kids in the band were really giving it some welly, while the rest were dragging their heels. The tune's correct tempo existed somewhere in the gulf between the two, so if you could somehow average it all out, you could argue that, mathematically speaking at least, they were nailing it.

Your ears, of course, would very much beg to differ.

"Christ, right, I'm not standing here listening to that," Hoon said, setting off towards the escalator that led down to the floor below. "I need to run for a pish. You head out the doors round that corner, and then hang a right. Station's there. I'll meet you there in five minutes."

He stood on the top step of the escalator, and ran a hand

across his stomach as he began gliding downwards. The gurgle it gave bode ill.

"Actually," he said, wincing back over his shoulder at Iris. "Better make it ten."

At the bottom of the escalator, Hoon hung a left towards the toilets, while Iris, following directions, headed right.

Iris wasn't a fan of crowds. He wasn't big on public buildings, either, and generally didn't get on well with exposed, wide-open spaces. The former food court ticked a lot of those boxes, and had the added disadvantage of the mezzanine level above, where he and Hoon had just been standing, and which he knew would offer a gunman perfect sight lines on him as he passed below.

Narrowing his shoulders to better slip through the gaps between the shoppers, Iris took the long way around the old food court, sticking close to the big wall of 'coming soon' signage. He glanced upwards a few times in search of snipers, and let his eye linger a few moments on the three men in Santa suits he saw standing up there, scanning the crowds below.

He picked up the pace as he neared the edge of the big circular space, and hurried towards the doors that would lead out onto Falcon Square. There were several tall windows on the left as he approached the exit, but a team of men in grey *Eastgate Centre* polo shirts were just finishing covering them up with floor-to-ceiling static-cling posters, so he couldn't see out to check if it was still snowing.

The glass of the doors up ahead had been similarly covered over with Christmas-themed advertising. They cut out much of the light, and between them and the snow-covered glass dome, Iris felt like darkness was gathering itself around him.

Somewhere, deep among the gooey folds of Iris' frazzled, shell-shocked brain, an alarm began to ring.

He started to walk faster, head down, hands in his pockets. He counted his steps, dividing them into short bursts—*one-two-*

three, one-two-three, one-two-three—in an attempt to calm the rising panic in his chest.

Something was wrong, he thought. A lot of things, maybe. The phone. The Santas. The darkness.

He looked to his left again, where the centre staff had now fully covered the windows in an opaque sticky film.

"Can't see in. Can't see out," Iris muttered to himself, hurrying on. "Not good. Not good."

A passing Santa turned to look at him. Only a few inches of his face were visible between where the white fur trim of his hat met the wild hair of his fake beard, but in that space, his eyes narrowed.

Iris scratched at his arms as he walked, so hard that he left red lines on his skin, even through his jacket. He risked a glance back at the closest Santa, then whipped his head forward again when he realised he was still being watched.

"Not good, not good, not good!" he whispered. He had an urge to run, but he fought it, and instead kept walking on towards the doors. "Stay on target. Stay on target."

Behind him, with a heavy-sounding *clack*, the man in the Santa Claus suit lowered his sack to the floor.

Hoon was passing the disabled toilets when one of the doors was opened from the inside. There was some thumping and groaning, and a muttered, "Stupid bloody thing," and when the door failed to open more than a foot or so, Hoon realised someone was having problems.

"You alright, there?" he asked, taking hold of the handle and pulling the door open the rest of the way.

"Jesus!"

The woman on the other side of the door let out a gasp and

almost leapt out of her wheelchair in fright. She was in her thirties, Hoon guessed, and had her right foot in a stookie.

The stookie—or *plaster cast*, if you lived anywhere in the world that wasn't Scotland—had been decorated with brightly coloured, though not particularly accomplished, drawings of people, and animals, and sunshine. Presumably, her kids had been given free rein to use it as a canvas. Recently, too, given how vibrant the colours still looked.

"No, but people often get us mixed up," Hoon said.

She either didn't get the joke, or didn't appreciate it. Either way, she didn't laugh. Or smile. Or really do much of anything except look alarmed by his presence.

"Sorry, I was passing, and thought you looked like you were struggling," he explained. "Don't worry, I'm no' a fucking murderer or a rapist or anything."

This statement didn't appear to reassure her. If anything, it did precisely the opposite. On reflection, Hoon could see why.

He kept the door open for her, but stepped aside and gestured with a sweep of his arm.

"There you go. Just thought I'd help."

The woman inexpertly wheeled herself out of the bathroom, still watching him like a hawk. Or rather, like something scurrying around in the grass, watching the hawk circling in the sky above.

"Weirdo," she said, once she was clear, then her arms pumped frantically as she put as much distance between herself and Hoon as possible.

"Well, that's fucking charming!" he called after her. "That's the first and last fucking time I do a good deed for anyone."

She stopped wheeling herself just long enough to raise a middle finger back over her shoulder, and then she reached the end of the corridor, took the corner at speed, and was swallowed by the crowd.

"Unbe-fucking-lievable," Hoon remarked.

He started to close the door, then stopped. The disabled toilets were standalone, solo affairs. They were roomy, much nicer than the other bathroom facilities, and could usually only be accessed by pressing a buzzer and pleading your case.

And now, here he was, being presented with an opportunity.

Morally, it was wrong, of course. But then, morally, he'd done a whole lot worse.

"Never look a fucking gift horse in the mouth," he said. His stomach gave an ominous gurgle, so he stepped inside, locked the door, and hurriedly unfastened his belt.

CHAPTER FIVE

BERTA *SLURPED* the last of her tea, smacked her lips together, then let out a long, satisfied, *aaaaah.*

Then, and only then, did she look up at the two men standing across the table, one of them carrying a tray with both hands.

The man who she'd ejected from the very seat she was sitting on spoke to her through gritted teeth

"You done, then?"

"Uh..."

Berta lifted the lid of the teapot, peeked inside, then replaced it with a *clink.*

She studied the table, with its three dirty cups, saucers, spoons, sugar packets, and other associated mess, like she was trying to memorise it all.

She picked up a paper napkin, wiped her mouth with it, then noisily blew her nose.

"Yes," she said, tucking the napkin into her sleeve for later. "Yes, I think I am."

Bones creaking, Berta rose to her feet and indicated the

clutter with a wave of a hand. "Be a dear and tidy that up for me, will you? I can't be carrying trays at my age."

She smiled thinly at both men, almost daring them to object. Sensibly, they chose not to, and instead just quickly slid onto the closest two chairs so they could salvage the few degrees of warmth still left in their hot drinks.

Hooking her handbag over her arm, then tucking both arms beneath her bosom, Berta strode out of the café, quietly *pom-pom-pomming* below her breath in time with the music playing from the centre's speaker system.

Saviour's Day. Another Christmas classic from Cliff.

As she left the café, for the first time in as far back as she could remember, Berta realised she was feeling almost festive. She'd been alone in that big house for so many years, that she'd barely given things like birthdays or Christmas a moment's thought, other than to—very occasionally—dwell on the lack of anyone to celebrate them with.

This year could be different, though. This year, Roberta Hoon thought, Christmas might actually be tolerable.

She emerged from the café into the same foyer they'd all entered through earlier, and stopped when she saw the doors. While she'd been making the most of her tea, someone had taped what looked like black bin bags over the glass, blocking the view of the street beyond.

A row of yellow warning cones had been set out on the floor in front of the exit, and three men in matching grey security uniforms stood in front of the doors, gesturing for everyone coming down the escalator to head back up.

They all looked young. Ridiculously so. Berta wouldn't trust them to run a fucking bath, let alone a shopping centre.

"Sorry, folks," one of them was announcing. "Doors at this end are out of order. The *Markies'* doors, too. You'll need to back up and use the other exits."

There were some heavy sighs and muttered objections, but

when the people coming down the escalator reached the bottom, they quickly stepped onto the one heading upwards beside it. If all the doors at this end were closed, there were going to be major bottlenecks at the other exits, and they all wanted to get there before every other bugger did.

Berta's gaze followed them up to the floor above. Another security man was up there, stopping people before they could start heading down. A man in a Santa costume—presumably one of the horde she'd seen earlier—stood beside him, and when the last person had stepped off the escalator heading down, it was Santa who reached over and flipped the switch to turn it off.

"What the fuck's all this, then?" Berta demanded of one of the security men. "What's going on?"

All three men turned to look at her, then two decided she wasn't worth bothering about. Instead, they turned their attention to the steady stream of shoppers now emerging from *Marks & Spencer*, and began ushering them up towards the floor above.

"Doors are out of order," the third security guard told her. He looked even younger than the others, and had so many spots and boils on his jaw and neck that she'd initially mistaken them for a horrible beard.

"What's that supposed to mean?" Berta asked. "Out of order *how?*"

The man shifted his weight from foot to foot, squirming on the spot. "Just, you know, not working," he said. "All the ones at this end. Think it's maybe the snow. Or... or something. Or just the weather in general. It's cold."

"Of course it's bloody cold! It's Scotland," Berta fired back. "If doors stopped working every time it got cold, we'd never be able to leave the fucking house." She waved a crooked finger at the glass behind him. "What's all this about, with the black bags? Are we expecting a nuclear blast all of a sudden?"

"It's, uh, it's just a precaution," Acne Beard said.

"A precaution for what?" Berta demanded, but before the

lad could reply, the guard beside him butted in. This one wasn't much older, but he had a confidence that made him appear that way.

"Is there a problem here?" he barked. His accent wasn't local. English. Somewhere down south. This did nothing to endear him to Berta Hoon.

"Well, I'd sure as fuck say there is, yes," Berta replied, squaring up to him. "I think your spotty little chum here's full of shit, for starters. Maybe you'll give me a straight answer. What's going on?"

There was a hesitation from the Englishman. A flash of something crossed his face. Anger, maybe, or disgust, there and gone too quickly for Berta to fully register it.

He took a breath, and when he replied, you could barely even tell that he was struggling to control his temper.

"As we explained, the doors are out of order, ma'am. We're asking everyone to head for the other exit."

Berta's eyes became slits of suspicion. She regarded the two men directly before her, then checked out the third one, who was still directing the foot traffic.

"Bollocks. You're lying," she said. "There's nothing wrong with the fucking doors."

A look passed between the two men. The lad with the beard of spots looked worried, but his colleague's expression leaned more towards anger.

"Look, just go up the stairs, alright?" he hissed, leaning in closer.

The expression on Berta's face hardened like calcifying bone. She didn't have to say a word to make the guard realise that he'd taken completely the wrong approach with her. He forced an unconvincing smile, and moved quickly to correct his error.

"Sorry, it's been a stressful day," he told her, then he leaned in closer still and lowered his voice to a conspiratorial whisper.

"The truth is, we've got an incident happening outside. Police are on their way, but we need to get everyone upstairs and away from this level as quickly, and with as little fuss as possible. We don't want to risk causing any panic."

Berta's expression didn't change beyond the raising of one eyebrow. "What sort of incident?" she asked.

"I'm not at liberty to reveal that down here, ma'am, but it's serious. If you head up top, everything will be explained up there," the guard assured her.

His smile widened when he saw her resolve faltering. He indicated the escalator behind her, and she turned her head to look.

"I promise," he said. "You head on up there for me, and all will be revealed..."

CHAPTER SIX

IRIS WAS ALMOST at the exit. Almost outside. Almost safe.

He didn't know what the danger was, exactly, but it crackled in the air around him, and in the gaps between the shoppers. He could hear it reverberating in the notes of the school brass band. Could see it reflected back at him in the now completely covered windows.

Every instinct, every fibre and follicle in his body, was screaming, 'DANGER!'

Granted, that happened on a fairly regular basis, and it was usually the paranoia talking, but this was different. This was real. Whatever was happening was, for once, *actually* happening.

He'd get outside. He'd make plans there. Regroup.

Was it possible to regroup on your own? He wasn't sure. But he'd do his best.

He wished Boggle was with him. Boggle would know what to do. Boggle always did.

Shit. Boggle. He wouldn't know. He wouldn't know about the danger.

Iris faltered to a stop. Fear shoved him on another pace or two, but he held fast. Stood his ground.

He couldn't leave Boggle on his own. He couldn't just abandon him like this.

His heart raced at the very thought of turning back, crashing in his chest and stealing the air from his lungs until his head went light, and darkness crept in from the corners of his eyes.

The sounds of the centre became faint, tinny echoes. The people, and the shops, and the noise, and the hot, burning terror became a tornado around him, spinning and swirling, with him at the eye of the storm.

He had to run. He had to get out. What good could he do in here? If he stayed, with so many people around, there was no saying he could even get to Boggle, let alone warn him.

And what would he warn him of, exactly? He didn't know what was wrong. He just knew that his skin was on fire, and his head was filled with flashing lights and the drumbeats of war.

What would make Boggle believe that this wasn't just another paranoid outburst? What made this any different from his usual panic attacks?

Outside, he could figure out what was going on. He could warn people about the danger. Outside, he could help.

What good was he in here? What good would he be to anyone?

As if sensing his wavering resolve, his legs started to move, plodding him towards the exit—slowly at first, then faster.

Yes. This was the right call. Get out. Get help. Save his friend. Save the day.

They hadn't survived all those special forces operations by charging straight into danger. They'd planned. They'd been clever. They'd used strategy.

That's what he needed now—a strategy. And to do that, he first needed to remove himself from the battlefield.

Less than thirty feet separated him from fresh air and freedom.

Less than twenty.

Less than fifteen.

It was then that he noticed the build-up of foot traffic around the exit, as a dozen or so people who were trying to leave stopped at the motionless sliding doors. They looked up at the sensor and shuffled around a little, like they were trying to politely draw the doors' attention without making too much of a fuss.

Then, when that didn't work, a few of them raised their arms and waved, but the doors remained steadfastly shut.

The fear that had pushed Iris on now snapped him to a stop.

Oh, God. Oh, no.

"Uh, sorry, folks. I'm sorry. I'm really sorry."

A fifty-something man with short grey hair and a day's worth of beard growth appeared at the side of the growing crowd. He was dressed smartly in a shirt, tie, and waistcoat, but everything was creased and dishevelled, like he'd been wearing them for a while. His face had a similar look about it, too, his eyes carrying bags beneath them, and ringed with a circle of red.

On the breast of his waistcoat, a badge identified him as the centre's security manager. There was a big metal ring attached to his belt, like he was supposed to be carrying a big bunch of keys with him. He appeared to have left them somewhere, though.

Either that, or someone had taken them from him.

Iris didn't see where the man had come from, but the door to the *Burger King* next to the exit stood open, so presumably, he'd been in there.

Through the fog of his panic, Iris dimly recalled the restaurant having an on-street entrance, too. Maybe if he headed through there, he could still get out.

He started towards it, then stopped again when two men in ill-fitting Santa suits appeared in the doorway, blocking it.

"Why aren't the doors opening?" asked a woman near the front of the would-be leavers. "I need to get out."

"You can't," the man said. "Sorry. I'm really... I'm so sorry."

There was a hoarseness to his voice, like the words had to scrape their way up through his throat. He looked apologetically at the people standing by the doors.

They didn't seem to see it, but Iris did. Iris could see.

He could see the fear in the security manager's eyes. He could see the defeat in the shape of his shoulders, and the shame in the lines of his face.

He could see the lies, all jagged, and prickly, and pulsating in shades of purple and black, as they came tumbling out of his mouth.

"Something's happened. Um, out front. Outside. There's been..."

He glanced back at the *Burger King* doorway, and the two Santas stared back in silence.

"There's been a security incident," he said. "Police have asked us to stay inside and wait for their signal."

"A security incident?" asked someone else in the crowd. "Oh, God, it's not one of those van attack things, is it? Where they drive into crowds?"

"Oh, Jesus. It's not, is it?" gasped a woman near the back.

Another voice piped up. "It's happened at Christmas before. Germany, I think. Awful."

"Shite, yes. Is anyone hurt? Have they caught him? What's happening?"

The security manager raised his hands, trying to hold on to the group's rapidly evaporating sense of calm.

"We don't know, exactly. We've just been asked to get everyone upstairs and off this level. I'm told..." He stole another glance at the Santas. "I'm *promised* that it'll all be over soon, and we have nothing to worry about."

"No signal!" a man in the crowd announced. "My phone. I've got no signal. No bars. Nothing."

"They do that, don't they?" a woman replied. She sounded breathless, and quite excited by the whole thing. "The police. If there's a terrorist attack. They shut down the phone networks, don't they?"

"I think she's right," another voice concurred. "I've heard that's what they do."

"Mine's down, too."

"And mine!"

"Is that what's happened?" the first man asked. "Is that why I can't get anything?"

The security manager swallowed. Blinked. Shrugged. Shook his head. Each movement followed directly on from the one before, like they were all part of some pre-planned sequence.

"I don't know," he admitted. "Maybe. If we could just... If you could all just head up the stairs or the escalators..."

"My son's out there!" an older woman cried. "He's out there somewhere with his dad! What if something's happened? What if they've been hurt?"

The security manager flinched at the way her voice broke towards the end of her outburst. He offered her the most reassuring smile he could muster, though it wasn't up to much.

"They'll be fine," he said. "Nobody's hurt. Nobody's in danger."

A ripple of confusion passed through the group. Over by the *Burger King* doors, the two Santas set down their sacks.

"Then... what's the problem? Why are we stuck in here, if there's no danger outside?"

The security manager tugged at his collar, like he was trying to cool down by getting some air in about him. Judging by the beads of sweat on his brow, though, it didn't help.

"I don't... It's just... The police, they said we needed to..."

A large, bald man took a step towards the door and gave it a shove. His neck, cheeks, and forehead all bore crudely drawn tattoos that could only have been done by himself, or as part of some bizarre assault. No way anyone was paying for them, anyway. He looked, Iris thought, like his old school desk.

"Just open the doors and let us out, then," the guy grunted. "Stop pissing about and let us go. You can't keep us here."

"Listen, please, I just... The police said."

"Fuck the police!" the tattooed man barked, spinning to face the security manager. "Now, open this door, before I use your face to break the fucking—"

The poster covering the door behind him was suddenly spattered with reds, and pinks, and lumpy blobs of goo.

At first, thanks to all the tattoos on the man's face, Iris didn't notice the ragged red circle on the left side of the big man's forehead. It was only when a rivulet of blood pumped out and ran down the side of his face that it all made sense.

The crowd, shocked into silence, stepped back as the tattooed man dropped to his knees, then fell forwards so his face slapped against the vinyl tiles of the floor.

Iris' whole body locked on him, his arms pinned to his sides, his head sinking down between his shoulders, like it was trying to take cover inside his chest. He shuffled around, frozen like that, until he could see the man in the Santa suit standing just a few feet behind him and to his right.

He held an FNX-45 Tactical handgun in his right hand, a suppressor fitted to muffle the sound of the bang.

He'd pulled down his beard, revealing a face that even a mother would struggle to love. Not because of the burn-like scarring that had marked much of his skin, but because of the expression he wore—hatred and contempt made up most of it, but there was a gleeful, sneering sort of arrogance to it, too, which was where the true horror lay.

He was smiling, his eyes ablaze with excitement as he watched blood pooling beneath the head of the man he'd shot.

Iris' gaze crept down to the open sack on the floor beside the gunman. He could see other weapons in there. A *lot* of other weapons.

In the *Burger King* doorway, the other two Santas produced firearms of their own from their sacks. Another silenced handgun—a *Beretta*, this time—and, even more worryingly, a *Brügger & Thomet* submachine gun. The latter weapon was Swiss-made. The Santa holding it, going by his accent, came from even further afield.

"Any of you motherfuckers scream, and you're all dead!" he barked. The accent was from somewhere in the old Soviet Bloc, Iris reckoned, but oddly American sounding, too, like he'd learned his English from Hollywood movies.

Accent or not, his warning did the trick. The crowd backed away from the men with the weapons, sobbing and whimpering, but not screaming. Not daring to.

Down on the floor, the man with the holes in his head let out a low death rattle, then farted loudly and pissed himself, as all the muscles in his body fully relaxed for the very last time.

"You didn't have to do that!" the security manager said, his voice wobbling as he stared down at the dead man on the floor. "I could've stopped him! I could've sorted it!"

"Shut the fuck up," the shooter said.

There was no venom or anger to the way he spoke, but a calmness that was even more unsettling. This guy sounded American, born and bred, the words drawing out in a Deep South sort of drawl.

"You just... You didn't have to..."

The gun was raised so it pointed directly at the security manager's face.

"Shut. The. Fuck. Up. Your job here is not to talk back to me, buddy. Your job is to do what I tell you, when I tell you. Is that clear?"

The security man's gaze flitted back to the man on the floor, then across to the huddled crowds cowering against the blacked-out windows.

Finally, he looked past where Iris and the shooter stood, to where the sounds of sobs and cries echoed around the rest of the centre.

This was happening everywhere. The whole building. Every part of it, all at once.

"Yes," the security man croaked. "Yes, that's clear."

"Well, alright!" The Santa with the burned face lowered his weapon. "Right now, your job is to keep all these people alive. How do you do that? Easy-peasy. You do that by making sure they keep their mouths shut and do what I tell them. If they do, if they behave and follow orders, they'll all have one hell of a story to tell over Christmas dinner."

He cast his gaze across the group, letting it linger on those who looked like they might pose him problems.

"Round up the cattle," he instructed, waggling his gun carelessly in the direction of the terrified crowd. "Bring them upstairs. Nice and calm."

His smile broadened, showing a mouth full of more gaps than teeth. The stumpy pegs that remained were yellow and brown, and stuck out from his gums like headstones of the long-forgotten dead.

"Then, we'll explain exactly what will happen if they *don't* behave."

The Santas in the doorway surged forwards, guns raised, barking orders. Iris turned his good eye towards the doors of the other stores on this level, where cowering, stooped-over shoppers were being marched towards the central staircase by armed Santas and men in security uniforms.

There were at least a dozen men with weapons that Iris could see in this one section alone. Whatever was happening, the centre's security team was in on it, as several of those had snaffled firearms from the Santas' sacks, and were using them to herd the sobbing crowds up towards the floor above.

Or, more likely, Iris thought, whoever had organised this whole thing had swapped out the security staff with their own guys. That meant this was big. This—whatever this was—had taken some serious planning and preparation. These guys clearly weren't amateurs.

He realised then that there was a gun being pointed at his face. He tried to focus on the end of it, but it was too close, so it remained a blur.

The same, unfortunately, could not be said for the face of the man holding it. This close up, Iris got a proper look at the scarring, though he wished he hadn't. It looked like an acid burn had completely ravaged the skin on the left side of his face. It had twisted up the fat and muscle, which explained his permanent sneer.

He was missing his eyelids on that side of his face, and the eye itself had a milky look to it that suggested he saw out of it about as well as Iris saw out of his glass one.

Iris almost felt sorry for the poor bastard, right up until the point that he spoke.

"Are you fucking listening to me?"

"Eh, no," Iris admitted. Then he blurted, "I mean, I wasn't just then, but I am now, obviously. Sorry. You were saying?"

The gunman regarded him curiously for several seconds. Around them, his fellow Santas ushered the stumbling hostages towards the stairs.

And then, all of a sudden, the muzzle of the gun was pressed against Iris' forehead.

"I could kill you. I killed that guy. You saw that. Right, boy?" the scarred Santa asked.

Iris almost pointed out that he was older than the gunman by quite a number of years, so the 'boy' comment didn't really make sense. He decided, though, that it probably wasn't the best time.

"I saw it, yeah. It was quite a good shot, actually," Iris said.

"Why, *thank you*. I been practising." The gun was pressed harder against Iris' head, until either metal or bone gave a faint *creak*. "You want me to shoot you, too?"

"Um... God. Wow." Iris blew out his cheeks. "I mean... there's a question. When do you need to know?"

The look of curiosity tipped over into confusion. "What?"

"I mean, do I have to tell you now, or can I think on it?" Iris asked.

"Are you trying to be fucking funny?" the Santa demanded.

"No. No, I'm just... Sorry. You asked a question, and I just thought... You know, it's a big one. It's probably *the* big one, isn't it? I don't think you should rush into these things, you know?" Iris babbled. "Like, maybe if you'd asked me a couple of months ago, I'd have said, 'Yeah, sure, go for it. Might as well. Not like I've got anything else on.' But that was before the house, and Boggle, and then, you know, Bamber was there, and it was nice to see him, and I got to blow stuff up, and all that, so... I just...."

He shrugged and huffed out a big breath, as if to stress the difficulty of the decision he was being asked to make.

"Can you give me half an hour to think about it?"

The man with the gun appeared to have no response to that. No verbal response, at least. But his finger went tight on the trigger, and the rotten pegs of his teeth clamped together in the twisted line of his mouth.

Something *bleeped* inside his suit, and his finger relaxed. He reached in through the opening at the front, took out a phone, and checked the screen.

Then, stepping back, he waved the pistol, gesturing for Iris to follow the others.

"Up the stairs," he muttered, his attention now split between his phone and his prisoner. "Get up the stairs with the rest of them."

Iris nodded, gave a thumbs up, then trotted ahead until he'd caught up with the panicked masses, and let himself be swallowed by their ranks.

Back near the door, the scarred-faced Santa raised his voice to a shout, glowered at a couple of men in security uniforms, then waggled his gun in the direction of the dead man on the floor.

"Someone drag that piece of shit upstairs," he commanded. "And let's use him to make an example."

CHAPTER SEVEN

TUCKED AWAY in the disabled bathroom, Hoon gave the toilet another flush, and watched glumly as it failed to clear for a third time.

"Jesus fucking Christ," he muttered. "Why's that no' going anywhere?"

He gave the cistern a slap, ordered it to sort its shit out—literally—and then he grabbed the big paddle-like lever with both hands, so he could really put his back into the fourth flush.

The cistern gurgled as it finished refilling, but just as Hoon prepared to push down on the lever, he heard a raised voice from out in the corridor. It was a man. He sounded Russian. He also sounded royally pissed off.

"Do as you are fucking told, all of you, and nobody gets hurt. Fucking shut up. No crying! Move! Move!"

"The fuck?" Hoon muttered.

Abandoning the clogged toilet, he crept over to the door and listened. There was movement outside. People rushing right past the door. Muffled sobs. Stifled cries. Distant shouts from somewhere deeper inside the shopping centre.

The brass band had stopped, he realised. He'd been forced

to listen to them while sitting there on the toilet, their tuneless trumpeting barely drowned out by his own.

Now, though, they had fallen silent.

The Russian voice came again, from right on the other side of the door this time.

"I said *move*! Get upstairs. Do as you are told, or we shoot! Children first!"

There was some crying—a woman, he thought—then the *crack* of a slap, and an attempt at silence.

Another voice cut in from further back along the corridor, closer to where the main toilets were. This one also belonged to a man, but the accent was French.

"You see what happens? Get up top, or we fucking kill you. Or worse!"

Hoon stepped back from the door, took out his phone, and checked the screen. Up the top, where the bars of the signal strength indicator should be, was a small X.

"Fuck's sake!" he tutted.

He gave it a shake to see if that would fix it. He rapped his knuckles on the back of it, but quietly, so as not to draw the attention of the men outside.

When those failed to summon any sort of signal, he took the nuclear option.

He turned it off and back on again.

Still nothing.

"Fuck's *sake*," he said again, but with slightly different emphasis this time, so as to keep things interesting.

This couldn't just be the snow, could it? The signal in the Eastgate was never great, but it was never non-existent.

But if it wasn't the weather blocking the phone's reception, then that presented him with a truly horrifying prospect.

Maybe Iris was right.

Maybe that mono-eyed fucking headcase was actually onto something for once.

"No," Hoon whispered. "No, I'm not having that. No way he's actually fucking correct on something."

It had to be the weather, that was all. That was why he couldn't call for help.

Of course, he wouldn't need to. Shopping centres and big public places like this all had protocols in place for this sort of thing these days. An alarm would already be going off somewhere at the Burnett Road Police Station. Jack Logan and his wee team of minions would probably be fucking creaming themselves with excitement right about now.

All Hoon had to do was sit tight and wait for the cavalry to arrive.

That was all. Just sit there and bide his time.

He didn't have to get involved. He shouldn't. He had quite a comfortable wee hidey-hole here, after all. Running water, space to stretch out—even toilet facilities, albeit partially blocked.

There was absolutely no reason—no fucking reason whatsoever—for him to open that door.

He closed the lid of the toilet, took a seat, and crossed one leg over the other.

There was no point in him getting involved. None.

If he went out there, he might get someone hurt or killed.

Very possibly himself.

And for what?

If this was some sort of hostage situation, then there was absolutely no reason why it couldn't end peacefully, just as long as everyone kept their heads down, did as they were told, and didn't do anything stupid, or do anything to anger the...

Hoon groaned.

"Aw, fuck!"

He sighed and rose to his feet, aware now why he couldn't just stay here until help arrived.

Aware of the one thing that would inevitably fuck up this whole situation for everyone.

"Berta."

"Right, then. Which one of you bastards is in charge?"

A young man in an Eastgate Centre security uniform blinked frantically, like he'd had sand thrown in his face, then drew back from the woman in the tweed coat who'd just come thundering towards him.

Things had gone relatively smoothly down his end of the centre. They'd spread word of an 'incident' outside, and had encouraged everyone downstairs to head to the upper floor and wait.

They were herded into the long stretch of the centre that ran from *Boots* at one end, to *Next* at the other. It was lined with shops on both sides and, crucially, had no windows, so nobody could see out.

And, more importantly, nobody could see in.

Packed in close together, they filled around a third of the space, and were stopped just past *Starbucks* by another row of security guys.

It had all gone surprisingly smoothly, but then people had started to flood in from the other direction, and it was immediately clear that things were no longer going to plan.

This lot were wide-eyed and sobbing, hugging each other, stumbling along, breathless and terrified.

There were kids in the mix, too. There weren't supposed to be kids. Kids were supposed to be in school. But a whole squad of them—twenty or more—came around the corner by *HMV* together, their faces wet with tears. A bearded teacher shuffled behind them, arms spread wide, like he could shield them all with his body.

"Hello? Anyone home?"

Bony knuckles rapped against his forehead, drawing him

back to his more immediate concern.

"Um, yes. Sorry. I mean..." He shook his head and drew down his eyebrows into a scowl. "What do you want?"

"I want to know who's in fucking charge here," Berta demanded. "Because I'm going to go out on a limb and say it isn't fucking you."

"What? I don't..."

"What's your name, lad?" Berta asked.

He blinked again. "What?"

"Your *name*! You do have a name, yes? Or did your parents decide that you weren't worth the fucking bother? Because, frankly, I wouldn't blame them."

"It's Mark," the young security man said, then his eyes widened in shock and he shook his head. "No. It's..." He hesitated, just for a moment, like he was struggling to bring himself to say the word. "Shaggy."

Berta's nostrils flared, like she'd just smelled something unpleasant.

"I beg your fucking pardon?"

"Shaggy," he said, doubling down. "It's... I'm Shaggy. Shaggy Goat."

"What sort of shite are you blethering, lad?" Berta demanded. "That's not a name. It's an adjective and a fucking noun."

"That's what I have to... I was... Just..." The young man sniffed and stood a little taller, trying to scrape back an ounce or two of authority. "Shaggy Goat. It's a codename. That's what you can call me."

Berta crossed her arms over the front of her big coat. Her tongue wiggled around inside her mouth like she was tasting every letter of the name.

Finally, she shook her head.

"No. I'm not calling you that," she decided. "It's fucking ridiculous. I'll call you Mark."

Panic flashed across his face, and his eyes shot over to the other security men, then to the four men in Santa suits who stood at the fringes of the crowd.

"Please don't," he said, his voice becoming a strained whisper. "Don't call me that. Please."

Berta's eyes narrowed, then they retraced the route that the security man's gaze had just taken.

"Why? What is this?" she asked. "What's going on?"

The man calling himself Shaggy Goat stood up a little straighter again. He spoke more confidently now, like he was back on more familiar ground.

"As we've explained, ma'am, there's been a security incident outside. The police have asked us to make sure that everyone stays—"

Berta flapped a hand at him. "That's quite enough of that. I know the sound shite makes, sunshine, and I'm hearing it coming out of your mouth right now," she said. "What's really happening here? What's actually going on? Why are all those maudlin fuckers up the far end crying? I want to talk to whoever's in charge."

Shaggy Goat swallowed. His gaze darted wildly again, then he met her eye, and lowered his voice so that nobody else might hear.

"Trust me," he said. "You don't. You really, *really* don't."

"I'll be the fucking judge of that, *Shag*," Berta replied.

"Shaggy," he corrected.

Berta shot him a warning look. "You'll take what you're given. It's Shag or Mark, you choose. No skin off my fucking nose, either way."

"Uh, Shag, then."

"Good. So, *Shag*, like I said, I'll be the judge of who I want to speak to. And I want to speak to whichever of you bastards is in charge."

Shaggy let out a wobbly sort of gasp, and took a big backward step away from Berta.

"Then you're in luck," he muttered, standing to rigid attention. "Because here he comes now."

Berta turned in the direction the lad was looking. At first, it was hard to see what he was staring at. The crowd of people in this section of the centre had more than doubled. It didn't quite reach all the way to *Next*, but it wasn't a kick in the arse off it.

"Who am I meant to be looking at?" she asked, scanning the crowd. She finally settled on a red hat with a white fur lining, and watched as a beardless Father Christmas climbed up onto a bench halfway along the concourse. "The ugly fucker in the Santa suit?"

Beside her, Shaggy nodded in an absent-minded sort of way that suggested she was no longer his main concern.

Up on the bench, the Santa turned slowly, looking out across the heads of his captive audience. His mouth was pulled into a lop-sided smile, like he was *quite* pleased with what he saw, but not delighted.

He was holding something in his left hand. It wasn't until he raised it to his mouth that Berta realised it was a radio or walkie-talkie of some kind.

"Hello? Hello? Is this on?"

She heard him directly at first, then again a fraction of a second later through the same speaker system that had, until just a few minutes ago, been blasting out Christmas hits.

"Can everyone hear me?" He shot a questioning look out at the crowd, but got no response. His smile spread further across his face as he brought the radio back to his mouth. "Come on, y'all, don't be scared. Speak up, now."

"Christ, a fucking American. As if things weren't bad enough already," Berta muttered, then she raised her voice to a shout. "Yes, we can hear you. Now, get on with it. What's all this about?"

A ring of empty space appeared around her, as everyone who had been standing nearby shuffled further away, making it clear she wasn't with them.

The Santa on the bench raised a hand above his eyes, shielding them from the lights as he searched for whoever had spoken.

When he finally settled on Berta, he regarded her in silence for a few seconds, then pointed at her and gave her a thumbs up.

"Thank you, old woman at the back," he said into the radio, and the words echoed around the concourse. "Very good question. I'm going to get to that in just a moment. But first, I need to make sure that everyone is paying close attention."

He made a beckoning motion behind him, and a couple of men in Santa suits began moving through the crowd. Yelps, and cries, and screams rose up as people raced to get out of their way and clear a path.

"Something very unfortunate happened downstairs," the lead Santa said. He sniffed, and ran a sleeve across his eyes. When he continued, his voice wobbled, but it was a bad parody of grief, and nothing like the real thing. "Someone didn't do as they were told. Someone thought they knew better."

Behind him, the two Santas drew closer, and Berta saw that they were carrying something. The sound of crying was spreading through the crowd like a virus now. Some people were shielding their eyes or burying their faces in their hands, while others just stood frozen, staring in horror and disbelief.

The bearded teacher was trying to pull all the children to him, to turn them away from whatever was passing just a few feet in front of them. The Santa on the bench noticed this, and brought the radio back to his mouth.

"Eyes open," he instructed. "I want everyone to see this."

"Please. Please, they're kids," the teacher begged. "They're just kids."

The Santa's right hand reached into his big red coat, then

emerged holding his silenced pistol. He pointed it at the group, letting his aim wander lazily from child to child.

"They watch, or they die. I'm gonna go ahead and let you decide on which."

"Oh, God! Oh, God! No, no! OK, OK!"

The teacher frantically turned the pupils back to face the man with the gun, but pulled them in close, his arms around the shoulders of as many of them as he could reach.

"It's going to be OK. It's going to be fine," he assured them, though the crack in his voice didn't really sell the promise.

"That's right! You kids listen to your teacher!" Santa said. He twirled the gun on his finger like a cowboy from an old Western, then went back to addressing the crowd at large. "Like the man says, everyone is going to be just fine. Nobody is going to get hurt. Not unless they ask for it. And y'all look like a bright, sensible bunch, who ain't gonna cause us no trouble."

He returned the gun to the inside of his coat, then put a hand on his heart, lowered his head, and sighed theatrically.

"I just wish I could've said the same for this fella right here."

With some difficulty, the two other men in Santa suits hoisted a third figure up into the air, so his head was visible to most of the assembled audience.

Or what was left of his head, anyway. The front was mostly intact, though streaks of blood marked it like war paint.

He was turned around slowly, like he was being presented at auction, and Berta's lips pursed tightly when she saw that the back of his head was almost entirely absent.

Those around her—the ones who had, despite the threats, and the guns, somehow still been under the illusion that the security guards' cover story was legitimate—were not quite as stoic in their reactions.

They surged, stumbling and screaming, trying to get clear, get away, get safe, only to find a wall of armed resistance behind them.

"Nobody fucking move!"

"Face front! Look at him, not at me!"

"Stop fucking screaming!"

Unsurprisingly, none of this had the calming effect the security men had presumably been hoping for, and fear surged through the crowd, turning it from a lot of distinct individuals to one big panicked animal.

Two shots rang out, the sound thundering off the windows of the shops on either side of the concourse. The window of a clothes store exploded into fragments, sending everyone around it ducking for cover, and filling the centre with their screams.

A wall of men with weapons blocked every exit, staring the crowd down, barking at them to get back. To stand still. To face front, or face the fucking consequences.

The animal panic was still there, still raging through the hostages, still palpable in the air, but the sight of all those guns cut through the terror, and the instinct for survival proved stronger. With some prompting and cajoling, the huddled masses gradually turned back to the man with the radio.

"Thank y'all for making the smart choice. Running? Well, that ain't gonna work out well for anyone," he drawled.

He waved the back of his hand at the other two Santas, and they set off, dragging the corpse back through the crowd. They looked around for somewhere to dump the body, then settled on the doorway to *Vision Express*.

"OK, so, getting down to business," their leader continued. "Today, my name is Santa Prime. In the highly unlikely chance that any of you needs to address me directly, then that's what y'all can call me."

His tongue flicked out, licking across his scarred lips. His smile widened. Clearly, he was enjoying this.

"And, I'm sure all you fine folks are wondering just exactly what the hell is going on…"

CHAPTER EIGHT

HOON LURKED JUST inside the bathroom door, gripping the handle, listening to the voice ranting over the PA system. The sound was being piped all through the centre, by the sounds of it, including through a speaker mounted in the ceiling directly above the toilet.

From what he could gather so far, at least one man was dead, and some shots had been fired. By the sounds of it, the terrorists were well-armed.

They were serious, then, whoever they were. Organised, too, if they'd managed to take the whole centre like this. That sort of thing took planning and resources. It took brains.

Something about that wasn't sitting right with him, though, because the man currently talking over the PA system sounded like he was the result of several generations of unchecked inbreeding.

"This here. All this that's happening right now, it ain't about you. It ain't about any of you," he said, his voice hissing a little through the speaker. "It's about money. Plain and simple. They got it, we want it, and you folks are how we're gonna get it."

He paused for a moment to let them think on that, and Hoon

heard enough muffled sobs to tell him there were a *lot* of hostages up there.

"Y'all don't need to panic about nothing," the voice from the speaker continued. "Long as everyone sits tight and does as they're told, and as long as we get what we came for, then all you folks'll be tucked up in your beds back home by nightfall, none the worse for wear. That's a promise. That's a goddamned pinky swear."

Hoon pressed an ear to the door and listened for any movement out in the corridor. The gents' and ladies' bathrooms were out the door and to his left, and beyond those was a dead end.

There were lifts on his right, but if this place was locked down, then they had to have someone up in the security room watching the camera feeds. If he jumped in a lift, they'd see him immediately, and an assortment of armed bastards would almost certainly be waiting to riddle him with holes when the doors *pinged* open.

"Now, I'm gonna be honest with y'all," the voice from the speaker continued. "The police, they're gonna send people to talk us down. They're gonna try to *negotiate*."

He snorted out that last word, like it amused him.

"But we ain't here to negotiate. We ain't gonna broker a deal. We're just here to get what we came for. That's all. No more, no less."

There was something gleeful behind his words, Hoon thought. Like he was struggling to contain his laughter.

"Now, don't y'all worry. See, the police, they'll figure out sooner or later that there's only one way this ends, and they'll give us exactly what we want. And, once they do, then, good news, it's Merry fucking Christmas for all of us. You folks get to go on home, we get to take our money and go buy ourselves a nice tropical island somewhere, and everyone lives happily ever after."

"Aye, that'll be fucking right," Hoon muttered, still listening at the door.

"It might'n not feel like it right now, but I promise y'all that someday—someday not too far in the future—today's just gonna be one hell of a story you get to tell at parties. All y'all will be able to tell folks that you were here. Right here. Right now. Right in the goddamn thick of it. Right on the front fucking lines of a moment in history."

The guy clearly liked the sound of his own voice, which was one way in which he and Hoon very much differed. Hoon had heard quite enough from the fucker and, once he was reasonably confident there was nobody lurking outside, he pushed the door open a crack and peered out into the corridor beyond.

To his left, as expected, the hallway was empty all the way to where it stopped at the far wall.

Twenty feet or so on his right, the corridor opened up onto the circular food court area. If he headed that way and hung a left, there would be a door leading outside. But, since the terrorists, or hostage-takers, or whatever the fuck they were, seemed to have full control of the centre, the exits would be locked down. Probably guarded, too.

He knew from experience that there were a lot of ways in and out of the building. A dozen different doors across multiple levels, from the underground car park and loading bays, to the roof four storeys above.

In fact, there were probably far more than a dozen ways in. If they had any hope of keeping control of the place, they'd have to have secured all of them, along with the security station up on the top floor.

Christ, this thing must be huge.

Out in the corridor, the voice from the speakers was louder and boomed as it echoed off the narrow walls.

"Here are the rules. They aren't difficult, so I want y'all to memorise them," the American announced. "Rule number one, you do what we say, when we say it. No questions. No whining.

No backtalk. We say, you obey. Simple as that. If you step out of line, if you fail to do what we tell you, then you pick out one of these here little kiddies to watch die. You will look them straight in their eyes as I blow their brains clean out of their adorable fucking skulls, and then I'll do the same to you, and anyone you came here with. Anyone you care about. Anyone you love."

Hoon's stomach did a full flip.

Kids. They had kids.

Shite.

"Rule number two, do not try to contact anyone on the outside. You can't. It's pointless. We already took care of that."

Hoon checked his phone. The little 'x' where the signal strength should be was still there, taunting him.

"But if we see you so much as try, then there are gonna be consequences. Y'all want to know what those consequences are? That's easy. See rule number one."

Hoon opened the door a little further, then quickly shut it again when he heard footsteps approaching. He left just a crack to look through, and watched as a man dressed in a cheap Santa coat and matching hat went strolling past the entrance to the corridor, a sawn-off shotgun resting on his shoulder.

He whistled cheerfully as he walked—a flat, yet piercing rendition of some Christmas hit or other that Hoon couldn't quite place. Whatever it was, he was mangling every note.

Still, it wasn't anything by Cliff Richard, so small mercies...

"Rule number three," the redneck on the PA system continued. "Respect works both ways. Me and my boys here, we got a job to do, same as anyone. Like I said, none of this shit is personal. We don't have nothing against any of you folks. Y'all just happened to be in the wrong place at the wrong time. We're aware that none of you asked for this, so, we're gonna treat you folks as fair as we can. We're gonna go out of our way to do right by y'all."

The suggestion of humour in his voice died away, and the

next few sentences came out as a warning.

"But that's a two-way street. Me? I got broad shoulders. I can take it. But, I hear you disrespecting my boys? I hear you talking shit about them? Well, then we're all the way back to rule number one."

Hoon waited until the guy with the shotgun had passed, then widened the gap in the door just enough so he'd be able to slip out through it.

There was a camera on the ceiling further along on the left, but this corridor was unlikely to be a hotspot for criminal activity at the best of times, so it probably wasn't being monitored live. There were scores of such cameras all around the inside and outside of the centre, and nowhere near enough screens in the security room to watch them all at once.

He'd been through the centre plenty of times before, both out front and behind the scenes. The emergency services used the place for training exercises every couple of years, simulating everything from active shooters to towering infernos.

Funnily enough, though, a hostile takeover by Father Christmas had never been one of the chosen scenarios.

"Now, this fourth rule might not seem as important as the first three..."

"Fuck's sake, is that prick still going?" Hoon muttered, sticking his head out through the gap in the door. He could still hear footsteps, but further away now. Still, if the guy with the shotgun was walking a circuit, he could reach the doors and double back into view at any moment.

"And, I guess it ain't," the American continued. "But I wanted to throw it out there for y'all to think about. Rule number four—try and have some fun. I'm sure it ain't every day all your humdrum, run-of-the-mill, pointless little lives get caught up in exciting shit like this. Try to *enjoy* it. I mean, hell, I know I am!"

Hoon slipped out of the bathroom, and eased the door closed

just far enough that it rested on the latch, and didn't shut all the way. If he needed to dive back in there, he could. If things got crazy and out of hand, and he needed somewhere to hole up, then at least he'd have—

The weight of the door proved too much for the latch, and it shut itself fully with a definite *clunk*.

"*Fuck!*" Hoon hissed.

So much for that plan.

Out there on his right, beyond where the corridor opened up into the ground level of the shopping centre, the footsteps scuffed to an abrupt stop, and the tuneless whistling died away into silence.

Hoon tried the door behind him, just on the off-chance that it hadn't completely screwed him over.

It had. Of course it had. Just his fucking luck.

The footsteps returned, but they were growing louder this time. Getting closer, moving faster, picking up the pace.

He thought about running to the toilets along the corridor and taking cover in there, but they were too far away. There wasn't time. He'd be seen. He'd be shot.

The lifts, then? No. Even if there was one there waiting for him, the same problems as earlier applied. He'd be spotted right away. He'd be dead the moment he reached the next floor.

The redneck was still droning on, but Hoon wasn't listening. All he could hear were those footsteps, and the faint *clack* of a shotgun being taken down from a shoulder.

There were two vending machines directly across from the disabled toilets—one for drinks, one for snacks. The gap between them was narrow, but it was his only chance.

Hoon launched himself across the corridor, turning sideways as he ran, and squeezed himself into the narrow space between the two machines just as the *squeak* of shoes on polished floor reached the opening of the corridor, and a man with a sawn-off shotgun silently surveyed the scene.

CHAPTER NINE

THE MAN with the burned face turned on the spot, addressing every corner of his captive audience. Only around half of them were watching him, the other half cowering away, shielding their loved ones with their bodies, or just avoiding his gaze for fear it might settle on them for too long.

He didn't mind. Looking at him wasn't necessary. He wasn't about to demand that. They were listening, that was the main thing. Even over their pathetic sobs and whimpers, they were hanging on his every word.

"Here's what's going to happen," Santa Prime announced, raising his voice to really hammer home the importance of this next part. "Y'all are gonna wait. You're going to stand or sit—but let's not be selfish and think about lying down, we just don't have the space for that—and you're going to wait. That's all you gotta do. Stand. Sit. Wait. *Quietly*."

He gave that last word a moment to sink in, and continued turning around, his gaze sweeping across the audience.

"I don't want to hear anyone complaining. I don't want to hear anyone asking to go to the bathroom. And I sure as shit don't want anyone saying they're hungry," he warned. "That shit ain't our problem. We ain't responsible for you. We ain't your babysitters, we're the badass motherfuckers who've taken you hostage. Do as y'all are told, and I guarantee your survival. But, I give zero fucks for your welfare. Is that clear?"

Nobody chimed in to confirm, which seemed to simultaneously please and anger him. He grinned, but he jerked the radio closer to his mouth and snarled into it.

"I can't hear you. Is that clear?"

There were a few gasps and cries of fright, but a general murmur of agreement came back to him from amongst the crowd of hostages.

"Good. That's music to my ears. Now, does anyone have any questions?"

There was a dangerous look in his eyes as his gaze swept across the crowd like a searchlight at a prison camp, hunting down the defiant.

Or the foolish.

"No, I didn't think—"

He stopped on a raised hand in the crowd. From the way his eyebrows met, it was clear he had not been expecting anyone to dare ask him anything.

"Yes, boy?" he spat, after a pause. "You have a question?"

At the edges of the crowd, Santas and security men alike bristled and adjusted their grips on their weapons, all eyes focused on the raised hand.

"Uh, yeah. Yeah, just a quick one."

At the other end of the concourse, upon hearing the Scouse accent, Roberta Hoon shut her eyes and sighed.

"Oh, for fuck's sake. I might have guessed."

Back along near *HMV*, under the shadow of the musical clock, Iris lowered his arm back down to his side.

"I was just wondering, and don't take this wrong way, or nothing, but what happened to your face?"

The man standing on the bench looked taken aback. He

touched a hand to his cheek, and for a moment, all his authority left him, and he stood there looking like a wee boy, all exposed and ashamed.

Only for a moment, though. The mask quickly slipped back on, and he drilled a glare into Iris like it could punch a hole clean through his head.

"What the fuck did you say to me?"

"Your face. I hope you don't mind me asking," Iris replied. "But what went on there?"

For a man who spent his days imagining danger around every corner, he appeared completely oblivious to the fact he was now staring it in the face.

"It's just it's pretty... I don't want to say 'fucked up,' because that might come across as rude, like. But, it's not nice. From our perspective down here, I mean. Looking on." He shrugged. "Don't get me wrong, like, I'm sure it isn't exactly a barrel of laughs from where you're standing, either, but..."

Iris became aware of a circle of space around him. People had been standing there just moments before, he thought, but now a perfect circle of exposed floor surrounded the spot where he stood.

"What?" he asked, looking at the faces of the people who'd backed away. Most of them didn't return the look, averting their gazes, instead. "He asked if anyone had any questions, so... I mean, we were all thinking it, right?"

He glanced around, seeking confirmation, but finding no one to back him up.

"No? Just me? Wow. I find that surprising," he said. "I thought we'd all be wondering, because it's so..." He shuddered, stuck out his tongue, and grimaced all at the same time. "*Ugh*! I mean, no offence, mate. It's not your fault, like. I just think, maybe, you know, put the beard back on, or something. Take the edge off it for us. I'm sure we'd all appreciate it. Right?"

He looked around again for backup, but the circle on the

floor had only grown wider. Iris now resembled an island, standing alone in a deep and dangerous ocean.

Santa Prime's boots smacked down on the vinyl flooring with a *thack* that made half of the gathered hostages jump. The crowd parted between him and Iris, who appeared increasingly confused by this response to what had been a perfectly innocent and genuine question.

The boots *squeaked* as the man in the Santa suit closed the gap between them. He still clutched the radio in his left hand. In his right, he held the gun that he'd used to threaten the school children with. The same one he'd pointed at Iris earlier.

"So, looks like you made your mind up, after all, boy," Santa Prime drawled. "I guess you decided you do want to die."

"What? Oh, no, I'm still going back and forth on that," Iris told him. "I need a bit more time, if that's alright?" He winced as the man with the gun drew closer, gritting his teeth in a sort of horrified sympathy. "Is that sore? It looks sore. I've seen guys with burns like that before. Not alive, though." He grimaced and shook his head, like he was trying to expel a thought from his head. "Well, not *all the way* alive. Not for long, anyway."

His one good eye went almost as glassy as the other one for a few moments, then he gave himself another shake and brightened.

"But, look at you! You seem to be doing alright with it! You've got yourself a little gang, and everything." Iris stared with absolute sincerity into the other man's eyes. "Can I touch it? Would that be weird?"

There was another glimpse of that vulnerability hidden between the scars of Santa Prime's face, then it was swept aside when he brought up the gun and pressed the silenced muzzle against Iris' forehead.

"Wait! Don't shoot! Hold your fucking horses," harrumphed a voice from the crowd.

Berta finished elbowing her way through the sea of hostages, and emerged into the still-widening clearing around Iris and Santa Prime.

"Sorry about him. He's simple," she announced, stopping beside the two men. A number of guns had turned to train on her, but she didn't appear to care. "Got the brains of a fucking door knob. He was dropped on his head as a child. Repeatedly. From a height."

"What? No, I wasn't!" Iris protested.

"Don't listen to him. His head's like a pound of fucking mince. Doesn't know what he's saying half the time, and believe me, the other half's not exactly worth writing home about, either. Absolute waste of fucking space."

Santa Prime's scarred forehead creased. He kept the gun trained on Iris, but shifted his gaze to the woman in the bulky tweed coat. "So, he's a friend of yours?"

"What? No. Christ, no, I cannot fucking abide him," Berta replied. "But, as his dear old mother always said, God rest her soul, 'He's more to be pitied than scolded.'"

"Since when did you know me mam?" Iris asked, but Berta steamrollered straight over the question.

"Would shooting him be a blessing for the poor, one-eyed, gormless fucker? Maybe. Maybe it would. Would it be better all-round if someone went ahead and finally—*finally*—did the decent thing and put him out of his misery? Put us *all* out of our misery, in fact, by which I mean everyone who's ever met the fucker?"

She wrinkled her nose and pursed her lips, then nodded.

"Probably, yes."

"Are you trying to talk me out of killing him, or talk me into it?"

Berta hesitated, like she wasn't quite sure, then she grunted and shrugged her broad shoulder. "I suppose what I'm saying is, why waste the bullet? He's a pain in the arse, aye, but he's harmless. And I'll make sure he keeps his fucking mouth shut from now on. He won't bother you again. If he tries, I'll throttle him for you myself."

Santa Prime looked from Berta to Iris and back again, his finger still on the trigger, his ravaged skin all contorted with contempt.

"He shouldn't have spoken to me like that," he said. "That shit can't be allowed to stand."

Berta drew in a deep breath. Then, she nodded, and patted Iris on the back.

"Ah well, can't say I didn't try."

She stepped back into the crowd, smoothed down her coat, then crossed her hands in front of herself, ready to watch the show.

"I mean, you're making a big mistake," she said. "But, whatever you think yourself, son. You're in charge. Just you fire away."

Santa Prime pressed the muzzle of the gun more forcefully against Iris' forehead. Iris' good eye looked up at the weapon, while the glass one continued to stare straight ahead.

He didn't pull the trigger, though. Not yet. Instead, he turned to look at Berta.

"What do you mean, it's a big mistake?" he demanded, his eyes narrowing.

"Oh, come on. Fucking think about it," Berta replied. "You shoot him, what happens? To this lot, I mean? Look at them, they're already halfway through shitting themselves inside out. What happens if you kill him now? They'll stampede like a herd of fucking cattle, that's what.

"Aye, you've got guns, but it's not going to be easy to fire when your skull's being trampled into the floor." She gave another shrug. "And aye, sure, maybe you'll get them back under control eventually. Maybe you'll kill enough of them to restore order. But I'm guessing the whole thing would be a big fucking inconvenience all round. Right? You look like you've got a plan.

Do you really want to throw that all away for this empty-headed jug of rat's piss?"

"Steady on, Berta," Iris protested.

"Give me your eye," Santa Prime said, his mouth contorting upwards into the beginnings of a snigger.

Iris blinked. "My eye? What do you mean?"

"I want your eye," the man with the gun told him. "For talking to me like that. That can't go unpunished. Your lady friend's right, though. I don't want to shoot you. Not here. Not right now. But I do want your eye. I'd say that's a fair compromise."

"Bit weird, though, innit?"

"Oh, just give him the fucking thing," Berta urged.

Iris glanced over at her, then around at all the faces of the people watching on. None of them made any move to help him. Many of them had turned completely away, but a few were watching, fascinated, to see what would happen next.

"Right. Fine!" Iris huffed. He pulled back from the gun, bent his head to the side, and began to extract the ball of coloured glass.

The gun was pressed against his temple. The hammer was drawn back.

"No," the man in the Santa suit drawled, and something wicked etched lines of glee into his disfigured face. "I meant the other eye."

"What?" Iris half-laughed, not understanding. "But that one's not glass. That one's..."

The penny dropped. He stopped fiddling with his glass eye, and turned as far as the gun would allow him to look at the man on the other end of it.

"Good one. Dead funny. You got me there, like."

"It isn't a joke, son. Give me your eye, or we go back to rule number one, and you pick one of them little kiddies to watch die. Then, I shoot your lady friend here."

"You can't do that!" Iris cried. "The kids, I mean. I'm not all that fussed about her. No offence, Berta."

"None taken. Believe me, the feeling's very much fucking mutual."

"Uh, sir?"

A man in a security uniform had been making his way through the crowd for the last few moments, and now arrived on the scene. He hung back from the man calling himself Santa Prime, and bowed his head slightly in deference.

"I'm busy right now, Private," Santa Prime said, all his attention still fixed on Iris.

"Uh, yes. I, um, I see that, sir. It's just... Well... It's just..."

He took a breath so deep it inflated his lungs and made his whole chest swell.

"We think we have a problem."

One of Santa Prime's eyes twitched.

"You *think* we have a problem?"

"We, um, we know we have a problem. Sir. It's, um... Well... We think you should see."

The gun remained pressed against Iris' temple. The tendons in the gunman's wrist *creaked* as he tightened his grip.

And then, with a grunt, he jerked the weapon away, and held it by his head, pointed upwards at the snow-covered skylights overhead.

"To be continued," he told Iris. "Y'all don't go nowhere."

And then, he spun on the heels of his polished black boots, and went stalking off through the crowd.

"Well," Iris breathed, once he was out of earshot. "He seems nice."

CHAPTER TEN

HE HELD HIS BREATH, though the space between the machines was even tighter than it had looked from across the corridor, so it wasn't like he had a lot of choice in the matter. The metal sides of each machine pressed against him, pinning him in place.

If he was spotted, there would be nothing he could do about it. Getting out of here quickly was going to be difficult.

Getting out while maintaining even a shred of dignity was going to be impossible.

"*Allo?*"

French accent. One of the guys he'd heard outside the bathroom door a few minutes earlier.

"Is there anyone there?"

The absurdity of the question almost made Hoon want to say, "No," just to see what would happen.

He didn't, of course. But he did take some comfort from the fact the question had even been asked in the first place.

The terrorists may have been able to lock down the entire shopping centre, but it was reassuring to know that at least one of them had the brains of a fucking cabbage.

The footsteps drew closer. Slowly. Warily. Sensing danger.

Hoon inched himself deeper into the gap, until his right shoulder was pressed up against the wall. There was nowhere else to go, but maybe, if he tucked himself in enough, the shadows would swallow him up.

Remaining hidden was his only chance. There was no way he could get out fast enough to launch an attack. The fucker would get off a couple of shots *and* have time to reload before Hoon could extract himself from his hidey-hole.

He saw movement. The Frenchman crept into view, shotgun held ready to fire. He was looking at the doors of the disabled toilets, though, so Hoon and the vending machines were behind him.

Stopping at the first of the two bathroom doors, he reached out with his left and tried the handle, keeping the shotgun trained with his right.

The handle gave a *thunk*. The door remained locked. Hoon watched, breath held, as the Frenchman pressed a button on the wall between the doors. A buzzer sounded, a moment passed, then a voice crackled out from a panel on the wall.

"Yeah, what?"

Whoever was up in the security room didn't sound best pleased about the interruption. He was Scottish—east end of Glasgow, or thereabouts—and Hoon got a clear mental image of a manky wee fuckwit of a ned.

"It's me," said the man with the shotgun. "It is *Père Noel*."

"Aye, I can see that. I can see you on the *hing*. What ye wanting?" the voice on the other end demanded.

"Can you open these doors?"

"Jesus Christ. You needing a shite? Seriously? Now?"

"Non. I want to check them," the man identifying as Père Noel replied. He, too, sounded irritated now, the neddy wee bastard's impatience proving infectious. "I don't know if they were checked in the roundup."

A grunt of exasperation was ejected from the speaker. Hoon half-expected it to be followed up with a rant of, 'I hate you! I wish I'd never been born!' but, instead, another buzzer sounded, and both bathroom doors unlocked.

Pére Noel turned the handle of the first door again, inched it open enough to slide the shortened barrel of the shotgun through the gap, then threw it wide with a shove from a big black boot.

"See anything?" crackled the voice from the wall.

Pére Noel checked inside the bathroom and behind the door, then let it close again.

"Non. That one's empty. One more."

The next door along was the one Hoon had been hiding behind. He watched from between the vending machines as the same process was repeated—the door was widened enough to let the gun lead the way, then the bathroom was checked for signs of life.

"Nothing," the Frenchman concluded.

"Right, well hurry up and get your arse around to the main doors. We've got a problem."

"What sort of problem?"

"We've got a crowd building up outside. Bunch of arseholes trying to get in, wondering what's going on. They're going to draw attention. Find that security prick—the manager guy—get a few of our boys out there with him, and get everyone telt tae get tae fuck."

Pére Noel shut the door and turned away so he was standing side-on to Hoon, still squeezed between the vending machines. Hoon had already been holding his breath, but somehow he found a way to hold it *more*.

"Since when did you give the orders?" the Frenchman asked.

"I'm no' giving the fucking orders, pal. This came fae the fucking big man. This came fae Santa Prime. You want tae fucking argue wi' him aboot it?"

Pére Noel gripped his shotgun, his fingers drumming on the

shortened barrel.

Then, after a moment, he shook his head.

"Non. I will go take care of it," he said, bringing the weapon back up so it rested on his shoulder.

"Aye. See that you fucking do."

The panel on the wall whined, like speaker feedback, then fell silent. The man calling himself Pére Noel muttered something in French, and set off along the corridor, back in the direction of the food court.

Hoon slowly exhaled as far as the heavy machines would allow, then froze again when he heard the Frenchman turning around.

There was a *bang* and a *crash* from the machine at his back. Fragments of glass hit Hoon like hail. It rattled against the other machine, and scattered across the polished vinyl floor.

Christ. What now?

It hadn't been a gunshot. It wasn't loud enough for that, and the damage would've been much more catastrophic at this range.

What, then?

Reflected in the dented metal of the freestanding unit in front of him, Hoon saw a warped, funhouse-mirror version of the Frenchman reaching inside the now glassless vending machine, and helping himself to a bottle of *Coke*.

"Don't mind if I do," Pére Noel muttered.

Then, without another word, he turned and crunched across the carpet of broken glass, and off into the centre proper.

"Fucking hell," Hoon whispered. He let his head rest against the machine in front of him for a moment. The cool metal was soothing, but the faint vibrations of the refrigerator motor soon spoiled the effect.

He needed to find somewhere to get his head together. He needed a place to make a plan. The disabled bathrooms were off the cards. Ironically, now they'd been searched, they were probably the safest place in the whole centre, but there was no way of getting inside them without buzzing the bastards upstairs and asking politely, and he was fairly sure he knew how that would end.

He'd managed to avoid detection where he was, but 'standing jammed between two heavy vending machines' wasn't a long-term solution to anything. Besides, now that one was broken, you could bet the other bastards would soon be at it like flies round shite. One of them would be bound to see him. He had to move, and fast.

Hoon cast his mind back to the training exercises he'd been involved in here before. It wasn't easy, because a lot had happened since then, including the consumption of a not-insignificant amount of alcohol.

And it wasn't like he'd been paying a lot of attention at the time, either. He'd been spending his days behind a desk at that point, dishing out orders. The likelihood of him being on the front lines of a live incident had been all but non-existent, so he'd sort of coasted through the training courses, paying them very little attention.

In hindsight, he was starting to wish he'd listened a bit more.

Or even just listened a bit.

He dimly recalled that the security cameras were largely confined to the customer-facing parts of the centre, and to a couple of the loading bays. Very few of the behind-the-scenes areas were monitored. Or not by cameras, anyway. Opening the doors would trigger a wee flashy light somewhere, but by the time anyone came to investigate, he'd be sure to be elsewhere. Other than that, and assuming the back corridors and stairwells weren't hoaching with big angry armed bastards, he should be able to move around relatively freely.

So, he had the beginning of a plan. He knew where he was going. That was something, at least.

Now, all that he had to do was figure out how the fuck he was going to get there.

CHAPTER ELEVEN

"YOU. WHAT IS NAME?"

The security manager, who was trying to steady his hand enough to slot a key into the locking mechanism of the automatic doors, didn't hear the question at first. It was only when the Russian caught him by the ear and yanked his head back that he realised it had been addressed to him.

"I said *what is name?*"

"Nigel! It's... it's Nigel!" the guard cried, fighting to keep his footing as the much larger man dragged him backwards.

"Nigel! *Da.* You look like a fucking *Nigel*. Little fucking *Nigel* face."

He twisted the ear, drawing a yelp of pain from the security man. This brought a sickly sort of smile to the Russian's lips.

He was dressed all in red, but had removed the white beard and hat he'd been hiding behind, revealing a face pitted with the scars of old teenage acne.

Although, Nigel thought, as he looked helplessly up the other man's flared nostrils, not *that* old. The brute couldn't have been out of his teens for more than four or five years. Most of that time, judging by the size of him, he'd spent lifting weights and living on a diet of anabolic steroids and raw steak.

"I bet you have little *Nigel* wife, yes? Little fucking uptight, nagging *Nigel* wife waiting at home? Lounging around all fucking day, leaving fucking dishes in sink? Making you make own dinner after hard day's work? Yes?"

Nigel kept his mouth shut. Partly because he didn't quite understand the line of questioning, but mostly because he was concerned about getting himself killed.

"*Yes*?!" the Russian bellowed, and the smell of cheap beer and expensive cigars was forcibly inserted up Nigel's nostrils.

"I'm divorced!" he replied. "I'm not... I don't have a wife."

"Ha!" This seemed to please the Russian. He released his grip on Nigel's ear, and slapped him so hard on a shoulder that he was sure he felt his spine go out of alignment. "This is good. Fuck that bitch, yes? Fuck your *whore* wife!"

Nigel rubbed the side of his head, and gently cleared his throat. He shot a look over to another Santa, who stood nearby with a sawn-off shotgun, watching the exchange through narrowed eyes.

If he was hoping the other one might offer some sort of backup, though, he was sorely disappointed.

"She, uh, she wasn't actually... It was mutual. The split. I wouldn't call her... I wouldn't say she was a... a... You know, a 'whore,' exactly..."

"Come on, Nigel. Don't be fucking pussy!" the Russian spat. "They are all whores. Every one of them. Yes? Yes?"

"He's right," the other Santa said, in a thick, French-sounding accent. He took a swig from a can of *Coke*, then tossed it onto the floor behind him. "All women, they are whores."

Nigel had always considered himself a bit of a feminist. He had two daughters, after all, so what sort of father would he be if he wasn't willing to fight for women's equality?

But fighting for it was one thing. Dying for it was quite another.

The Russian was so much bigger than he was, and had what looked to be quite a serious rifle slung over one bear-like shoulder. The Frenchman didn't have the same size advantage, but the shotgun he carried more than made up for that.

"Um, yes," Nigel said, coming to the conclusion that it was better to say goodbye to his principles than to the contents of his skull. "Yes. They're all... You know."

"*Whores.*"

"Yes. Exactly!"

The Russian grinned, showing a lot of squint teeth. "I like you, Nigel. Maybe I try and not kill you."

The security manager swallowed and smoothed down the front of his shirt. "Uh, well, I'd appreciate that."

"I am Ded Moroz." The man with the gun gestured down to his Santa suit. "*Grandfather Frost.* You like?"

"It's, um... Yes. It... it suits you."

Ded Moroz ejected a laugh that came all the way from his toes. "Ah, Nigel, you fucking spineless ball of shit! You are funny man!"

The laugh faded. The smile fell away. The Russian pointed to the locking mechanism Nigel had been trying to get his key into.

"Now, get out there and get rid of all those people outside."

Nigel looked down at his hand, and appeared surprised to see his keys there.

"Uh, right. Yes. But... what do I say?"

Ded Moroz slapped a big hand onto his shoulder again, but this time kept it there. He pulled Nigel in close against him, and lowered his voice to a growl.

"You will think of something," the Russian told him. "We have faith in our little Nigel. Don't we, Pére Noel?"

The Frenchman nodded. "Oui. We have total faith in our petit Nigel."

"What the fuck is the hold up here?"

The Frenchman straightened quickly, like he was snapping to attention.

Nigel was manhandled around by the Russian until they both saw Santa Prime storming across the food court towards them, a couple of security guard lackeys scuttling along behind him.

"No hold up," Ded Moroz said. He gave the security manager's shoulder a squeeze that drew a faint whimper of pain. "We are just giving Nigel here a little *pep talk*."

Santa Prime thudded to a stop just a pace or two away from Nigel, who was still trapped in the big Russian's hug.

"Oh, really? Well, we got a whole lot of inquisitive motherfuckers gathering outside, and we need them gone. So, how about this for a *little pep talk*, Nigel?"

He brought up his gun and aimed it between the security manager's eyes.

"Get the fuck out there and make them all go away."

"Uh, uh, yes. Yes. But... I mean... how?" Nigel squeaked. "What do I tell them?"

"You know, Nigel, I looked at your resume," Santa Prime announced.

The remark caught Nigel off guard, and he could only babble out a whispered, "What?" in response.

"When we were planning all this—when we were figuring it all out, getting all our little duckies in a row—I went through all your records. I wanted to get the measure of you. Get to know you. And on your resume, Nigel, I seem to recall you referring to yourself as 'a problem solver.' You put that in there as one of your strengths. Correct?"

"Um... Um, I don't remember."

Santa Prime's scarred face twisted in a sneer. "You got two little girls. You remember them?"

Nigel's face paled. "What?"

"*Do you remember your children, Nigel?!*" Santa Prime demanded, anger burning white hot behind his eyes.

"Yes! Yes! God. Yes, but please, please—"

"Good. So your memory works just fine. You're a problem solver, Nigel. You said so yourself, right there in black and white." Santa Prime pointed to the door with his gun. "So, get your ass out there, and solve our problem."

Nigel grimaced as the Russian squeezed his shoulder again, and then he was suddenly cast adrift, standing on his own two feet, the other man's bulk no longer holding him up.

He looked down at the keys in his hand again, then turned towards the door. The sound of the pistol's hammer drawing back made him stop.

"Out there, you're gonna feel the urge to do something stupid," Santa Prime said. "You'll feel like you can run. Like you can get away. Get somewhere safe, warn people, call the police. And, you know what? You're absolutely right. You could do those things. There ain't nothing we could do to stop you."

Nigel held his breath. Had the bastard been reading his mind?

"But we have a lot of innocent people in here, Nigel. And them? Well, they can't run. These people? In here? With us? They ain't going anywhere. Not without my say-so. Not a one of them. Not one man, not one woman, not one child. You run? You go? Then, I cannot guarantee that bad things will not start happening to them. *Real* bad things."

The voice was low and flat, yet the words seemed to echo around the vast cavern of the centre.

"So, when you go out there and you think about running, Nigel? You do them all a favour, and you think about *them*."

The voices berated him from all sides. Impatient. Annoyed.

"What's going on?"

"Why can't we get in?"

"I've got stuff to pick up!"

"My car's down in the car park!"

The outer door to the centre stood open at Nigel's back as he raised his hands, calling for calm and for quiet. The inner doors, just a few feet further in, had been secured from the other side by one of the armed men.

The snow was getting heavier now. It was early afternoon, yet Falcon Square had the lustre of late evening about it. The lights twinkled on the big Christmas tree, cheerfully oblivious to what was going on within the Eastgate Centre's walls.

The chill of the air pinched and snapped at him through his shirt. He felt himself start to shiver, though he wasn't convinced the cold was entirely responsible for that.

Nigel looked back at the locked doors, then ahead at all the colourful lights and festive decorations. Schools must be out now, because a few kids were laughing and kicking up clumps of snow as parents rushed on by, pulling them along by the hand.

He could smell hot chocolate and melting marshmallows from somewhere nearby. A waft of gingerbread. A suggestion of nutmeg and spice.

The sights and smells of Christmas.

He thought of his two daughters. They'd be at home with their mother, getting excited for what the next few days would bring. They were all spending Christmas Day together. He was cooking lunch.

Out there somewhere, out beyond the curtains of falling snow, his life was waiting for him. Out there lay freedom.

"Well? What's happening?" demanded a woman near the

front of the crowd. "I've got a list a mile long to pick up this afternoon. I'm not going to get another chance before Christmas!"

She was local—Nigel recognised her as a regular visitor to the centre—and looked thoroughly annoyed at having her plans disrupted. Judging by the nods and mutterings of agreement from the rest of the group, she wasn't the only one.

Nigel looked ahead through the snow at the twinkling lights of the Christmas tree.

He looked back over his shoulder, to the locked doors of the centre, and the dangers that lurked beyond.

None of it was his fault. None of it was his problem. He wasn't responsible for those people trapped inside. Not really. Not by law.

He faced the crowd. He smoothed down his shirt. He straightened his back.

"Sorry, folks," he said, plastering on his best smile. "Sprinkler malfunction. The place is a mess. We're doing what we can, but it's looking like we're going to be shut for a while..."

The door slid closed at Nigel's back. He exhaled shakily, while the big Russian turned the key that locked the inner door.

Nobody spoke. Not at first.

And then, Nigel watched as Santa Prime brought his radio to his mouth, thumbed the button, and said, "Well?"

There was a delay of several seconds before a voice crackled back.

"Aye, they're fucking off. That seems to have done the trick."

Santa Prime continued to hold eye contact with the security manager as he returned the radio to his belt. Then, he took three big, lurching paces, and grabbed Nigel by the back of the neck.

"No, wait, no, please!" Nigel sobbed, then he stopped when a kiss was planted on his forehead.

"Nigel, the fucking problem solver! See? I knew you had it in you!" Santa Prime whooped, grinning so broadly that his lips looked like they might split wide open. "Congratulations. You just kept a whole bunch of people alive."

He spun on the spot and whistled through his teeth, summoning his lackeys to his side like they were well-trained dogs.

Nigel's legs wobbled as he watched them marching back towards the escalators, and he'd almost certainly have collapsed to the floor had the man called Ded Moroz not caught him by the shoulder again.

"Good for you, Nigel!" the Russian boomed. He cackled, and the stink of his breath hit the security manager square in the face again. "Maybe you not such total pussy after all!"

CHAPTER TWELVE

THERE WAS A DOOR, Hoon thought, down by the gents'
bathroom. He was sure he'd seen it before. There was a chance
he'd even used it during one of the training exercises, while
moving around the building behind the scenes.

There was also a chance that he was imagining the whole
thing, and that where he thought a door was located might just
be a cupboard—or worse, a blank patch of wall.

There was movement out in the centre, though. Raised
voices beyond the food court. Waiting here was getting him
nowhere. Well, nowhere that didn't end with him being repeatedly shot in the face, at any rate.

There was a door. There *was*. Down by the guys' bogs. He
was fucking sure of it.

What was that? A five-second sprint along an open corridor?
The coast was clear at the moment, but he had no way of
knowing if the camera had been switched back, or if it was still
staring along the bathroom hallway. He could step out from
between the vending machines and directly into the view of the
gobshite up in the security room.

Where would he be then?

Right on the High Street of *Royally Fucked*. That was where.

He couldn't stay here, though. It wasn't just the thought of being caught, either. He was getting cramp in his arse. His right buttock and the back of his thigh were seizing up. His left leg, below the knee, was falling asleep. His mad dash to the door was already going to be more of a Quasimodo lurch. Leave it any longer, and he'd be dragging himself along the floor on his elbows.

"Right, fuck it. There's a door," he said, sounding determined, like he was trying to will it into existence. "There's definitely a door."

He'd have to take his chances with the camera. Hopefully, given there had been some sort of drama going on out in the centre proper, all eyes would be on that. All he needed was a count of five. Five seconds of good luck. Five seconds of the whole damn world not being against him. Was that really too much to ask?

He exhaled a little, shrinking his chest so he could more easily squeeze out of the tight gap. Glass *crunched* beneath his feet as he emerged from between the machines. Fragments of it fell from his head and his shoulders, like crystalline flakes of dandruff.

He stood for a moment, gazing up at the camera, like he might be able to reverse it somehow, and see if anyone was watching from the other end.

And then, from behind him, back out beyond the food court, he heard a voice raised in celebration, and the bark of a big man's laughter.

"Good for you, Nigel! Maybe you not such total pussy, after all!"

Footsteps padded on the hard, polished floor. Two people, maybe three, headed towards the escalator, where they'd be able to see straight down the corridor where Hoon was currently standing.

"Fuck, fuck, fuck," he whispered.

No time to duck back into cover. Nowhere to hide. Nothing to do but run.

He broke into a clumsy, lumbering dash, his dead leg and sore arse slowing him down even worse than he'd feared.

Voices muttered, drawing closer. He couldn't make out the words, but he recognised the Southern drawl of the American he'd heard over the speakers.

They were close. Too close. He had seconds, maybe less.

He hurpled towards the gents' toilets, where he knew he'd find the door that led into the labyrinth of corridors, storage rooms, and loading bays that most people never got to see.

Or, where he *thought* he'd find the door. Instead, there was only a blank wall. A blank, featureless, smug-as-fuck looking wall.

"Bastard!" he hissed.

Back along the corridor, the voice was louder. The footsteps closer.

He could hide in the toilets, but the entrance was still too far away. No way he could reach it before they spotted him. No chance at all.

And then, from the corner of his eye, he spotted the door he'd been looking for, on the wall directly across from where he'd expected to find it.

He grabbed his aching arse cheek and held it, like he was trying to stop it falling off, and hobbled as quickly as he could towards his only hope of escape.

Like most of the other doors that led through to the back area of the centre, this one wasn't locked. Aye, it would trigger that wee flashy light somewhere on the security console, but it was a risk he'd have to take.

It was a swing door that opened inward. Lucky. For once.

He shouldered through it and grimaced at the piercing *squeak* the hinges made.

Not *that* lucky, then.

He tumbled through into darkness, caught the door, and closed it slowly to minimise the noise. Hoon crouched there in the dark, listening for movement as he shook the feeling back into his sleeping left leg.

At the bottom of the escalator, just as he was about to step on and be carried up to the floor above, Santa Prime stopped. The two lackeys dressed as security guards hurriedly retreated as he took a step back and peered along the corridor that led to the bathrooms.

"Y'all hear something?" he asked.

"Uh, no. No, don't think so," one of the lackeys said. He turned to the other. "You hear anything?"

"I thought maybe, like... Something. But maybe not."

Santa Prime tutted. "Well, ain't you two just a whole power of help?"

He led the way towards the corridor, taking his gun from his big red Father Christmas coat. He flexed his fingers on the grip, caressing the wood.

Slowing as he entered the mouth of the corridor, he surveyed the shards of glass on the floor, and the shattered vending machine.

"Now, what have we here?" he muttered.

"Uh, my apologies." Père Noel joined Santa Prime and the others in the corridor. He smiled, but it was closer to a grimace. "I, uh, I got thirsty. That was me."

Santa Prime turned his head slowly until he was staring the Frenchman straight in the eye.

"Did we come here to break their shit?" he asked.

"Uh, non. Non. We did not."

"Did we come here to steal their fucking sodas?" The words were a hiss of barely contained rage. "Is that why all that planning and all those resources went into this thing? So we could quench our fucking thirst?"

Pére Noel lowered his head and shook it, not daring to speak.

"We are here to do a fucking job. If you ain't working with us, you're against us."

He caught the Frenchman by the back of the neck, just as he'd done with Nigel, then leaned in so their foreheads were pressed together.

"So, which is it, boy? You on our side?" He gestured upwards with a finger and twirled it around, like he was indicating the rest of the world at large. "Or on theirs?"

"Ours. Our side. Always," Pére Noel whispered. "Always. I am sorry. I will not fuck up again."

Santa Prime ran his fingers across the back of the Frenchman's head, and through the tufts of hair that stuck out below the fuzzy white band of his hat.

"Oh, I know you won't. I know. I know," he whispered, rolling their foreheads together.

It was an oddly intimate moment. The two lackeys in security uniforms shuffled their feet uncomfortably, and looked in every direction but that one.

Finally, Santa Prime breathed out slowly through his nose, patted the other man's cheek, then stepped back and pointed with his gun along the corridor. "I thought I heard something. Go check it out."

"Yes, sir. Oui. Merci, sir. I will, yes," Pére Noel gushed.

Santa Prime's voice became a roar that rolled like thunder along the corridor. "Well then, why are you still fucking standing here? Go!"

The Frenchman ducked as he ran off, holding his shotgun in one hand, and clutching his hat to his head with the other.

Santa Prime watched him go, then unclipped his radio from his belt and thumbed the call button. "Security room. You there?"

The response came almost immediately, the same Glasgow accent as before, but this time with a slightly breathless sort of deference to it.

"Yes, sir. Here, sir. Everything alright?"

"Downstairs. Bathrooms. You watching?"

"Uh..." There was a click of a mouse button. "Wasn't, but am now, sir. I see you. Everything hunky-dory?"

"You tell me. That's why you're up there."

"Eh, right, aye. Sorry, sir," the voice on the radio replied. "I'm, um, I'm not seeing anything dodgy. Everyone on the upper floor's behaving themselves. Crowd's thinning out front. Might be worth putting some sort of notice up, though. There's still a few people trying to get in."

"And what about the staff doors?"

"Uh, staff doors? I'm no' sure what you mean."

Santa Prime watched the man with the shotgun continuing down the corridor. He was creeping now, crouched low, his shotgun gripped in both hands.

"What the fuck do you think I mean? Has anyone used the doors the staff use to go out back? Do we have rodents scurrying around where they ain't meant to be?"

From over the airwaves came the unmistakable sound of a man blowing out his cheeks.

"There's a load of wee lights, but they're on and off pretty much all the time. Our guys are coming and going a lot, getting everything sorted oot, an' that. So, eh, I'm no' seeing anything unusual."

Santa Prime kept the radio to his mouth. Kept his eyes on Pére Noel.

And then, with a nod, he gave one last command.

"Keep your fucking eyes peeled."

Then, he turned back towards the escalators and headed up to join his hostages on the floor above.

CHAPTER THIRTEEN

PÉRE NOEL INCHED OPEN the door, shoved his shotgun through ahead of him, then nudged his way through into a long, narrow corridor that stopped at a T-junction thirty feet ahead.

Long fluorescent strip lights cast a sickly yellow glow across the scuffed grey stone floor and the masonry blocks of the walls.

Going from the customer-facing part of the centre to the stairwells and passageways behind the scenes was like slipping into another world. It was still the same shopping centre, but it was like all the colour and life had been drained out of it, leaving a dead husk of a place behind.

He looked up at the hanging fluorescent bulbs burning away high above him. All the lights back here worked on motion sensors. Had the opening of the door triggered them, or had they been on before that?

Was someone else moving around in here?

"*Merde*," the man with the shotgun whispered, and he adjusted the shotgun in his hands, firming up his grip.

The door squeaked closed behind him. He checked the corners of the corridor on his left and right, but saw nothing.

Wait. No.

Not quite nothing.

There were fragments of broken glass in one corner. Two larger pieces, and a handful of diamond-sized chunks that glinted in the light as he crouched to examine them.

Turning on his haunches, he looked along the length of the corridor. A scattering of shards shone along the floor. An uneven line of them, stretching on.

A trail.

Pére Noel stood, but kept low as he crept along the corridor, following the glass. His heavy boots made it hard to sneak, but he moved slowly, step by step, shotgun sweeping left and right like it was a scanner in search of a target.

There were two doors ahead, one to the left, one to the right, both set into alcoves in the walls.

Pére Noel slowed, squatted again, and checked the trail. It curved to the left, headed for the door on that side of the corridor. He brought the shotgun up, crept to the edge of the alcove, then jumped out, ready to fire.

The alcove was empty. The door was closed, but he could hear something inside. Something mechanical. Beneath the door, down by his feet, he saw a thin line of light seeping out from the room beyond.

He took a moment to roll his head around on his shoulders, stretching his neck. He flexed his fingers. He took a breath. And, as quietly and as carefully as possible, he turned the handle of the thick, sturdy wooden door.

As soon as the door was off its latch, something fast and heavy hit him from behind, slamming him against the wood and propelling him into the room beyond. He cried out in shock, but the sound was swallowed by the clanking and whirring of half a dozen shed-sized heating units, all working to pump warm air through the shopping centre.

His momentum carried him on, too quickly, too fast. He

couldn't stay upright, and threw out a hand to cushion his impact as he fell, face-first, towards one of the big heaters.

"Non, non, non! You'll kill us bo—" he started to scream, then the metal wall of the unit *bonged* like a big cymbal as he slammed against it. The pain of the impact jolted through his arm and into his shoulder, then his skin *hissed* against the heat of the metal. Yelping, he pushed himself away with such force that he lost his balance in completely the opposite direction, and landed on his arse on the ground.

He watched, helplessly, as the shotgun clattered across the floor and skidded just out of his reach. Before he could make a grab for it, there was a click, and the lights went out, plunging the room into near-total darkness.

A moment later, there was a second click. Not the lights, this time, but the sound of a heavy door being locked.

Someone was trapping him in here. Someone was locking him in!

He reached out in the direction he was sure the shotgun had gone, slapping at the floor, searching for it in the dark.

Nothing.

Gone.

He rose to his feet as quickly as he could, hissing at the pain when he pressed his hand against the floor to help him get up. It wasn't a bad burn, but something was grinding in his wrist, jagged bone carving into meat.

His breath wheezed. He blinked through the burning of the perspiration that ran down his forehead and into his eyes. The temperature in the room was already becoming unbearable. Sweat slicked his back, darkening the red of his cheap, flimsy Santa coat.

He searched for the door, but the darkness disoriented him and the hand he'd stretched out found only a wall full of hot copper pipes that scorched his fingertips and made him spring back once again.

This time, he hit something. Something not quite solid. Something that grunted with annoyance at the impact.

"Here, ye fucking snail-munching horse-botherer," growled a voice in the darkness. "How about you watch where you're fucking going?"

Père Noel spun, swinging wildly with a big right hook. It connected with nothing and no one, and he once again found himself thrown off balance, the force of his own punch spinning him on the spot.

A fist connected hard with one of his kidneys. Once. Twice. A forearm was pressed against the back of his neck, and he was forced forwards until his whole body slammed against the side of one of the heating units.

A *bong* rang out, like the chime of Big Ben.

"Non, non, non, non!" Père Noel ejected. He tried to push back, kick free, but the man behind him was too strong and had leverage working on his side.

His face was pressed against the hot metal. He felt his skin burning, heard his sweat sizzling like oil in a frying pan.

Frantically, he grabbed for the radio on his belt.

Gone. Just like his shotgun.

"Looking for this, pal?"

He heard the creaking of the plastic as the walkie-talkie was waved around beside his head.

"I'm afraid I had to fucking confiscate it. I hope you don't mind."

"P-please. Please, don't!" Père Noel pleaded. "Let me go. You will kill us both. You will kill us both!"

"Both? What would be the fucking point in that? I'm no' going to kill us both, son," The man holding him leaned in closer, and spoke directly into his ear. "But you? Well, that's another fucking matter entirely..."

CHAPTER FOURTEEN

"AYE, I know. I'm not arguing with that. We *have* spent a lot already. I'm just saying, we should probably get the boss something. You know, like, nothing big, just something wee."

In the passenger seat of the car, Detective Constable Sinead Bell pulled a face. It was quite a hard face to describe, but it was one that her husband, Detective Constable Tyler Neish, had become increasingly familiar with over the course of his wife's pregnancy.

She had grown in size considerably over the past seven months, while her reserves of patience had shrunk at an even faster rate.

Usually, that face was a good indication that he should stop talking. And, to be fair, he did consider keeping his mouth shut as he sat there behind the steering wheel, waiting for the lights to switch from red to green.

He just didn't consider it for very long.

"You don't think we should get him just a wee something? He is the boss. And it *is* Christmas."

"Aye, I'm well aware it's Christmas. And I know you're excited—you've already spent a fortune on presents for babies that aren't going to be born for another two months," Sinead pointed out.

"Some of them are technically from your brother," Tyler countered. "You know, I think Harris is really excited about being an uncle."

Sinead shot him a sideways look. "I don't think he gives a shit," she said. "And, anyway, we still paid for all of them."

Tyler conceded that point with a nod, then looked ahead through the windscreen. The wipers were working hard to keep the glass clear, but the falling snow was making visibility poor. The flakes reflected the whites and the reds of headlights and tail lights, and they dazzled briefly on their way to becoming a dirty grey slush on the road.

"I know I've gone a bit overboard. I'm just, you know, excited." He turned to look at her again. "Are you not excited?"

Sinead smiled. His hand was on the gearstick, ready to start moving. She placed her hand on top of his and squeezed.

"Of course I'm excited," she assured him. "Excited. Exhausted. Borderline broke..."

The colour of the falling snow changed from red to green. The procession of traffic up ahead began to slowly crawl forwards.

"Aye, maybe we shouldn't bother getting the boss anything," Tyler conceded. "I mean, there's nothing he wants, is there? If we got him something, it'd probably just annoy him. And one of us might get him in the Secret Santa, anyway."

Sinead didn't answer. She was looking out of her side window at the snow-covered Falcon Square, where the big city centre Christmas tree was passing on their left.

Young kids were running around trying to catch the snow in their mittens, or kicking gleefully at it with their chunky Welly boots. A few older ones were tossing snowballs at each other, cackling whenever they scored a direct hit.

The Eastgate Centre, where she and Tyler were headed,

looked busy as they crept past in the slow-moving line of traffic. There were a lot of people coming and going through the front doors.

"Hang on," she muttered. "No, they're not."

Tyler took his eyes from the road ahead long enough to fire her a questioning look.

"Who's not what?" he asked.

"Huh? Oh. Sorry, thinking out loud," she replied. She craned her neck to try and look back at the entrance as the car curved around the side of the building. "I think it's shut."

"Shut?" Tyler frowned. "What do you mean? Like *shut* shut?"

"No. Just shut," she clarified. "Think the doors are locked. People are turning away."

"The lights are on," Tyler said. "It can't be shut. It's one of their busiest days of the year. They won't be shut. They can't be."

He indicated left to turn onto the ramp leading down to the car park beneath the building, then slammed on the brakes when a young man in an Eastgate Centre security uniform stepped out in front of them, waving his hands.

"Sorry, mate!" the security guard shouted to them. "We're shut!"

He had an English accent. Newcastle, or that neck of the woods. His hair was blond, with a centre parting that formed it into curtains on his forehead. He looked like a pop star from the 90s.

It was quite a good look, Tyler thought.

Pressing the button that wound down his window, Tyler leaned his head out. "What do you mean?"

The security guard didn't come closer. He stood with his head down and his shoulders up, like he was trying to stop the snow going down the back of his shirt.

He didn't have a lot of meat on his bones and stood shivering slightly in the cold.

"I mean we're shut."

"Aye, but you're not *shut* shut?"

The security guard looked confused by the question. "What do you mean?"

"Well, I mean, you're not *shut* shut," Tyler said, clearly hoping that just repeating the same words would somehow make the meaning clear. "Like, not permanently shut."

"No. Of course not," the guard replied. "Just shut for a little bit. Technical problems. Health and safety, and all that bollocks."

Tyler looked to Sinead, but she was staring at the security man like he was the most fascinating human being to have ever walked the face of the Earth.

He leaned out the window again. "When will you be back open?"

"When it's fixed."

"And when's that going to be?"

The security man shrugged. "Well, how should I know? I'm not the one fixing it." A suggestion of a smile played across his face. "But you'll know when we're ready. We'll make a very big announcement. You won't be able to miss it."

With that, he waved them back towards the road, and ducked in close to the building, taking shelter from the snow.

"Well, that's a pain in the arse," Tyler said, shunting the car into first gear and turning back towards the junction.

"Aye," Sinead confirmed. She studied the reflection in her wing mirror as the car swung around. "Is it just me, or did that guy seem really young for a security guard?"

"People say we're both young to be detectives," her husband reminded her.

Sinead couldn't really argue with that. And yet...

"They're quite often young, aren't they?" Tyler reasoned,

only half-listening as he tried to reinsert them back into the flow of traffic. "Much easier to run after a shoplifter if you've got both your own hips."

"Suppose, aye," Sinead admitted. She watched the scrawny security man lighting up a cigarette. "But I don't think I've ever seen one *that* young before..."

CHAPTER FIFTEEN

HOON STOOD, arms folded, face fixed in a boggle-eyed scowl as he addressed the Frenchman. The man in the Santa suit was now lying on the floor, half-choking on one of his own socks. Hoon had been forced to stuff it in there to stop the bastard shouting for help.

Well, 'forced' was a bit of a stretch. He'd mostly just liked the idea. He'd then used the man's other sock to hold the first one in place, by wrapping it across his mouth and tying it tightly at the back of his head.

A length of insulated wire that Hood had ripped from one of the heating units had turned out to be perfect for tying Père Noel's hands behind his back. Hoon had taken the trouble to form loops around the other man's thumbs in such a way that any attempt to wriggle free would result in a lot of pain and, if he persevered, permanent damage.

"Well, now, this is a bit of a fucking pickle you've found yourself in here, pal," Hoon said, putting his hands on his hips. "There you were, minding your own business, just taking a fucking shopping centre hostage with a load of your wee fuckwit pals, and now look at you. Lying there, couple of dirty socks in your mouth, at the mercy of a big mad bastard." He smiled toothily. "That's me, by the way."

He bent and picked up the shotgun that he'd leaned against the wall behind him, then turned it over in his hands like he was admiring the craftsmanship.

"Sawn-off. Old school. I like it. It's a classic, but it's a classic for a reason. You could do some real fucking damage with this. But then, I suppose that's why you brought it."

He cracked the mechanism open, checked one of the cartridges, then nodded his approval as he returned it to the chamber.

"All loaded up and ready to go, too. No fucking messing around, eh?"

He snapped the gun shut with a *clack*, and pointed its stubby barrels at the Frenchman's head.

"What's up, *wabbit*?" he asked, then his grin broadened. "Elmer Fudd. You know him? The wee baldy cartoon fucker wi' the giant heid? He had a shotgun, too. No' a sawn-off like this, mind you, but still."

Hoon ran his tongue across his exposed teeth, tracing the points of them as if checking their sharpness.

"Always fucking cracked me up that name. I mean, poor bastard. Being called Elmer's probably no fucking picnic at the best of times, but *Fudd*? Elmer fucking *Fudd*? I mean, Christ Almighty. Good fucking job he didn't go to the same school I did, or never mind Bugs Bunny, it'd be his own fucking head he'd have blown off with that shotgun."

He pressed the barrels of the gun against his captive's head and pressed down, drawing a strangled whimper from the man on the floor.

"But that's what I'm going to call you. You're Elmer Fudd. And I'm..." He thought for a moment, then shrugged. "Whoever the fuck it is that Elmer Fudd's scared of. I'm Big Daddy Fudd. I'm the fucking Fuddmeister General."

He pressed harder with the gun, underscoring his point, then removed it from the Frenchman's head, leaving a sideways figure-of-eight etched on his skin in red.

"I've got a few wee questions for you, Elmer. I'm no' going to bore your arse off and tell you what'll happen to you if you don't answer them. I'm sure you can use your fucking imagination. All I'll say is that it'll be very much in your best interests to answer promptly, and without any pissing about."

He leaned the gun against the wall again, then squatted down next to the man on the floor. The Frenchman's eyes were bulging with terror, or possibly through lack of oxygen. Either way, it should help loosen his lips.

Hoon lightly cracked his knuckles, holding eye contact.

"Me? I'm sort of hoping you don't answer. Cos, I'll be honest, see places like this? Shopping centres? I fucking hate them. The idea of spending hours wandering around them is my idea of hell. Generally, I try and keep as far away from the fucking things as possible, and I only stopped in here for coffee and a shite. That was all. In and out. Job done. That was the fucking plan, anyway."

He tapped his captive on the forehead, right in the centre of one of the conjoined circles that were now fading on his skin.

"But you and your wee fucking Santa pals had to go and put the kybosh on that, didn't you? So, I'm kind of hoping you stick to your guns and keep your mouth shut," Hoon said. "Because I am fucking itching for an excuse to demonstrate my displeasure."

Grabbing him by the hair, he dragged the Frenchman up into a sitting position. Then he dug his fingers in under the sock that was tied across his captive's mouth, but he didn't pull it down yet.

"Whatever you fucking do, don't shout," Hoon warned.

He gave the other man a moment to imagine what the conse-quences of doing so might be, then he pulled the first sock away from the Frenchman's mouth, allowing him to hack and cough up the second. It landed on the floor between his legs with a damp-sounding *thuck*.

Pére Noel retched, his stomach heaving in a big, violent spasm. Once it passed, he shook his head, dislodging the stringy tendrils of saliva that had been hanging like bunting between his mouth and the ejected sock.

Finally, he raised his eyes to meet Hoon's. Sensibly—and perhaps a little disappointingly from Hoon's perspective—he chose not to call out for help.

"Very wise, son. That's a good sign. That's encouraging. That tells me you know how to follow orders, and you know what's in your best fucking interests," Hoon told him.

"Who are you?" the Frenchman whispered.

"Whoa, whoa, steady there, Elmer! I'm the one asking the fucking questions here," Hoon said. He stood up, rocked on his heels, then shrugged. "Although, I suppose fair's fair, and all that, and I'm sure you're a bit fucking concerned about what might be happening to you here. So, here's what we're going to do."

He pointed between them, first at himself, then at the man tied up on the floor.

"We're going to take turn about. Asking questions, I mean. I'll ask one, and if you answer to my satisfaction, then you get to ask one, too. That's fair, isn't it?" He held up an index finger. "That wasn't my question, by the way. This is my question coming now."

He squatted again, bringing his face closer to Pére Noel's. There had been some levity in his voice until then, but that quickly became a thing of the past.

"Who *the fuck* are you pricks, and what do you think you're fucking playing at?" He raised the same index finger again, but this time it was a warning not to try his patience. "I know that's two questions, but good luck finding someone who gives a fuck to complain to."

Pére Noel's eyes flitted to the door, then to the shotgun, then to the radio that sat on the floor beside it.

Hoon slapped him on the cheek, drawing his attention again.

"Don't even fucking think about it, son. I suggest you concentrate on staying in my fucking good books. Who are you, and what the fuck do you want?"

"We, uh, we... Money," Pére Noel said. "Ransom. We want money."

Hoon sat on the floor and crossed his legs, sizing the other man up.

"Money? That's it?"

Pére Noel nodded.

"Bollocks. You're lying."

"What? Non. We want money."

"You've got money," Hoon replied. "All this, this whole thing, this would've cost a fucking fortune to pull off. You'd need a big fucking ransom to even break even."

"We're demanding ten million," Pére Noel said.

"Jesus fuck!" Hoon sucked air in through his teeth. "Aye, that's quite a fucking healthy payday, right enough," he conceded. He shrugged. "I mean, you'll never get it. No fucking way. But, you know, well done on the fucking ambition."

"Is it my turn?" asked the Frenchman.

"Is it fuck. You still haven't told me who you are."

Pére Noel shrugged. "We are the people who are going to leave here ten million richer," he said. "Does it matter who we are?"

Hoon drummed his fingers on his knees, considering the response.

"See, you've got me curious," Hoon said. "I mean, look at you, you're nothing but a streak of frog's piss in a funny hat. Your man in charge sounds like his mum's his sister, his first cousin, and his high school fucking sweetheart all rolled into one, and from what I've seen so far, I wouldn't rely on any of you to be able to hold up a banner with 'We're all useless bastards,' written on it, never mind a fucking shopping centre two days before Christmas."

He rubbed his chin, his fingers rasping across his stubble as he studied his captive.

"And yet, here we fucking are. So, I'm going to ask you again, nicely, one more time, son. After that, you can kiss goodbye this carefree fucking attitude you're currently enjoying, and we'll start doing things the hard way."

Hoon gave him a moment or two to consider his options, before asking the question.

"Who. The fuck. Are you?"

This time, the Frenchman stared back at him, almost matching Hoon's intensity.

"We are no one," he said.

Hoon slapped his hands on his thighs. "Right, then," he said, starting to rise. He stopped when the man on the floor continued.

"You walk past us in the street. You overlook us. You all do. You choose to ignore us in favour of mutts and mongrels. In favour of freaks. Of *abominations*."

"I try my best to ignore everyone, son, you're no' exactly narrowing it down for me," Hoon told him.

"You want to know who we are? We're the majority who no longer wish to be silent," the Frenchman said, his face contorting now, his skin flushing with righteous rage. "We are the most oppressed, most disadvantaged, most put-upon group in all of society."

"Come on, now," Hoon grunted. "I'm sure being French isn't all *that* bad..."

Pére Noel jerked his head forwards, hissing the rest of his reply through his teeth.

"Straight white men!"

Hoon raised his eyebrows. He regarded the man in the Santa suit for quite a long time, then finally clicked his tongue against the roof of his mouth.

"Right," he said, really dragging the word out.

"You should not be fighting against us, you should be fighting with us!" Pére Noel insisted. "You should stand with us before it's too late. Before they make it a crime to be us! For us simply to exist! They're already trying. They're already trying to replace us—to wipe us out in favour of blacks, and whores, and queers!"

"Jesus Christ! I'm starting to wish I hadn't fucking asked," Hoon retorted, but the Frenchman was in full flow now.

"Do you know the head of police in this city is all three?"

Hoon frowned. "All three what?" he asked, then the penny dropped. "Wait. A gay black woman? Aye. I believe I might've heard that somewhere, right enough. Although, I also hear the guy she replaced was a bit of a fucking legend."

"Well, there we are!" The Frenchman sat back, pulling a smug wee face like he'd successfully proved his point. "She replaced him. Like they wish to replace us all. He lost. She won."

Hoon scratched his chin for a moment, then shrugged.

"Fuck it. Good enough for him, I reckon. The bastard had it coming," he said.

"My point still stands," Pére Noel insisted.

"Does it fuck. Aye, she might've won the triple rollover on the diversity lottery, but none of the rest of them did. The polis up here, I mean. Ninety fucking percent of them are straight white guys." He thought for a moment. "Well, I'm no' sure about Boyband. I mean, he's definitely white. And he's married, though that could all be a fucking sham. I mean, look at Philip Schofield."

The Frenchman frowned, struggling to follow what was

being said. "Pardon?"

Hoon shook his head. "Doesn't matter. Oh, and here. How come I've got no fucking phone signal, by the way? How did you pull that off?"

"Easy. Signal jammers. Downstairs. On roof. All over. We have cut almost all landlines, too. No calls. No internet. No communication with the outside world, unless it goes through us."

"Fucking hell. You're on the ball with it all, I'll give you that much."

"Oui! We are in complete control."

"Says the man with his fucking hands tied behind his back, who was just choking on his own socks," Hoon shot back.

"Oui! You are in charge here. In this room. But out there? Non. Out there, we set the rules."

Hoon sniffed. "Aye, well, we'll soon fucking see about that."

"You could join us," Père Noel urged. "Take up arms with us. Stand with us. Stand with your brothers!"

Hoon winced. "Oh, fuck no. Not a chance. I've already got a sister, and she's hard enough fucking work as it is. The last thing I want's a load of brothers, too. Especially a coven of snivelling, pillow-shagging, rancid wee fuckwits like you. I mean, what's the initiation ceremony? Do you all sit around in a big circle, furiously wanking each other off with tweezers and foaming at the mouth about how the whole fucking world hates you?"

Hoon leaned in closer, as if sharing a secret.

"Well, newsflash, son—you're right. The whole fucking world *does* hate you, but it's no' because you're straight white men." He shook his head, and said the next few words slowly and deliberately, as if explaining something to a child. "It's because you're cunts."

Seeing an opening, Père Noel threw himself at Hoon, snapping his head forward hoping to strike with a head-butt. Hoon leaned back, avoiding it, then brought up a knee that connected hard with the Frenchman's jaw.

Despite the shock of the pain—or perhaps because of it— Pére Noel tried again. He rocked himself up onto his knees, throwing his body weight on top of Hoon, trying to force him back onto the floor.

He realised, too late, that Hoon's foot was still up. The sole of it pressed into his stomach, and Hoon gave a grunt of effort as he extended his leg to full stretch, launching the Frenchman backwards towards the closest heating unit with a, "Fuck... *off!*"

The force of the kick propelled Pére Noel all the way back onto his feet. A look of triumph flashed momentarily across his face, then his backwards momentum slammed him hard against the shed-sized metal heating unit, and his whole body contorted with the force of the impact.

Hoon jumped up, fists clenched, ready to give the bastard the leathering of his life.

"Right, you weasel-eyed, mum's-pants-sniffing, virginity-riddled wee fuck," he hissed. "Now you've gone and made me—"

But, what the man in the Santa suit had *gone and made* him was destined to remain a mystery, as the end of the sentence was drowned out by the sound of the Frenchman exploding.

It happened without warning—one moment, he was standing there, the next, a small fireball tore through him, turning his torso into hot chunks of burning meat, and spraying Hoon in sizzling innards, bits of bone, and smouldering fragments of festive red fabric.

Hoon stood there, mute with shock, watching as Pére Noel's legs shuffled around like a drunk auntie on a wedding reception dance floor.

Then, finally accepting that there were no more signals coming from the brain—and no more brain, for that matter—the legs toppled forwards, spilling a slop of intestinal gloop onto the floor.

Hoon blinked. Something that had, until recently, made up part of the insides of Pére Noel, slid off his shoulder and landed wetly in the bloody puddle at his feet.

"The fuck...?" he muttered.

He turned and looked behind him, as if hoping to find someone else there with which to compare notes about what in the name of God had just happened.

He found no one, of course, although there *was* the shape of a man there. It was his own perfect outline on the door—the only part of it that hadn't been splattered with a viscous coating of satin red.

He hadn't been given an answer the first time, so he asked the question again, only with more emphasis on the second word.

"The *fuck*?!"

The smell hit him then. For most people, the aroma of burning human flesh would be the scent of a nightmare. It was for Hoon, too, though not so much for the horror of it, but for the nostalgia.

They all smelled the same, young men who'd been blown to bits before their time. Even the ones playing for the other team.

Hoon put his hands on his hips, took another long look around at all the gristle and carnage, then puffed out his cheeks.

"Well, this is a fucking new one on me," he said to nobody in particular.

It hadn't been much of an explosion. There hadn't been much of a flame, and even less of a noise. Hoon would've called it more of an *implosion*, were it not for the way the Frenchman's entrails had been fired in all directions around the room.

Parts of the guy were sizzling away on the hot metal of the heating units now, adding to the room's smoky aroma, and making Hoon think, just for a moment, about burgers on a barbecue.

Hoon cautiously prodded the Frenchman's legs with the toe

of a boot, though he wasn't quite sure why. The chances of the fucker getting back up were slim, after all.

Still, his top half had spontaneously combusted. There was no saying his legs weren't about to take it upon themselves to detonate, too.

Once he was satisfied that the limbs weren't plotting anything, he squatted to get a closer look. As he did, he came eye to eye with part of a head that had found its way under the closest of the heating units. Roughly a quarter of the Frenchman's face was still attached to the chunk of skull. The expression wasn't easy to read, but there was definitely a note of surprise somewhere in the mix.

"You and me both, pal," Hoon said, then he turned his attention to the grizzled, char-grilled remains of the torso.

He reckoned, at a push, he could hazard a guess at what might have been a couple of ribs. And, with a bit of imagination, he thought he could identify a section of spine. Beyond that, though, he was struggling.

"Where's that fucking pathologist when you need her?" he muttered.

Not that he was struggling to pinpoint the cause of death—the man had exploded, plain and simple—but it would've been nice to know why.

He saw, among the human debris, a piece of wire, blackened at both ends. He picked it up and studied it. It was thinner than the cable he'd used to tie his captive's hands behind his back, so it wasn't that.

Something else, then.

Something that worried him immensely.

He decided it was best not to hang around here thinking about it for too long. The Frenchman's unexpected detonation was quiet, but it wasn't completely silent. The tussle beforehand hadn't been, either.

Even if nobody had heard a thing, they were bound to come

looking for the bastard, sooner or later. Best if he wasn't around when they did, or he was going to have a lot of explaining to do.

He was about to turn to leave when he caught this reflection in the metal of one of the heating units. It was blurry and indistinct, but the main thing that jumped out at him was the colour red.

Looking down, he quickly concluded that his suit jacket was ruined. The front of it was caked in blood, and there appeared to be a small amount of brain matter in the breast pocket. No amount of dry cleaning was going to get those stains out.

The jacket had shielded his shirt from the brunt of the gore-spray, apart from an exposed strip, a few inches wide, that ran from his neck to his crotch. He lifted his tie—a navy one, with little pineapples on it for old time's sake—and revealed a near-pristine outline of it on the pale blue of his shirt.

"Well, this is all fucked," he decided, shrugging the jacket off. He used the inside lining to wipe as much of the blood off his face as he could, then he stuffed the jacket under one of the heating units, out of sight.

He took off his tie, considered disposing of it the same way, then decided it might come in handy later. You never knew when you might need to strangle some bastard to death.

At least, *he* didn't. For most people, it probably wasn't even a consideration.

His good trousers were also beyond saving. His shoes were leather, though, and should polish up fine. That was something.

Slipping his tie in the back pocket of his trousers, he picked up the shotgun and the walkie-talkie from where he'd sat them. The gun felt reassuringly heavy in his grip, although he only had the two cartridges it was currently loaded with. If the Frenchman had been carrying any others about his person, then, just like most of his person, they'd have been completely obliterated in the explosion.

Still, on the bright side, two shotgun cartridges was still

infinity times as many shotgun cartridges he'd had until now, and he had the radio so he could...

Shite.

The casing of the radio was cracked wide open, a sliver of metal having speared clean through both the plastic and the battery pack inside. Hoon tried to squash all the broken parts back together, but he was wasting his time. The radio was well and truly kaput.

He shot Père Noel's legs a look of reproach, shook his head, then tossed the walkie-talkie on the floor. The impact finished it off for good, splitting the casing all the way open, and sending components pinging off in all directions.

"Right, then," Hoon muttered. "Off we fucking go."

Holding the shotgun at the ready, Hoon turned the door handle, took a deep breath, and slipped out into the corridor beyond.

CHAPTER SIXTEEN

DCI JACK LOGAN turned in his chair to look at the two detective constables who'd respectively walked and waddled into his office, then reluctantly set down the half-eaten *Tunnock's Caramel Wafer*, which he'd been hoping to give his undivided attention.

It was, as far as he, and anyone with any common sense was concerned, among the top tier of chocolate biscuits. He'd gone to his office on the pretence of catching up with some paperwork when, in fact, he'd just planned on tucking into the biscuit alone, and in absolute silence, so as to savour every bite.

So much for that idea.

"It's shut?" he asked, responding to the announcement they'd made when they entered the office.

DC Tyler Neish nodded. "Aye, boss."

"What do you mean, it's shut?" Logan asked. "It's no' *shut* shut?"

"Oh no, boss," said Tyler. "No, it's not *shut* shut. It's just shut. Technical difficulties."

"Technical difficulties?" Logan frowned. "It's a shopping centre, no' a bloody PC."

Tyler shrugged. "Something about health and safety, the security guy said."

"'Or some such bollocks,'" added Sinead.

Logan turned to look at her, eyebrows raise. "Eh?"

"That's what the guy said."

"The security guy? For the centre? He said it was shut for...?"

Sinead nodded. "'Health and safety, or some such bollocks,' sir. Aye."

Logan picked up the mug of tea he'd been planning to wash the caramel wafer down with and took a big, thoughtful slurp.

"Bit weird that," he mused.

"Not exactly professional, sir, no," Sinead agreed. "He was young, too. Like... stupidly young."

"Aye, well, people say that about you pair," Logan reasoned.

"That's what I said, boss."

Logan grunted. "Aye, well, they might be right in your case." Using his feet, he twisted his chair left and right, while his fingers drummed on the desktop.

His biscuit was right there beside him, and yet something told him it was getting further and further beyond his reach.

"What's your gut telling you?"

"It's telling me I fancy a caramel wafer now, boss," Tyler said, his eyes drawn to the half-eaten, foil-wrapped biscuit on the desk.

"I wasn't talking to you, son," Logan said. He gave Sinead a nod. "Well?"

Sinead ran a hand across her bulging stomach, almost like it was a crystal ball feeding her visions of the future.

"It's probably nothing, sir."

Logan waved a hand for her to continue. "But...?"

"But, I don't like it," she admitted. "I don't know why, exactly, but I can't shake the feeling that there's something up."

Logan gave a non-committal sort of grunt, then looked longingly at his biscuit.

"What's the name of that guy there?" he asked. "Did all that training stuff with us a few months back? Head of security."

Tyler's face scrunched up in thought. "I want to say Norris, boss."

"Nigel," Sinead corrected.

Tyler still managed to look pleased with himself. "Come on, though, that's pretty close!"

"Give him a ring," Logan instructed. "Ask for him by name. See what's happening."

"You think there's something up, sir?"

"Me? No. But you do, and I trust your instincts," Logan said. He took another gulp of tea. "And besides, I learned a long time ago that it's best no' to argue with a heavily pregnant woman."

"Very wise, boss," said Tyler, who had clearly learned similar lessons over the past few weeks and months.

Logan waved them out, his gaze creeping back to the biscuit on his desk.

Just before they left, though, a thought occurred to him.

"Oh, Sinead?"

"Sir?"

Logan chewed his bottom lip for a moment, deep in thought. "Maybe don't mention you're polis, eh?"

The place was like a rabbit warren. Grey masonry block corridors and passageways branched off on Hoon's left and right, then zigzagged away into darkness.

Staircases led up and down into oceans of shadow. The concertina doors of cargo elevators stood silent and solemn, patiently waiting to be put to work.

He imagined this area would usually be bustling with shop

staff and security guards, all hurrying about, making sure every-thing was going smoothly for the ongoing Christmas rush.

Now, the whole place felt dormant. Dead. Hoon felt like a mote of bacteria in the corpse of a giant, creeping through the decaying veins and arteries, trying to find the storeroom for *Tres-pass* or *Next*.

OK, he'd be the first to admit that the analogy sort of lost its way at that point, but it had been pretty good up until then.

He was looking for the clothes shops so as to cut down on the number of squelching noises he was making as he walked. Stealth and the element of surprise were about the only things he had going for him at the moment—well, aside from the shot-gun, obviously—and his entrail-soaked trousers and blood-sodden shoes weren't helping on either front.

The leather shoes hadn't been stained on the outside, but the insoles had absorbed their fair share of blood, so he'd kicked those and his socks off, and stuffed them behind a big padded ventilation pipe on the corridor wall. He refused to take his trousers off, though. No bugger was going to take him seriously if he rocked up in a nylon shirt and bloodied grey Y-Fronts.

Although, there was also the possibility that this would make them take him *very* seriously indeed.

But, no. He drew the line at losing his breeks. What he needed was a clean set of clothes and a pair of decent trainers in his size. After that, he could take on the world.

Well, the part of the world currently made up of angry, women-hating, racist fucks, at any rate.

The big problem with that plan was that he had no idea whereabouts in the centre he was. The second biggest problem was that he had no idea where those shops were, either, so he was sort of wandering blindly, hoping a well-signposted stock-room would suddenly draw itself to his attention.

That was looking unlikely, though. There were plenty of doors about, but they seemed to be sworn to secrecy about what lurked behind them. He'd tried a couple, but they'd either been locked, or full of equipment and machinery he could only guess at the purpose of.

He pressed on, taking a couple of random turns when the notion took him. Each corridor he stepped into remained in darkness for a second or so, before motion sensors brought the lights on with a *clunk*.

A few seconds later, he'd hear the lights go out behind him in the corridor he'd just left. On the one hand, it meant he'd know if anyone was following him. On the other, it might alert someone up ahead to his presence.

"Swings and fucking roundabouts," he muttered, as he took another turning, and another set of ceiling lights came to life ahead of him.

Just a few feet ahead on the left, this corridor opened up onto a set of stairs that ran up and down from this floor. There were two cargo lifts on the wall across from the staircase. The door of one was jammed open by a wheeled cage stacked with boxes, like someone had abandoned it in a hurry.

He checked the label stuck to the side of one of the boxes. *Superdry*. That was a clothes shop, wasn't it? He was sure it was.

After listening at the stairs for a few moments to make sure nobody was moving around on them, he set down the shotgun, then carefully wheeled the cage back far enough that he could offload the topmost box.

It was well taped shut, so he felt around in a sodden trouser pocket until he found his keys, and used his front door key to rip through the layer of brown packing tape that secured the top of the box.

"Fuck's sake," he muttered, when he found an assortment of women's underwear waiting for him inside. That was no good. He couldn't exactly swing into action in a frilly bra and matching knickers.

Although, again, it might make them take him *very* seriously indeed.

He slid the box aside, ignored a near-identical one that had been stacked in the cage beside it, and instead went for the bigger one on the layer below.

This one felt heavier as he heaved it down onto the floor. Not women's underwear, then.

Well, maybe for someone Berta's size.

He used the key again, hacking and ripping at the tape with the metal teeth until the cardboard flaps sprung upwards.

He was right. Not underwear. Proper clothes. Men's clothes. He'd hit the fucking jackpot.

Although...

He took out the first garment he found, pincering the shoulders between the fingers and thumbs of both hands, and stared at it in much the same way as he'd stared at the gelatinous innards of the exploding Frenchman.

"You have got," he groaned, "to be fucking kidding me."

When Sinead and Tyler returned to DCI Logan's office, he had fully polished off his caramel wafer and necked the rest of his tea. It hadn't been the momentary escape from reality that he'd planned, though it had still been tasty, all the same.

"Well?" he asked, before Sinead had a chance to report. "You get him?"

"No, sir. Spoke to someone called John. Says Nigel's not in today."

"John?" Logan asked. He sat back in his chair, interlocking his fingers on his stomach. "Can't remember a John there, can you?"

"No, sir."

"Nor me, boss," Tyler added.

"Aye, well, you thought Nigel was called Norris, so you don't count," Logan told him. He turned back to Sinead. "You get his second name?"

"Smith."

"John Smith? Bloody hell. No wonder we can't remember him. With a name as generic as that, the bugger probably just blends into the paintwork." He puffed out his cheeks. "What are they saying? What's going on?"

"He says there's been a sprinkler system malfunction," Sinead explained. "They're trying to get it under control and get the place cleaned up so they can reopen."

"He give an estimated time?" Logan asked.

"No, sir. Couldn't tell me."

"Seems fishy."

"Definitely does, boss," Tyler agreed. "When I heard Sinead say that on the phone—about the sprinklers, I mean—I got in touch with one of the lads at the fire station. Place like that, big public building, it's all linked up, innit? Sprinklers go off, alarm triggers, whatever, then they know about it."

Logan nodded. "And?"

"And they didn't know about it, boss. First they'd heard. They asked me if they should go round."

"What did you tell them?"

"I told them to hang fire, sir," Tyler said. He scratched the back of his head, looking a little embarrassed. "Bad choice of words, in hindsight. I think they thought I was taking the piss. They sounded quite annoyed."

Logan shut his eyes, just for a moment, not for the first time wondering how DC Neish managed to function in day-to-day life, let alone as a member of the polis.

Then, he rose to his feet, the shadow of his enormous frame falling across both junior officers.

"Right. Good. If there's something going on, I don't want a

fuss. No' yet, anyway." He looked down at the floor. "You seen the dug?"

"He's out there with DI Forde, sir," Sinead said, jerking her head back towards the office door. "Think he's sleeping."

"Aye, well, he'd better shift his arse and get himself wakened," Logan said. He reached for his coat, which hung on a hook by the door. "Because he and I are going for a wee daunder into town."

CHAPTER SEVENTEEN

IT HAD TAKEN SOME TIME, and the assistance of three able-bodied men, to help lower Berta into a sitting position on the floor. It wasn't that she wasn't flexible—she prided herself on still being able to touch her toes from a standing start—but the way everyone was packed in so tightly together meant her landing zone wasn't much bigger than her backside, and nobody around her relished the thought of being sat on.

She'd picked a spot beside the children, who sat huddled in a tight orbit around their teacher, just across from the entrance to *Starbucks*. This spot was also, not entirely by coincidence, adjacent to a set of swing doors that led through the back somewhere, away from the watchful eyes of the Santa squad.

Iris had tried to stay standing beside the exit, but a wave from a submachine gun, and a nod of a head, had directed him down onto the floor beside everyone else. Now, the only people standing were the ones with weapons. They paced slowly through the seated crowd, heads scanning left and right, like farmers checking their crops before the start of the harvest.

"So, how are we all?" Berta asked, addressing the children.

They were aged between twelve and fourteen, she reckoned.

Not usually an age group she enjoyed interacting with. In fact, she'd generally go out of her way to avoid them. Today, though, she felt compelled to make an exception.

"Having a nice time?" she pressed.

The kids all looked to their teacher, but Berta tutted.

"I wasn't asking him. I was asking you."

"Please," the teacher said. "They're scared."

"Course they're scared!" Berta retorted. "We're all fucking scared. Well..." She adjusted one of her breasts with a forearm and sniffed. "...not all of us, but most. But we shouldn't be scared. Not of these fuckwits. I mean, aye, they're strutting about like the cock of the walk right now, but believe you me, they'll get their comeuppance. We'll get the last laugh, not this gaggle of arseholes."

She fired a two-finger salute in the general direction of the terrorists, though none of them saw it.

"Anyway, what good does being scared do us, eh? How does that help? What's the point in us sitting here pissing in our knickers? Is that what they teach you in school these days?"

"Funnily enough, we don't cover terrorist attacks in the curriculum," the teacher fired back at her.

Berta rolled her eyes and leaned in closer to one of the children sitting nearest her. She was a girl with red hair and green eyes, and the sort of haunted expression you generally only saw on the battlefield.

"Christ on a bike. I bet he's hard work, is he?" Berta asked. "What's his nickname?"

The girl blinked and shook her head. "I don't... I'm not..."

"Oh, come on! He must have a nickname! What sort of teacher doesn't have a nickname?" Berta sized the music teacher up, her eyes narrowed in thought. "Eggy Stan?"

The teacher frowned. "Why would they call me—?"

"Because your head's shaped like an egg, boy!" barked Berta, so sharply and fiercely that the teacher shrunk back a little, and gingerly touched the top of his skull like he was searching for a pointed top.

"My name's not Stan," he protested weakly.

Berta tutted. "Well, I don't know what your bloody name is, do I? I'm shooting in the fucking dark here."

She looked around at the children. They were mostly staring back at her, but their terrified expressions were now sliding more towards confusion.

"Big Colonel Shit-His-Pants?" she guessed. "Ludwig van Knobholden?"

The teacher's mouth fell open. He looked around, like he was hoping one of the gunmen might come rushing to his defence.

Nobody but the hostages sitting closest to the group was paying them even the slightest bit of attention, though. He was on his own with this madwoman.

"No? Not that?" Berta asked. She tapped a finger against her chin, then turned to Iris. "What about you? Any ideas what his nickname could be?"

"How do you know he's got a nickname?" Iris asked.

"Because he's a teacher. If he doesn't have a nickname, he's got no business being in the bloody job."

"Oh. Right. Yeah." Iris looked the other man up and down. His brow furrowed in concentration like he was grappling with some newly discovered mathematical concept. "It might be..." He grimaced with the effort. "Joe..."

Berta, the children, and the soon-to-be recipient of the nickname all sat in expectant silence, waiting for more.

Eventually, though, Iris exhaled and shook his head. "No. That's all I've got. Just Joe."

Berta glowered at him like he was a piece of shit on her shoe, then she shook her head and turned back to the kids.

"OK, my dears, here's what we're going to do. We're going to ignore this man, and with a bit of luck he'll go away," she said.

There was no response from the children at first. And then, from the girl with the ginger hair, there came the faintest suggestion of a snigger.

That was all the cue that Berta needed. She folded her arms, leaned back a little, and gave the teacher another long, lingering look.

"Beardy McTwat?" she eventually posited.

"Oi!" the newly christened Beardy protested.

Then, beside him, on his left, a boy who looked a little younger than the others had to fight to suppress a giggle.

The teacher's eyes widened in surprise. He turned to look at the boy, only to find him biting his lip, trying very hard not to laugh.

"Gavin?" he whispered.

"Sorry, sir," the boy squeaked, his shoulders shaking with the effort of holding back his giggles.

Berta gave Beardy a nod of encouragement as he turned back to her. He scowled and wagged a reproachful finger in her direction.

"I'll have you know that it's *Mr* McTwat to you."

A smile tugged at one corner of Berta's mouth. A look of understanding passed between them, then she held up both hands in surrender. "Aye. OK. Fair's fair. Bit of respect. Mr McTwat it is."

Behind her, Iris clicked his fingers, his face lighting up with excitement. "Got it! Joe the Kiddie-Fiddler!"

The children gasped. Mr McTwat clutched at his chest, almost fainting clean away.

"Jesus Christ, man!" Berta hissed. "You've got to take things too far, haven't you? You can't say that. We don't know he's a kiddie-fiddler."

"I'm not," the teacher was quick to insist. "I'm not a kiddie-fiddler."

"Well, I mean, to be fair, you're hardly going to admit it if you are, are you? If you were, you'd deny it," Berta reasoned. "But I'm sure you're not. I mean, they do checks and things, don't they, these days? I'm sure they've looked into you."

"They do, yes, but they didn't need to," Beardy insisted. "I wasn't... I've never been... No one's ever suggested that..."

Berta gestured with both hands, appealing for calm. "Look, let's not protest too much, shall we? Or we'll all start having our fucking doubts."

Before the teacher could say any more on the matter, Berta looked along the line of kids. Her nostrils flared, like she was appraising them and was finding them wanting.

"So, you're what passes for a choir these days, are you?"

"They're actually a brass band. But they're good at singing, too," said Mr McTwat, leaping to their defence. "Aren't you, guys?"

The children didn't appear to share in his conviction. They mumbled a bit, heads down, like they didn't want to commit to an answer.

"Well, good," Berta said. "Personally, whenever I find myself trapped by armed men—this is not my first spin of that particular wheel, I should say—I find a wee sing-song helps no end. Takes the mind off of things. Lifts the spirits. What do you say?"

"What? No. God, no," Beardy whispered, his gaze darting over to the closest Santa Claus. "They told us to sit here and shut up. So, that's what we're going to do."

"That's what *you're* going to do, maybe," Berta said. "Me? I think a song's in order. Feel free to join in if you know the words."

She cleared her throat, stretched her mouth a few times like an anaconda unhinging its jaws before a big meal, then she began to sing.

"Silent Night, Holy Night, all is calm..."

"Hey! Hey!" The closest Santa stopped in the crowd, and turned to face her. "Quieten down."

"...all is bright. Round yon virgin, mother and child..."

The man in the Father Christmas costume began marching towards her, forcing the seated crowd to scramble out of his way. Further along the concourse, a couple of armed security guards and another Santa turned to see what was going on.

"Did you hear what I fucking said, love?"

The lad storming towards them was English. Liverpool area, his accent not dissimilar to Iris', though a little rougher, like he was throwing in a rasp to make himself sound more intimidating.

It wasn't working. From where Berta sat, he was about as scary as a deflating balloon, even when he stopped just a pace or two away from her, and pointed his gun at her face.

"Sing another fucking word," he said. "See where it gets you."

Behind her, before Berta could carry on, Iris took up the challenge.

"Holy infant so tender and mild."

The gun shifted, taking aim at Iris, instead. Undaunted by it, he continued.

"Sleep in Heavenly pea—eace..."

Metal *clacked*. A round was slammed into a chamber. The rest of the verse, to everyone's surprise, came as a strangled whisper from the girl with the ginger hair.

"Slee-eep in Heavenly peace."

"I am fucking warning you all!" the Santa hissed. He swung with the gun, but stopped short of pointing it at the girl, like some shred of decency deep inside him jerked his arm to a halt. "You'd better cut this shit out. Now."

"Alright, alright, keep your beard on, son. We've finished," Berta said. She waved the back of her hand at him, *shooing* him away. "Off you go. Back you go to pacing around and feeling like you're important."

His knuckles whitened as he tightened his grip on the gun.

He stared pure hatred at Berta, who just smiled patronisingly up at him as she made the *shoo* motion again.

Finally, with a tut, the gunman turned and stormed off, taking kicks at a couple of people who weren't fast enough to get out of his way.

"See? What did I tell you?" Berta said to the children. "Nothing to be afraid of. Just a lot of wee men pretending to be bigger than they are."

"That was incredibly dangerous," Mr McTwat whispered. "They could've killed you! And Sarah, you shouldn't have done that. You shouldn't have joined in."

"Oh, quit your fucking whinging," Berta replied. "You can't just let people like that push you around, guns or no bloody guns. You've got to slap them back down."

She caught the eye of the girl with the ginger hair and winked at her. Sarah smiled back, blushing a little.

"Now," said Berta, slapping both hands on her thighs. "What's say we give the bastards a good old-fashioned blast of *Jingle Bells*, and *really* noise them up?"

CHAPTER EIGHTEEN

IT WASN'T Taggart's first time seeing snow, but you wouldn't know that to look at him. The wee dug had come exploding out of the polis station, snuffling and snorting away at the covering of powdery white, before rolling around in it and trying to eat it at the same time.

Eventually, he calmed down enough to make the short walk into town. He looked up at everyone they passed, tongue out, tail wagging, like they were all old friends who just hadn't yet noticed him.

When Logan reached Falcon Square, he stopped by the big Christmas tree, and let Taggart sniff around at the base of it while he scoped out the front doors of the Eastgate Centre.

Sure enough, just like Sinead and Tyler had reported, the place was shut. He saw a few would-be punters go striding up to the entrance, then watched them frantically aborting to avoid a humiliating collision at the last second, when the doors refused to swish open at their approach.

After that, they tended to stand around looking confused for a bit, then set off around the side to try the other door—presumably only to be met with the same result.

It was no different across the road, where the *Marks & Spencer* entrance was seeing a similar pile-up of people, albeit to a lesser extent. Those doors were manually operated, and even over the hustle and bustle of pedestrians and traffic, Logan heard the regular *thunk* of another failed attempt to gain entry.

"Right. What's the story here, then?" he muttered.

Taggart looked up at him, cocked his head to one side, and gave a little *whuff*, as if to say, 'Don't look at me. How the hell should I know?'

The snow was getting heavier now, and finding its way down the back of Logan's neck. He adjusted his collar to try to keep the worst of it out, then lowered his head and went striding towards the centre's front doors.

Just like with the other people he'd watched approach, the doors remained steadfastly shut. Unlike them, he'd been prepared for it, so didn't have to resort to a panicky last-second retreat to avoid smashing his face into the immobile glass.

"I think it's shut," said a woman who'd narrowly avoided that very fate just a few moments before. She gestured to the doors with a sort of weary disdain. "I don't know what's going on. I'm meant to pick stuff up for my grandson. It's nearly Christmas!"

"Aye, I'd heard rumour of that, right enough," Logan grunted.

The woman continued to stare at him for a while, like he might offer some sort of explanation. Or, better still, a solution.

When he didn't, she tutted, took out her phone, and went marching off in search of another way in.

Logan gave the door in front of him a long, lingering look. The glass had been covered on the inside by big static cling posters advertising that the centre's January sale had started in early December.

"It's no' a bloody January sale then, is it?" he muttered. Taggart gave another wee *whuff* as if in agreement.

The posters were custom fit to the glass, and no matter where he looked on the door, it was impossible to see inside.

He started walking towards the railway station, passing the *Burger King* and *Subway* restaurants. The front doors of both opened onto the square, but they were both still part of the centre, with entrances through other doors at the side and the back.

Both places were empty. No customers. No staff. No signs of life at all.

He cupped a hand around his eyes and peered in through the *Burger King* window. The tables were a mess. Whole meals sat uneaten and unattended. He could see a tray on the floor. It had landed upside-down, scattering chicken nuggets, fries, and a couple of large soft drinks all around the drop zone.

Nobody had bothered to clean it up.

Nobody was around to.

He tried the doors, but found them both locked. That didn't come as any surprise, and yet the hairs on the back of his neck stood on end, and something rumbled deep down in his gut.

He returned to the main centre doors, where a couple of young men had just avoided rearranging their faces thanks to a skin-of-the-teeth retreat.

Logan watched as they both stood there in mute confusion for a while, scratching their heads. Then, after a brief discussion, they followed everyone else around the side to try and find another way in.

They were wasting their time, of course. From what he could tell, the whole place was locked up tight.

And he was yet to see any water cascading from the sprinkler systems.

He decided that the best way to get to the bottom of it was the direct approach. That was how he went about most things, and he saw no reason to make an exception here.

Raising a hand, he rapped his knuckles on the glass, and

looked up to where he knew a security camera would be staring down at him.

He considered holding up his warrant card, but decided to keep his powder dry on that one for now. Aye, it was good at opening doors, but sometimes just being a big bastard who wouldn't go away was even more effective.

He knocked again, a slow, heavy, *rat-tat-tat* on the glass. Taggart barked once, adding his support, then got distracted by a big snowflake that landed on the end of his nose, and almost did a backflip trying to get his tongue around it.

Logan looked back to the camera, and kept eye contact with it while he thumped on the door for a third time. He wanted them to know that he wasn't going anywhere. He wanted whoever was in there to realise the only way of getting rid of him was to come out and face him.

He was here. He was knocking. And he wasn't going away.

"He's not going away."

The big Russian, Ded Moroz, raised his eyes from his walkie-talkie until he found Nigel sitting slumped against the centre's inner doors, his head buried in his hands.

"Who is he?" the Russian asked.

"How the fuck should I know?" came the response from the security room. "Big bastard with a dog. Keeps eyeballing the camera like he knows I'm here."

"You don't recognise him?"

"How the fuck would I recognise him?" The voice on the radio crackled as it was raised. "It's not like he's fucking Robert Downey Jr or someone. He's just some guy who won't fuck off. We need to get him gone before he draws more attention. Send your man out to him."

Nigel realised he was now the subject of discussion, and let his hands fall away from his face. "No, please, don't," he begged. "They'll go away. Whoever it is, I'm sure they'll go away. I don't want to... I don't want to mess it up. I don't want to risk anything happening to anyone."

Ded Moroz brought the radio closer to his mouth. "We take care of it," he said, then he grinned at Nigel and jerked a thumb upwards. "On your feet. Up. Get out there and tell big man to piss off. Tell him same as others. Make him go."

"Please, no, listen, please. What if I mess it up, though?" Nigel whispered. He clasped his hands in prayer, and used his legs to push himself up the door into a standing position. "What if it goes wrong? I can't be... I can't be responsible for something happening. I just... I can't."

"Nigel! Nigel! Relax. Shh. Relax." The Russian put an arm around him again. Nigel felt the bones in his shoulders *creak* under the strain. "You do this? For me? Happy time. You, me? We become good friends. Yes? Solid friends. *Best friends?*"

He stuck out his bottom lip and cocked his head, considering this.

"No," he decided. "Not best friends. Best friends too much. But you do this for me, and we are solid. Like rock."

He tightened his grip, and Nigel suddenly found himself lacking the ability to breathe.

"You don't do this? You let me down? We are not friends. We are opposite of friends." His voice became a low rumble, like distant thunder heralding an oncoming storm. "You know what I do to such people, Nigel? You know what I do to opposite of friends?"

Nigel swallowed and shook his head. He stiffened as Ded Moroz leaned down, bringing his mouth right in close to his ear.

"Nor me. I hope we do not have to find out together." He gave another squeeze of Nigel's shoulders, then released him and pointed to the door. "Now, do as you are fucking told, and make big man out there go away."

———

Logan had just finished knocking for the fifth time when he heard the sound of movement on the other side of the covered glass. He stepped back, wrapping Taggart's lead around his hand so the dog couldn't go charging inside the moment the doors were opened.

"Just a second!" a voice called from inside.

Logan glanced up at the security camera again, then turned his attention back to the door just as it was manually slid open. Not fully—not all the way—just enough for a worried-looking man with a fake smile to stick his head out.

Logan recognised the head of security right away. Nigel had been heavily involved in the polis training sessions that had taken place inside the centre. He looked simultaneously relieved and horrified to find Logan standing outside.

"Um, hello? Can I help you?"

Nigel had recognised him, Logan was sure of it. He wasn't an easy man to forget.

And yet, the security man didn't seem to want to let on.

Once again, and very aware of the camera watching them, Logan decided to keep his cards close to his chest.

"Eh, aye, hello there," he said. He nodded past the man in the doorway, and noted that the inner doors had been secured shut behind him. "I was just wondering, can we get in? Got a bit of shopping to do."

Nigel stared blankly back at him for a moment or two, before eventually asking, "What?"

"We've just got a bit of Christmas shopping to get done," Logan said. He gave a jiggle of Taggart's lead. "Well, no' so much him. Mostly me. Can we get in?"

"Uh... Um..." Nigel looked back at the door behind him, then faced Logan again, his false smile really straining at him now. "No. Sorry."

"How come?" Logan asked.

"We've had an, uh... We've had a sprinkler system malfunction."

"Sprinkler system malfunction? Christ. Sorry to hear that," Logan said. He looked the other man up and down. "You seem pretty dry, though. You know, considering."

"What?" Nigel looked down at himself, then snapped his head back up. "Uh, yes. It's not everywhere. Just a few areas. But, you know, we've got to stay closed until we can get it under control."

"Right. Right, aye, makes sense," Logan said. He pretended to think for a moment, then pointed to the other man, his eyes narrowed in concentration. "Norris, isn't it?"

"What?"

"Your name. I think we spoke before. The dog got loose and ran riot. You gave me a bit of a bollocking for it."

"Oh. Oh, yes. Yes," Nigel said, catching on. "The dog. Yes."

"Norris."

Nigel's eyes crept upwards, just for a moment, to the camera mounted on the ceiling right above his head.

"That's right, yes," he said. "Norris."

Logan nodded slowly. The leather of Taggart's lead creaked as he further tightened his grip.

"Fire brigade?" he asked.

Nigel blinked. "I'm sorry?"

"Fire brigade. I'd imagine they'll be here any minute, right? I mean, I assume they get called out for that sort of thing? Technical faults, and whatnot."

"Oh. Yes. That's right," Nigel confirmed. "Any fault is flagged with them automatically. Lights up on their system right away. So, I'd imagine they'll be here any time now."

"Right. Well. Good luck with that, then," Logan said. "And, I suppose I can't get in any of the other doors, either? All locked up tight, is it? Whole place secured?"

"That's right," Nigel told him. "Whole place. Top to bottom."

"Damn. Well, that is a shame," Logan said. He fixed the other man with an intense look, but kept his voice relaxed and light. "And is, eh, is everyone alright in there? You know, with all that water pouring out and everything? Everyone's in good shape?"

Nigel swallowed. Smiled. Nodded. "Mostly," he said. "For the moment, anyway."

"Right. OK. Well, that's something, at least," Logan said. He started to move away. "So, eh, I'll leave you to it. For now. Best of luck."

"Thank you," Nigel said, stepping back from the door.

"Oh, and Norris?" Logan said, snow crunching under his feet as he turned back to the centre.

"Yes?"

"You take care and try to keep everyone dry in there, alright?" the DCI said. His eyes scanned the front of the building, then settled back on the man in the doorway. "I'm sure help's on its way."

With a tug on Taggart's lead, he set off across Falcon Square, not looking back at the centre, or its cameras.

It was only when he was around the corner, passing the main entrance to the railway station, that he took out his phone, punched in a number, and pressed it to his ear.

He marched on through the snow, listening to the ringing tone, then the *click* of a connection.

Detective Superintendent Suki Mitchell's voice was short and clipped when she answered.

"Jack. I'm just heading into a meeting. Can it wait?"

"Sorry, ma'am, I'm afraid it can't," Logan told her. "And I think you're going to want to give that meeting a miss..."

CHAPTER NINETEEN

HOON HAD A PLAN. It was not, admittedly, a great plan. Nor was it particularly detailed. But it was a plan, all the same.

The plan was this: Get to the roof.

The roof, he reckoned, would open up all sorts of possibilities. The signal jammers would be less effective up there, so he could probably get a call out. Failing that, he could just shout down to someone on the street below. Or, if it came to it, he could climb down the outside of the building, then go round up the fucking cavalry himself.

The roof gave him viable options—something he was otherwise currently lacking.

He'd been on the roof before, back during the training sessions. Once again, he wished he'd been paying a bit more attention, because he had only the vaguest notion of where the doors that led out there were.

There were at least two of them, he thought, one on each side of the centre, though try as he might, he couldn't map out their location in his mind. Still, 'up' was a good direction to start with, he reckoned.

His footsteps were no longer accompanied by the *schlop* of

blood oozing from his shoes and socks. He'd found replacements for both back in the cage of boxes. The socks were inoffensive enough, but the trainers weren't really the sort of thing he'd usually wear.

Or, for that matter, be seen dead in.

They were orange, for a start—a bright, near-neon shade of the colour that kept catching his eye and making him look down in surprise, wondering what the fuck he'd just seen.

He'd found a pair of jeans in his size, but they were ridiculously, stupidly, *obscenely* tight, and clung to his calves and his thighs like whole-leg compression socks. They were so tight across the crotch, in fact, that as well as showing which direction he was hanging, they practically revealed his sperm count.

Fighting in the things was going to be a challenge. He could barely walk upstairs in them, and kicking anywhere above knee-height was going to be out of the question.

Still, they weren't caked with intestinal matter and bodily fluids, so they were still preferable to the trousers he'd ditched.

Albeit, only barely.

The long-sleeve polo shirt he wore on top was roomier and more practical. It made up for these advantages, though, by being eye-wateringly fucking hideous. It was a tie-dyed swirl of purples and greens, and when he'd first pulled it out of the box and looked at it, he was worried it might trigger a stroke.

It had a sort of 'wing' effect under the armpits—flappy, dangling swathes of material that served no apparent purpose other than to look daft—and a button collar that, if he'd fastened it, would've come almost all the way up his neck to right below his chin.

The piece came from the store's new 'Celebrity Design' range, and he could only assume that the celebrity who designed this piece was either mentally ill, or the singer Stevie Wonder.

He'd caught sight of his reflection in the glass of doors a few times as he'd passed, and each time had ejected some variation on, "Christ Al-fucking-mighty," at the sight of himself.

Mercifully, he'd made his way through the back area of the centre without bumping into anyone. He was less worried about the dangers of an encounter with one of the terrorists, and more about the abject fucking humiliation of being seen wearing this getup.

Mind you, a man dressed in a Santa outfit would hardly have much room to talk.

After a few wrong turns, he found himself at the foot of a staircase leading up. He listened at the bottom with his breath held and the shotgun ready.

Nothing.

Not a sound.

Maybe there was no one up there. Maybe the rooftop door had been left unguarded.

Or perhaps they'd heard him coming. Perhaps, there was a big bunch of the bastards up there, lying in wait.

Only one way to find out.

Slowly, step by step, Hoon began to climb the stairs up to the floor above. They were old and uneven, no two steps exactly the same height, like whoever had built them had left his measuring tape at home and just eyeballed the distances.

And not very fucking successfully, at that.

Hoon wasn't entirely sure that he'd find a rooftop door waiting for him at the top of the steps, but there was something vaguely familiar about the staircase that at least told him he might.

He kept the shotgun trained on the top of the stairs as he padded upwards in his bright orange shoes, the spongy soles allowing him to move in near silence.

There was nobody waiting for him up there. Nobody poised to open fire, or to jump out. There was just a square-ish little hallway with the stairs at one side and the doors to another cargo elevator on the opposite wall.

A fire extinguisher stood in a bracket on the floor by the corner, where the wall of the hallway turned at ninety degrees and became the wall of an adjoining corridor.

And there, above the fire extinguisher, was a green and silver sign, with an arrow pointing to the right, and a single four-letter word printed on it.

'Roof.'

"Now we're fucking talking," Hoon whispered, creeping over to where the hallway opened up into the corridor.

He stuck close to the wall, brought his head right to the corner's edge, then peeked out and quickly ducked back in. The movement lasted less than a second, but it was enough to put a big downer on what was already a pretty disappointing day.

Two guys stood down at the far end of the corridor—one in a Santa suit, the other wearing a security uniform. Both were armed, and both had weapons with a much longer range than Hoon's. He'd have to run about twenty feet straight towards them before the shotgun had even a chance of doing any damage. Plenty of time for them to fire off multiple rounds in his direction. Plenty of time for them to score a direct hit.

He chanced another look, checking out the ceiling this time.

Under normal circumstances, roof access would be a big weak spot in the centre's security. Fire regulations meant that the roof doors would have to be operable from the outside at all times, so nobody could get accidentally stuck up there.

If someone could climb up there from the outside, they'd find an unlocked door waiting for them. It was a big security gap, and it had been plugged by a three-sixty-degree camera and a motion sensor, both of which were mounted on the ceiling just above where the guards were currently standing.

So, even if he could somehow get along there and take out both guards without having holes shot through him, he'd be caught on camera. They'd know he was there, and they'd either send a squad after him, or start taking out the hostages. The first he could deal with, the second, though, even his conscience wasn't quite ready for.

Had there just been one of the bastards along there, maybe he could've lured him away from the cameras before panning his head in with the butt of the shotgun. With two of them, though, that wasn't going to happen.

There was still at least one other door somewhere, of course, but he was buggered if he knew how to find it. Stumbling upon this one had been mostly luck, and it could take him hours to find the other one.

Besides, if they had the common sense to protect this door so closely, chances were they'd done the same to any others. They'd be guarded, too. They'd have cameras, also.

The cameras...

Those were the biggest problems. There was a chance he could deal with the guards. Not a big chance, admittedly, but it was within the realm of possibility.

Those three-sixty cameras, though, would be feeding a high-resolution image directly to the main security console. They'd be up there on one of the screens right now, pannable, and tiltable, and zoomable—an all-seeing eye he couldn't possibly sneak past.

So much for that plan.

The roof wasn't an option. Not yet, anyway.

Not without making another stop first.

———————

Santa Prime stood by the security console, his hands tucked behind his back, his silenced pistol pinned by his thick black belt to the jolly red tunic of his outfit. His gaze flitted across the bank of monitors, ten different screens showing ten different pictures of the centre.

Six showed the insides, focused mostly on the sea of hostages down on the first floor. The other four were pointed at the outside world, but were struggling to see much of anything through the heavy snow.

Finally, after searching the monitors, Santa Prime turned his attention to the short, prematurely balding man slouching in the big swivel chair in front of the controls.

"I ain't seeing a damn thing," he remarked, making no attempt to mask his irritation.

"Aye, well, my point exactly," the other man said.

He took a bite of a sausage roll, flicked some flakes of pastry off the front of his uniform, then realised Santa Prime was waiting impatiently for more information.

"Oh. Right. Aye, sorry," he said, setting the sausage roll down on a napkin and turning to the monitors. "Your man. Your French guy..."

"Pére Noel?"

"Aye. Him."

The man with the scarred face then rolled his eyes. The damaged skin around them seemed to stretch impossibly tight.

"What about him, Bradley?"

"Well, I mean..." The counterfeit security guard, Bradley, gestured to the screens. "Where the fuck is he?"

Santa Prime's gaze flicked immediately back to the monitors, then darted between them. He watched as his underling pointed to a screen on the bottom row. It showed a broken vending machine and a set of wooden doors.

"He went in there. Right?" Bradley continued.

"Right," Santa Prime confirmed. "You're saying he didn't come back out?"

"Bingo. Didn't come back out of there. Didn't come out of any of the other doors, either. Not as far as I can tell."

"You tried his radio?"

Bradley turned in his chair, sucked in his bottom lip, and then spat it back out as he nodded. "Aye."

"Nothing?"

"Not a fucking cheep."

Silence hung in the air between them for a moment, then the man in the Father Christmas outfit unhooked his walkie-talkie from his belt and held it to his mouth.

"This is Santa Prime to Pére Noel. Santa Prime calling Pére Noel. Pére Noel, please confirm."

The low *burr* of static was the only response from the radio. Santa Prime checked the screens again, his gaze flitting faster between the monitors.

"Anyone seen Pére Noel lately?" he asked, spitting the words into the mouthpiece of the walkie-talkie. "Anyone got eyes on him?"

More static. More silence.

Eventually, a Russian-accented voice came back to him over the airwaves.

"He was here with me not long ago. At front," Ded Moroz announced. "You want I go look for him?"

Santa Prime chewed on a dirty thumbnail for a moment or two, then nodded.

"Do it. Find him."

"And what about security manager? What about my friend Nigel."

Up in the security room, Santa Prime shrugged. "Has he done what we wanted?"

"Da! Mission accomplished! Nigel was everything I hope for, and more."

"Good," Santa Prime said. "In that case, kill him."

"Wait, *what*?"

The voice in the background sounded frantic with fear. When the Russian spoke, his voice was quieter and further away, as he turned away from the radio.

"Sorry, Nigel. It is not personal."

"No, no, please, no, I have kids! I have kids, please don't—"

The sound of the shot came roaring from the walkie-talkie, forcing Santa Prime to quickly pull it away from his ear to avoid being deafened.

At the console, the man in the security guard uniform sat wide-eyed with amazement, his mouth twisted into something gleeful and wicked.

"Fuck me, that was badass!" he ejected. "That was fucking hilarious! You hear him? *Please, don't do this, I've got kids, an' that!*" He held out a clenched fist to the man in the Santa suit. "That was fucking epic!"

Santa Prime regarded the offered fist with a mix of disinterest and disdain, then got back on the radio to the Russian.

"Good job. Now, go find that French fuck. If he's lying sleeping somewhere, go right ahead and chew his nuts clean off."

"What if something's happened to him?" Bradley asked.

He tensed when Santa Prime put a hand on his shoulder.

"Let's try to stay positive, and assume he's just fine," he drawled. "Cause, if you let somethin' untoward happen to one of our boys on your watch..." He bent down lower, bringing his mouth close to Bradley's ear. "Well, now. In that case, we got ourselves a mighty big problem."

Bradley swallowed. His attention wasn't fixed on the man behind him, though, it had been caught by something being picked up by one of the external cameras. The snow was still falling, and a small mound of it had piled up against the camera's lens, but it was still possible to make out a couple of fire engines swinging up off the road and onto the pedestrianised Falcon Square, their blue lights swirling on their roofs.

"Um, speaking of problems..." he muttered.

Santa Prime followed his gaze and settled on the same screen. Both men watched pedestrians hurry to get out of the way as the fire engines rumbled to a stop in the snow.

They stopped parallel to the Eastgate Centre's Falcon Square entrance, twenty feet back from the doors. As the two men in the security room watched, half a dozen firefighters emerged from the trucks. Rather than move towards the building, though, they moved away so they were hidden from view by the fire engines.

Santa Prime straightened suddenly. He drew in a deep breath, then patted both hands on Bradley's shoulders.

"High fucking time!" he said, his ravaged face contorting itself with glee.

"What? But... I mean, it's the fire brigade. I thought it was the cops we were waiting on?"

"That *is* the cops."

Bradley looked back at the screen, frowning. "Eh, no. Maybe it's different in America, but they're fire engines. You know, for like, putting out fires, an' that?"

"Cops don't want us knowing it's them," Santa Prime explained. "They need to keep folks back, but they don't want to show their hand yet. They know we're watching, so they're hiding. But it's them, alright."

"Right. Aye." Bradley let out an unsteady breath. "Well, fuck. OK. So, it's all happening, then?"

"Of course it's happening. This was always happening. You knew what you were getting into. Don't you go losing your shit on me now," Santa Prime warned.

"No, no. No, I'm fine. My shit's no' going nowhere," Bradley assured him. "It's just... fuck. You know? I mean, after all the planning, an' that. It's like... It's happening."

"You bet your ass it is!" Santa Prime smiled, and almost skipped towards the exit. Just before he reached the door, he stopped and stabbed a finger at the telephone on the desk in front of Bradley. "Divert all calls to the satellite phone. When they make contact, they talk to me, and me alone."

"Eh, aye. Right you are, chief," Bradley said. "I'll do that now."

He stared at the phone for a moment. It was a big, complicated thing, with a stupid number of buttons. Judging by Bradley's confused expression, all the text printed on them might as well have been written in some ancient alien language.

"OK. So... How do I do...?"

With a tut, Santa Prime marched back around the desk, elbowed the other man aside, and tapped out a series of commands on the phone, before inputting a lengthy string of numbers.

That done, he jabbed a final button, stood back, and waited.

And waited.

"I don't think that's worked," Bradley remarked. "See, it's no' as easy as it looks."

A piercing series of *bleeps* rang out from one of the pockets of the Father Christmas suit. Santa Prime stabbed at the button on the desk phone again, and the ringing in his pocket stopped abruptly.

"I beg to fucking differ," he replied, heading for the door again. "You hear anything back on Pére Noel, you let me know."

"No bother. Will do, chief," Bradley said. He waited for the inner security room door to close, then listened for the outer one being pulled open before quietly adding, "Ya ugly big prick," below his breath.

Santa Prime threw open the outer door of the security room and stepped into another of the centre's grey, featureless corridors. He hung a left, headed for the walkway that passed behind the big musical clock.

From there, he could address his captives. He could let them know that things were proceeding according to plan. He could assure them that everything was going to be fine, and that they'd be home in no time.

And maybe some of the gullible fuckers might actually believe him.

He strode away, head held high, feeling pretty fucking pleased with himself.

So pleased with himself, in fact, that he failed to notice the figure in the tie-dye T-shirt slip from the shadows at his back and catch the door to the security room before it could automatically lock behind him.

CHAPTER TWENTY

DCI JACK LOGAN stood out of sight behind one of the fire engines, dishing out orders to the circle of plainclothes officers assembled around him. Most of his own team was there, with the exception of the heavily pregnant, just-about-ready-to-pop Sinead. If there was some sort of incident going on in the East-gate, a detective constable going into labour out front would only serve to further complicate matters.

"Right, where are we with Armed Response?" Logan asked.

"On their way, Jack," Detective Inspector Ben Forde replied.

Technically, he shouldn't have been there, either. His ongoing cardiac situation meant he was supposed to be desk-bound at all times. But there was something major going on here today. They could all sense it. And Ben was buggered if he was missing out on all the excitement.

He checked his watch. "Reckon they should be here any minute."

"Right. Good," Logan grunted. He pointed up towards the roof of the multi-storey car park that overlooked the shopping centre. "I want them high up. Get me clear lines of sight onto the roof. If anyone shows their face up there, I want to know about it."

"I'll let them know," Ben said.

He would, of course, though it wasn't necessary. The ARU guys were a reliable bunch, and they knew their job better than anyone.

Aye, some of them were somewhat unhinged—most of them, in fact, to some degree or another—but then, the same could be said for pretty much anyone doing front line polis work. After a while, it just had that effect on you.

Besides, there wasn't a huge amount of call for the Armed Response Unit in Inverness, so they had a lot of time on their hands. They'd mapped out the best sniper positions all across the entire city long before now.

"Good. I want as many eyes on the place as possible," Logan continued. "I want to know what's going on in there."

Beside him, Detective Constable Tyler Neish put his hands on his hips and drew a deep breath in through his teeth. "Tricky, boss. Windows are all covered," he observed.

"Aye, I'm no' blind, son, I can see that," Logan replied. "Maybe we can still see in, though. Get me thermal imaging cameras down here."

"Right. No bother, boss," Tyler said, taking out his phone. He stood there with his thumb poised over the screen for a moment, then looked up. "Is that the *Predator* ones?"

Everyone—Logan, DI Forde, Detective Sergeant Hamza Khaled, who stood a few paces away with his phone to his ear, and the three CID detectives who'd been dispatched from Burnett Road to assist—turned to look at the young detective.

"I'm sorry, what?" Logan asked.

Tyler smiled weakly. "Like, in the film? *Predator*. When he does the...." He held a hand up beside his eyes, like he was looking through a set of binoculars. "...thing. You mean like that?"

"They're no' going to ask you what bloody film it's from, Tyler," Logan barked. "They'll know what you're bloody talking about. Just get the request in. Thermal imaging cameras. That's all you need to say."

"Aye, boss. Right, boss. Sure thing, boss," Tyler said, half-saluting as he began scrolling through the contacts on his phone.

"And microphones," Logan added. "If we can't see, we at least need to hear what's happening in there."

"Are we sure it's even anything?" asked one of the CID guys who stood warming his hands on his takeaway coffee cup. "I mean, what do we actually know, aside from the fact that it's shut?"

Grover Depp was a few years older than Logan, but had been stuck as a DI for almost a decade. He felt some resentment over that, and didn't mind who knew it.

Nobody on the MIT had any idea what his real name was, but they all knew it wasn't really 'Grover'. He'd been saddled with that years ago, after some smartarse had remarked on how he looked like the wee furry blue bastard by the same name from *Sesame Street*.

And, sure enough, he did look like him. He was a different colour and texture, admittedly, and he didn't appear to be made of felt, but otherwise, the resemblance was genuinely quite striking.

"We know," Logan said. "There's definitely something wrong."

"But we don't know what it is?" Grover said. He gestured with his cup at the fire engines, and back around the corner to where several police cars were parked up out of sight. "So, all this could be overkill?"

Logan turned on him. "Aye. It could. And fingers bloody crossed that it is. But until I know for sure, I'm assuming the worst. If you've got a problem with that, pal, you can..." He thought for a moment, then shook his head and spun away. "Well, I don't give a shite what you do with it. Tyler!"

The shout almost made DC Neish drop his phone in fright.

"Jesus!" he gasped. Then, when he'd managed to grab hold of the handset again, he turned back. "Boss? It's only been about five seconds. I've not got hold of anyone yet."

"You said you and Sinead spoke to someone. Outside."

Tyler nodded. "Aye. Wee security guy. He's the one who told us the place was shut."

"Is he still there?"

Hamza took the phone from his ear, covered the mouthpiece, and shook his head. "We scouted round. Nobody there now, and the car park shutters are down."

Logan sighed through his nose. "Aye. That figures."

"Chopper's on its way, sir," Hamza continued. "Having problems with the snow, though. Still a couple of miles out."

"Tell it to stay as high as is safe," Logan instructed. "Don't want anyone inside getting wind of it, if we can help it."

"Will do, sir," Hamza confirmed, then he went back to his call.

"And we're *sure* this isn't just a big bloody waste of all our time?" Grover asked. "And that we're not standing here freezing our nuts off for nothing?"

Logan shoved his hands deep in the pockets of his coat. It was a trick he'd learned several years ago that stopped him from strangling people on pure instinct.

"Where'd you get that coffee?" he asked, nodding to the cup in the DI's hand.

Grover looked at the cup, then tilted his head back towards the town centre. "I got it at Costa. The Hamilton Street one."

"And you could find your way back there, could you? Through the snow?"

The DI looked a little confused by the question. "Of course, aye. It's just across the road and along. I could find it with my eyes shut, snow or no snow."

"Good. Glad to hear it," Logan said. He turned his back on the man for a second time. "DI Forde'll give you everyone's order. And if it gets here cold, I'll only send you back again." He looked back over his shoulder, and shot the DI a dangerous look. "So, I suggest you stop moaning, save your breath, and get your arse in bloody gear."

He turned away again, and looked past the fire engines to where the Eastgate Centre stood silently in the snow.

"I've a feeling we're all going to be in for a long, bloody night."

Behind him, Grover mumped and moaned as DI Forde scribbled down the team's usual tea and coffee order, ripped the page from his notebook, and handed it over.

"Mind and keep the receipt," Ben said.

The other DI didn't answer, though, and instead just set off through the snow, his crunching footsteps steadily fading away until they couldn't be heard over the sound of passing traffic.

Ben joined Logan in the shadow of the fire engine. The swirling blue lights danced across their faces.

"I'd be wary of drinking my coffee, if I was you," Ben remarked. "Knowing that bastard, he'll have gobbed in it on the way back."

"Aye," Logan agreed. "That's why I'm planning on swapping with you."

Ben chuckled. "I'd like to see you bloody try."

Both men stood in silence for a while. Around them, Hamza and Tyler spoke quietly but urgently into their phones. The other CID guys hung back a bit, like they were either waiting to be invited to join the conversation, or hoping not to be dragged into it.

"You look worried, Jack," Ben said.

"You know me. I'm always worried."

"More than usual."

Logan shot him a sideways look. "Aye. Maybe," he admitted.

Hamza finished his call, returned his phone to his pocket, then came over to join them. He'd grown up in Aberdeen, exposed to the harsh, biting winds that blew in off the North Sea.

Even so, he shivered in the cold as the snow swirled and danced around them.

"Right, you ready?" Logan asked.

Something close to panic flitted across DS Khaled's face. "Ready, sir? For what?"

"The phone thing. The recorder."

"Oh! That!" Hamza exhaled with relief. He opened one of the fire engine doors to reveal a bulky phone handset attached to digital recording equipment with a curly length of wire. "Aye. It's ready to go when you are, sir."

"Good," Logan said. He rolled his head around on his shoulders, stretching his neck. He flexed his fingers, cracked his knuckles, then finally gave a nod. "Then I think it's high time we got on the blower and gave whoever's in there a call."

Hoon slid silently in through the front door of the security room, and closed it gently at his back. He found himself in a short, narrow corridor that had been given much more care and attention than those on the other side of the door.

They had gone to the trouble of plastering the walls in here, for one thing, and the scuffed stone floor had been swapped out for some polished oak flooring.

The corridors beyond the door were for moving cargo around in, designed for functionality alone. People were expected to spend time in this area, though, so they'd made an effort to make it look less prison-like.

There were windows on either side of the hallway. Both offered glimpses into offices beyond—or they would've done, had blinds not been drawn across them both from the inside.

Keeping low, Hoon crept to the door on his left, listened for a moment, then turned the handle. He opened the door just an inch or two—just enough for him to peek in.

He smelled the gore before he saw it. Three bodies—a man and a woman dressed like senior staff, and what looked to be a wee ned who'd picked the wrong day to go shoplifting—lay piled on the floor, tangled together like they were one creature.

One very much dead creature.

Their throats had been slit. Their blood had fountained out in an arcing spray across the room, painting the walls, and the blinds, and the carpet, and the desk. The woman's eyes were open and staring blankly at him. Not pleading—it was far too late for that—just staring in a sort of idle curiosity, like she was waiting to see what he might do next.

Hoon closed the door. He wasted a moment or two leaning his head against the frame in silence, then he continued along the corridor and hung a left, heading for where he knew he'd find the inner door to the security room.

This one wouldn't be locked. The main door had enough reinforcement to it to stop all but the most determined of charging elephants, and was protected by a key code locking system.

The assumption was that no bugger was getting past that entrance, so those beyond it didn't need anything more than bog-standard locks. These would be secured at closing time, but otherwise remained unlocked for most of the day.

Handy, that.

Hoon dropped fully into a crouch as he closed in on the security room's inner door. A wide window that looked into the room started halfway up the wall, so he kept his head below that, staying out of sight of whoever was waiting inside.

He heard movement—the creaking of a chair, the tapping of a key—but nothing to indicate that anyone inside was aware of his presence.

Shifting the shotgun to his left hand, he reached up, carefully turned the door handle, then sprang to his feet as he rushed inside.

"Alright, nobody move a fucking..." he began, pointing the shotgun at a chair.

The chair was notable for the fact that it was slowly spinning, and even more so for the fact that it was empty.

"Muscle," Hoon concluded, then a sudden movement over on his right made him spin.

He was too late to get the gun between him and the charging security guard. Bent low, the guy hit him, shoulder first, roaring and gnashing his teeth, powering forward with every ounce of strength that he had.

Hoon was forced to take a half-step sideways. Less than that, even.

He looked down at the back of the man currently wrestling with him, muttered a half-embarrassed, "Oh, for fuck's sake," then drove an elbow sharply downwards between his attacker's shoulder blades.

The other guy went down hard, his face smacking off the floor with an audible, tooth-chipping *crunch*.

Almost at once, he began to thrash around on the oak floor like he was having some sort of spasm. He held his hands cupped protectively over his face, while his legs kicked, frog-like, in a largely futile attempt to propel himself to safety.

Hoon placed a violently orange trainer on the man's back, pinning him to the floor. The thrashing became more frantic, but a shifting of Hoon's weight soon brought the downed attacker under control.

By the time Hoon had placed both barrels of the shotgun against the back of his head, the other man was as still as a statue.

"Well, that was pretty humiliating all round," Hoon said. "I mean, Jesus Christ, son, what the fuck have you been feeding yourself up on? Cotton wool and fresh air? My fucking *sense of direction* is stronger than you are.

"But, listen, tell you what—I'll do you a favour, and promise never to speak of that fucking tidal wave of embarrassment again, if you do me a favour, and promise no' to spontaneously fucking combust like your wee pal downstairs."

He pressed harder with the shotgun, drawing a whimper from the man on the floor.

"I'm going to take that near-silence as agreement," Hoon said. "So, now that we've got that out of the way, I'm going to ask you a few rather fucking probing questions. And, between you and me, pal..."

He used the shotgun to roll the other man's head to one side, so a big, watery eye was staring up at him in terror.

Hoon grinned. It was the sort of smile usually worn by monsters in the nightmares of children.

"A big part of me's hoping that you don't fucking answer."

CHAPTER TWENTY-ONE

DED MOROZ HAD A NIGEL PROBLEM. He couldn't get the bastard off his boots.

He'd tried wiping the soles on the mat of the *Toymaster* store just around from the entrance he'd been guarding, but even after a full thirty seconds of shuffling around, he was leaving tacky red footprints on the floor behind him.

Nigel had got himself deep into the treads of the shoes like a big daud of dog shit. It was like a sort of low-level haunting, with the recently deceased doomed to follow his killer around until justice had been done.

Or until he walked through a puddle. Whichever came sooner.

The Russian *schlacked* his way across the food court, his gun cradled like a baby in his arms. He hummed as he walked, an old Christmas tune that reminded him of the homeland.

Not fondly. But then, he never thought fondly of anything.

The glass of the broken vending machine crunched under his feet. He stopped at it, took a moment to make his selection, then helped himself to a can of *Irn Bru*.

Cracking the ring pull, Ded Moroz tipped half the can down

his throat in one big gulp, then let out a burp that echoed all the way along the corridor to the toilets.

"What is this shit?" he spat, and he scowled at the can like it had personally offended him. "Fucking rat piss."

Despite his obvious distaste for the drink, he necked the rest of the can, grimaced at it, then crushed it in one hand, like Popeye with a can of spinach. It clattered loudly on the floor behind him, then he set off towards the doors where Pére Noel had last been seen.

He didn't bother with caution or stealth. When you were his size, you rarely had to concern yourself with such things. Instead, he placed a hand on one of the doors, palm flat, fingers splayed, and pushed it open until it banged against the wall of the corridor on the other side.

"Coo-eee!" he called in a sing-song voice. He pursed his lips together, making a kissing sound that was presumably meant to be enticing. "Here, kitty kitty."

He grinned into the darkness, like he was expecting it to laugh at his comedy genius. When it didn't, he tried again.

"*Heeeere,* kitty kitty. Do not be afraid. *Deddy's* here. Deddy will look after you."

The Russian stepped into the corridor, and looked up just as the lights began to *clunk* on one by one. The shadows were driven back, like the dark itself was afraid of him, and of what he might do.

He let the door squeak closed behind him, then advanced along the corridor, his SMG held in one hand, ready to spray a hot, fiery death at anyone who got in his way. With his other hand, he walked two fingers along the wall—a tiny figure advancing menacingly across the rough masonry blocks.

"Here I come, ready or not. It is not my fault if you get caught!" he sang.

There was a *thud* behind him. He spun on the spot, blind-

ingly quickly for a man of his size, his finger tightening on the
trigger of his weapon.

The door he'd come through finished settling back into
place, and silence rang out in the narrow confines of the corridor.

Ded Moroz waited long enough to be sure nobody was
coming through the door, then he turned and continued onwards
again, his machine gun panning left to right.

His left hand didn't go back to finger-walking along the wall.
The smirk that he'd been wearing was fading, too, the novelty of
the search already wearing off.

"Where are you, fucking piece of shit?" he muttered as he
stalked along the corridor. "If you are hiding like coward, I will
wring your fucking neck myself. Like chicken! *Buuuck-buck-
buck* little chicken."

A door on his left caught his eye, before something at floor
level demanded all his attention. A puddle of red had seeped out
under the door, and was pooling in an indent on the corridor
floor.

"What fuck is this shit?" the Russian asked, not yet moving
towards the door.

He unhooked his radio from his belt, brought it to his mouth,
then thought better of it before he thumbed the call button.

No point contacting anyone until he had more information.
No point causing drama without knowing what he was looking
at. A lot of these fuckers were amateurs. Drama would cause
panic. Panic would screw up the whole plan.

He returned the radio to his belt. He adjusted his grip on
his gun.

And then, with the overhead strip lights buzzing ominously
above him, Ded Moroz opened the door to a room marked,
'Heating System.'

He let the door swing open all the way until the room's
tableau of horror was fully revealed.

The first thing he saw was the blood. It covered pretty much every available surface, so it would've been hard for him to miss.

The next thing he saw was a pair of legs lying on the floor, intestinal matter spilling from the top of them like purple modelling balloons filled with day-old curry.

Displaying the caution that he'd been lacking earlier, the Russian carefully entered the room, and the Nigel in his boots became deeply acquainted with the viscous, congealing remains of Pére Noel.

The big shed-sized heating units were humming away, pushing warm air into the vents above. Ded Moroz sploshed through the puddle of Frenchman, his gaze darting around the room like he might be able to spot all the missing pieces that should be attached to the legs.

Technically, he did spot them—a few knobbly bits here, some charred flesh there—but most of it, aside from a couple of fingers and a patch of hairy scalp, was damaged beyond all recognition.

He stopped beside the heating unit that had been closest to the blast. He knew it had been closest because almost an entire side of it had been absolutely plastered with mushy red gore, which had darkened as it had cooked in the heat.

With a sleeve, he brushed off some of the drying innards, exposing the metal below. It was smooth and undamaged. He thought he felt perhaps the faintest of dents as he ran his fingers across it, but the temperature of the metal meant he couldn't let his touch linger there long enough to be sure.

But, that wasn't right.

That didn't make sense.

He made a number of remarks in guttural sounding Russian, ran a hand down his face, then reached for his radio again. The blood on his fingers, and the burns on their tips, meant the walkie-talkie slipped from his grip, clattered on the floor at his feet, then bounced twice in the blood puddle, before coming to rest up near the crotch end of the disembodied legs.

Muttering below his breath, Ded Moroz crouched, reached between the legs, and plucked the radio free. He was about to stand up again, when he spotted a bundle of material jammed beneath the heating unit.

Kneeling in the pool of gore, he reached in and rummaged around until he managed to get hold of the knotted fabric. Pulling it free, he ducked to see if there was anything else under there, then let out a string of Russian expletives when he saw part of a face staring back at him.

Recoiling, he stood up and squelched backwards, being careful not to trip over the legs. He swung his gun onto his shoulder and unfurled the fabric he'd recovered.

It was a suit jacket. A pretty nice one, too. Or, at least, it would've been, were it not quite so caked in blood and brain matter.

Ded Moroz looked at the jacket, then down at the mess on the floor. Clearly, this didn't belong to his now largely liquid former cohort. It had been stuffed in there post-explosion, too, which meant it almost certainly belonged to whoever was responsible for Pére Noel's grisly fate.

The Russian gave the jacket a shake. The weight was off, pulling it slightly to one side. The distribution of gunk and gore seemed pretty even, so it wasn't that.

Keeping hold of the back of the collar with one hand, he searched the front pockets, but found nothing.

The same could not be said for the inside pocket.

Ded Moroz dropped the jacket. It fell to the floor, flapping open, covering up some of the human debris that was lying there.

"Well, now," the big Russian muttered. He turned a slim black wallet over in one hand. "What do we have here...?"

CHAPTER TWENTY-TWO

SANTA PRIME STOOD on the bridge-like walkway behind the musical clock, listening to the hushed whispers and desperate sobbing of the hostages just a few feet below.

His hostages.

Granted, he hadn't done all this himself—there were far too many moving parts for that—but he was the key to it all. He was the driving force behind it. He'd created the group in the first place. He'd found others like him, others sickened by what the world was in danger of becoming, and he'd turned them into an army.

He'd taken the most downtrodden, most disrespected, most unfairly treated and marginalised group of people in the whole damn world, and he had taught them to rise up. He had given them what they needed to fight—not the tools, they'd come from elsewhere—but the desire. The urge. The strength. He'd given them all that, and more.

They called him their leader. But that was selling him short. He considered himself much more than that.

He wasn't their leader. He was their *Messiah*. And today, he was leading them to the Promised Land.

The back of his head rested against the rear of the clock. He could feel the mechanism turning through the metal casing, counting down to its next musical interlude.

He'd need to make a speech soon. He could hear the hostages getting restless. It sounded like one of them was even singing—*Rudolph the Red-Nosed Reindeer*, he thought, though she was mangling it so badly it was hard to tell.

A speech would get them back in line. He'd make some threats. Throw his weight around. Scare the shit out of them. They'd soon fall back into line.

He enjoyed the speeches. Those were fun.

And to think how much he used to hate doing that sort of thing back in high school. His stammer had meant it was difficult, but it was the constant sniggering and teasing from the other kids that had made it impossible.

Or worse—the pitying looks from some of the *nicer* kids, mixed with their relief that he was the one taking the brunt of it, and not them.

Back then, nobody had listened. Nobody had ever paid attention to him.

But they were listening now. Now, they'd hang on his every word.

It was amazing the difference a few years could make.

Plus the guns, of course. The guns almost certainly helped.

Before he could stand up and reveal himself to his audience, the front pocket of his Santa suit began to purr.

The phone. The satellite phone was ringing.

This was it.

His moment had come.

He'd let them wait a bit. Let them sweat it out.

Using the back of the clock for support, he pushed himself up on his feet, then took some time to peek down at the hostages below. He'd ordered a head count earlier, but nobody had fed it back to him yet. There had to be three or four hundred people there at least, though, all jammed in together. All trapped. All at his mercy.

All destined to be immortalised in the record books.

They wouldn't all be named, though. Not like him. His name would be at the top of the entry, in big bold print. His name would be the one that would be remembered.

He continued across the bridge until he found himself at the top of a staircase. There, he took a seat on the top step, removed the phone from his pocket, and placed it on the floor beside him.

The light on the simple, text-only screen flashed on and off. The phone continued to buzz.

Santa Prime fished around in the other pocket of his coat until he found a battered pack of cigarettes and a lighter. He lit one, took a few long drags, then picked up the phone.

"Who am I talking to?" he asked, not beating around the bush.

"That's funny. I was about to ask you the same thing," came the reply.

It was a man. That was something. Probably white. Santa Prime hadn't been here long, but he'd found the lack of racial diversity up here in the Highlands to be quite refreshing. He'd seen only a handful of black faces around Inverness, and the place was all the better for it.

"I asked you first," Santa Prime said.

There was a pause, though not a long one.

"Detective Chief Inspector Jack Logan, Police Scotland Major Investigations. I'd like to talk to Nigel."

"Well, I'm afraid I have some bad news for you, Mr Logan. Nigel can't come to the phone right now. He's, uh..." A smile played across his scarred face. "*Indisposed.*"

Another pause. There was some whispering, but too quiet for him to hear.

"OK. So, I suppose that brings me back to the question I was going to ask at the start. Who might you be?"

"I am the man who is going to fuck up your Christmas, Mr Logan. I'm the Grinch. I'm Ebenezer Scrooge. Think of me as your own personal Krampus." He flinched, annoyed. "Shit. *Krampus*. That would've been better than Santa Prime. Fuck!"

"What are you on about, son?" Logan asked.

"Do you speak for the city?" the man in the Santa suit demanded.

"What?"

"The city, *motherfucker*, do you speak for it?"

There were voices in the background, low and urgent.

"Well, I'm no' sure about that, exactly," Logan said. He started to say more, but Santa Prime shouted him down.

"Then you'd better hurry the fuck up and find me someone who can. Because I got four hundred very frightened people in here who ain't gonna live to see Christmas if I don't get what I want."

"What do you want?" Logan asked.

Santa Prime ignored the question. "I got your number now. I'm going to call you back in fifteen minutes. That's fifteen minutes to go sort your shit out, Mr Logan. Fifteen minutes to either get authorisation to speak on behalf of the city, or to find me someone who can."

He took a draw on his cigarette, then stubbed it out on the stone step.

"And I don't want to talk to that *mongrel* you got giving you orders. I ain't gonna debase myself by talking to someone like her," he said. He listened for a response, but got none, so he continued. "Fifteen minutes, or those four hundred folks I talked about? All those men, women, and kids? I start whittling them numbers down, one by one. And I whittle fast. I whittle real fast. Do we understand each other, Mr Logan?"

There was silence. He could almost hear the blood bubbling away in the other man's veins, all the way through the satellite link. An anger that coursed through outer space.

"We do," Logan confirmed.

"Good."

And then, without giving the detective a chance to say anything more, Santa Prime terminated the call.

He leapt to his feet, thrust both arms in the air, and let out a *whoop* of triumph.

"Hot damn!" he cried, adrenaline surging through his veins. "Hot *fucking* damn! This shit is happening! This shit is finally fucking happening!"

The call was perfect. It had been just like he'd always imagined. He hadn't just taken charge, he'd *dominated*. He'd owned every moment. The other guy hadn't known what hit him. He'd been outclassed, outmatched, outmanoeuvred, and outwitted. He'd been fucking *destroyed*!

"Yeah! Goddamn! I got this shit in the bag!" Santa Prime announced, his voice booming down the stairs, and echoing off the rough stone walls.

Everything was working. Everything was going *exactly* as planned. Everything was—

There was a squawk from the walkie-talkie on his belt.

"Ded Moroz to Santa Prime. Respond. Urgent."

Santa Prime unclipped the radio. "Prime. What do we have?"

"What do we have?" repeated the Russian. "What we have is problem," he said. "Big fucking problem."

Santa Prime listened as Ded Moroz explained what he'd found. The elation that had propelled him onto his feet became poisoned first by anger, and then—though he'd never admit it, not even to himself—by a creeping sense of dread. By a realisation that things might not be going perfectly to plan, after all, and by a fear that worse may be yet to come.

"Did you look him up?" he asked the man on the radio. "Do we know who this fucker is?"

"No. I cannot search him. We have no internet. Blockers are stopping connection."

"Well, then talk to the fucking security room. That's still online," Santa Prime hissed. "Jesus Christ, do I have to think of fucking everything? Call him up. Get him to run a search, and get him to cycle the cameras. If there's someone fucking around playing hero in here, I want him found. You got that?"

"Da. I got it," the Russian replied.

"Yeah, well," Santa Prime spat. "See that you fucking have!"

Ded Moroz held his walkie-talkie at arm's length, then silently raised a middle finger at it. With the press of a button, he digitally retuned to a different frequency, and put a call through to the security room.

"Security station, this is Ded Moroz. Pick up."

He leaned a hand against the corridor wall, and lifted first one boot, then the other, examining the soles. The amber-coloured rubber had been stained red. There were chunks of gristle, and a clump of matted hair wedged between the ridges. He used the stubby aerial of the radio to dislodge the worst of it, then brought the handset back to his mouth.

"Security station. What is holdup?"

Static hissed. The silence echoed.

A frown began a slow descent across the Russian's broad face.

"Security?" he said. "What is happening?"

This time, the silence was broken by a brief screech of feedback, and some frantic clattering.

"Sorry, aye. Sorry. Here now," came the slightly breathless reply from Bradley. "Had to go for a piss."

"Do not leave your fucking station again," the Russian barked.

"Eh, right, aye. Sorry. I was just... I was bursting."

"We have problem."

The man on the other end hesitated. When he spoke again, there was a sort of squeak to it. "Oh? What sort of problem?"

"We have interloper. Moving around behind scenes. I want you to check name."

"Name? What do you mean? Whose name? The guy's name?"

"Yes, fucking guy's name! What other name would it be?"

"Sorry, sorry. Aye. Go on."

Ded Moroz fished the driving licence from his pocket and checked the details. "Name is Robert Hoon. In photograph, he looks rough. Like old dog. Or like half-chewed dog bone, maybe. Like something dog shat out."

Bradley let out a shrill laugh that sounded almost pained.

"Haha! Yeah. Right. Aye, I get the picture," he said.

Across the airwaves came the sound of keys being tapped. Ded Moroz used the driving licence to pick some more scraps of flesh from his boots.

"Nah, nothing," said Bradley.

"What? What you mean, 'nothing'? How is nothing?"

"Like, I mean, I don't get anyone matching that name."

"Nobody? Nobody in whole fucking world?" the Russian demanded.

"Well, I mean, there's a teacher in Ohio..."

"Does he look like old dog shit?"

"No," Bradley replied. "He looks... I mean, he looks alright. Like, mid-thirties, maybe. Nice smile. Decent suit."

Ded Moroz shook his head. "It is not him. This guy looks like absolute fucking turd." He sighed. "Nobody else? Not Face-book, or nothing?"

"No. Nothing. Just that guy."

The Russian used the licence to ping a particularly stubborn piece of scalp from where it had been jammed in his boot tread.

It splatted against the wall beside him, then rolled slowly down to the floor.

"Fine. Prime wants you watching cameras. All cameras, one after other."

"Aye, no bother."

"And keep door locked. You need to piss, you piss yourself. You understand?"

"Yeah. Fine. Yeah, I get it," Bradley said. He swallowed audibly. "I understand. If I see anything, you'll be the first to know."

Bradley slowly held out the radio, being careful not to make any sudden movements. The last thing he wanted to do was startle the man who currently had both barrels of a sawn-off shotgun jammed against his testicles.

He had made his peace with death before coming here. That had been a big part of the training.

What he hadn't had the chance to make peace with was the idea of explosive castration. Death? Death would be glorious. Having his balls shot up through his arse? Not so much.

Hoon took the walkie-talkie and clipped it to the waistband of his painfully tight jeans. On-screen beside Bradley, a big list of search results showed all of the former detective superintendent's publicly available details, including—but not limited to—his employment history.

"Nicely done there, son," he said, withdrawing the shotgun from the younger man's crotch. "But what the fuck was all that about me looking like something a dog shat out? I mean, that was a bit fucking personal, wasn't it? Cheeky bastard. I bet he's no' exactly a fucking oil painting himself."

"They're looking for you now," Bradley said, still eyeing up the shotgun. It was no longer aiming at his testicles, but all it would take was a flick of the wrist to bring it back again. "You should get out. They'll find you. You should run."

Hoon put a hand over his mouth, his eyes going wide with worry.

"Shite. You think?"

Bradley quickly nodded. "Aye. Aye, I do. Like, just run. Just get out. I won't tell anyone."

"You promise?" Hoon asked. "You'd really do that for me? Even after I was going to shoot your cock off?"

The man sitting in the chair didn't reply this time. The levels of sarcasm were too high for him to miss.

"You're not going to run, are you?"

"Am I fuck," Hoon said. "We've still got that wee chat to have. Except now, we need to horse on and rattle through it. Because, like you said, your wee pals are going to be on the hunt for me now. So, bang goes all the getting to know each other small talk, eh? Shame. I was quite looking forward to finding out what a horrible, jazz-fingered wee bastard you are. But, you know, it is what it is, I suppose."

Bradley whimpered as his gonads were once again pancaked against the chair by the twin barrels of the gun.

"So, how about I just stand here in ominous silence, son, and you go ahead and tell me everything you fucking know?"

CHAPTER TWENTY-THREE

MILES CRABTREE SAT in a secure office at Inverness Airport, rubbing his chin, deep in thought. Samantha—or Suranne, as she still insisted on calling herself—sat cuffed to a table in the corner, a police officer standing on either side of her, and another two stationed outside the front door.

Suranne hadn't said much since the hearing. In total, in fact, she'd uttered just six words—"Shut the fuck up," and, "I'm hungry,"—with a gap of about two hours between them.

Now, she sat with her head back, shooting daggers at the ceiling like it had personally wronged her in some way. Occasionally, she'd let out a long, slow sigh, but otherwise, she remained pretty much silent.

Kevin, the assistant, sat across the narrow office from Miles, so they were face to face. He had his phone open in front of him and was peering over the top of the screen, waiting for Miles to give an instruction.

Up on the wall, the ticking of a clock marked each passing second.

Miles ran his tongue around the inside of his mouth, then fixed Kevin with a solemn stare.

"Shone," he said.

Kevin's gaze crept downwards to his screen. His thumb tapped six times.

"No. The S and the E are green, though."

"So, they're in the right place?" asked Miles, who still wasn't entirely sure on the rules.

"They're in the right place," Kevin confirmed.

Silence fell again. The clock ticked. Sitting at her table, Suranne exhaled slowly through her nose.

"Shame," Miles guessed.

Kevin continued to look at him over the top of the phone.

"Shame," the MI5 man said again, in case the assistant hadn't heard him.

"You sure, sir?" Kevin asked. "Because you know there's no H in it."

"Do we?" Miles asked, then he winced. "Oh. Yes. So we do. Don't put that then." He tapped his chin with a finger a few times, then said, "Slime. What about slime?"

"You want me to try slime?"

"Try slime," Miles confirmed.

He watched as his assistant punched in the letters, then tutted when he shook his head.

"It's not slime, sir."

"Any green letters?"

"No, sir."

"Any *orange* letters?"

"No green or orange letters, sir."

Miles thumped the heel of his hand against his chair. "Damn it! It's tricky, isn't it?"

"I mean... Yeah. That's sort of the point, sir," Kevin said. "Two guesses left."

"Christ. Just two?" Miles looked worried. He turned to the two uniformed officers flanking the seated prisoner. "What about you lads? Any ideas?"

One of the men, a heavy-set sergeant with his years of experience etched on his face as deep lines, gave a grunt and shook his head.

"Sorry," he said. "I wasn't listening."

Miles uncrossed his legs and sat forward. "Well, so far, we've guessed—"

"No, I mean I wasn't listening on purpose. It's not really my scene," the sergeant said, cutting him short. "I'm not interested in getting involved."

"Oh. Right," Miles said, taken a bit aback. "Well, I mean, thank you for your honesty, I suppose."

He turned his attention to the other officer. This one was larger, but younger. He was a constable and hadn't yet been afflicted by the world-weary demeanour of his senior officer.

"How about you? Any ideas?"

"Me?"

"Yes! You must have some ideas," Miles urged. "Let's hear them."

"Uh, maybe *spare*?" suggested the officer.

Miles frowned. "Spare?"

"Yes, sir," the constable said. "Like, as in 'spare prick,' sir."

His sergeant's body language didn't really change, and yet pride seemed to radiate from him.

"Aye. That's a good guess, Constable," he said, staring straight ahead.

"Cheers, Sarge. I thought so."

Miles sat back. "Yes. Well, I doubt it'll be that," he said, with as much authority as he could muster.

He placed his hands in his lap, touched the tips of his fingers together, and then gave the problem some more thought.

Finally, he said, "I mean, it can't hurt to try it, I suppose..."

"You want me to put spare, sir?" Kevin asked.

"As in 'spare prick,'" the sergeant added.

Miles side-eyed him, then gave Kevin a nod. The assistant

tapped away at his screen, waited for a moment, then slowly sat forwards.

"Ooh. Now. The P and the A are right."

Miles mirrored him, leaning closer across the gap. "Really? Shit! So, what does that give us?" he asked breathlessly.

"SPA—blank—E," Kevin told him. "One guess left."

"One guess left. God!" Miles said.

The clock on the wall continued its slow, steady tick.

"Spake," Miles said.

Kevin appeared taken aback by the suggestion. "Spake?"

"Yeah. Like the past... whatever of speak."

"Do you no' mean spoke?" asked the uniformed constable.

"No. It's a word. Spake. It's definitely a word."

Kevin nodded keenly. "Yes. It's a word. It's definitely a word, sir. I just think... Is it likely to be the answer?"

"Well, it can't be anything else, can it?" Miles reasoned.

The assistant pursed his lips, considering his reply.

"I mean... it could be space," he reasoned.

"Space! Shit. Yes. Space. It's probably space, isn't it?"

"Or spade," said the sergeant, finally getting involved.

"Oh, *God!*" Suranne ejected. "Can someone get me a spade so I can bury myself alive? Rather that than listen to this!"

Miles jabbed a finger at her in warning. "Button it, you," he warned, then he nodded to Kevin. "It's space. Put space."

"You sure, sir? This is your last chance."

"Do it."

Kevin tapped in the word.

He hit submit.

He shook his head.

"No. Sorry, sir. You were right. It was spake."

"See?" Miles cried, throwing his hands up in despair. "I bloody knew it! I said it would be spake, didn't I?"

"You did, sir," Kevin admitted. He bowed his head in deference. "I'm sorry I doubted you, sir."

There was a knock at the door, sharp and sudden. It was the sort of knock that wasn't asking for permission to enter, and was instead just warning you that someone was about to come in, so you should probably get dressed, if you weren't already.

The two Uniforms standing either side of Suranne both straightened, but neither one made a move towards the door.

Even Suranne herself looked interested by this development. There were a couple of hours until her flight. Nobody was meant to be coming for her yet.

Well, nobody official, anyway.

"Uh, yes? Come," Miles said, though the door had already opened before his mouth could.

One of the officers who had been stationed outside the room stepped inside, completely ignoring him as he addressed the other two officers.

"Sarge. A word."

The sergeant nodded curtly, and shot a look at the constable that seemed to designate him as the person now in charge. Then, without so much as a glance at Miles or Kevin, he followed the other officer out into the corridor and closed the door behind them.

"What's that about, I wonder?" Kevin remarked.

Miles kept watch of the door, waiting for it to open again. He could hear muttering from out there. It was too low to make out what was being said, but whatever it was, it sounded serious.

"I don't know," Miles admitted. He turned to the constable, who could only shrug.

"Don't look at me. No idea."

The door opened again. When the sergeant returned, Miles was sure there were another few lines on his face.

"We need to go," the officer said.

Miles and Kevin both jumped to their feet at the same time, like a man and his funhouse mirror reflection.

"What? Why? What's happened?" Miles demanded. "Are they here? Are they after her? Where do we need to go?"

"Not you," the sergeant said. "You three need to stay here. We... us." He pointed to himself and the other uniformed officer. "We need to go. Major incident in the city centre. Everyone's being called in."

"What? What sort of incident?" Miles asked.

"A big one," the sergeant said. "That's all I'm at liberty to say."

"What?! But what about us? What about her?" Miles asked. "We need to keep hold of her and keep her safe until the transport arrives."

"You've got your own guys, haven't you?" asked the sergeant. "The ones in suits hanging around out there in the airport, pretending not to be with you."

Miles stuttered out the start of a denial, then sighed.

"You're not supposed to know they're there."

"Aye, well, I do. We all do," the sergeant informed him. "So, either you can keep an eye on her yourself, or you can call them in. Because us—me and him? We're out of here."

Detective Superintendent Mitchell didn't much care for snow.

It was fine watching it from a distance. From her window, for example. Or, better yet, on one of the *Hallmark* Christmas movies she always became mildly addicted to at this time of year, despite the fact that they all had exactly the same characters and plot.

Up close, though? In person? She was not a fan of snow.

She was especially not a fan of standing out in it at dinner time on the day before Christmas Eve, surrounded by uniformed officers, and fearing for the safety of several hundred hostages.

It meant she was even more irritable than usual as she listened to the update from DCI Logan.

"So, what you're telling me, Jack, is that we know nothing," she said, neatly summarising the last couple of minutes' worth of conversation.

"We know they've got people in there," Logan countered.

"We *think* they've got people in there," Mitchell said. "Based on the word of one man you spoke to."

Logan shook his head. "Not quite, ma'am. We're starting to get reports coming into the station. People not coming home from work. A school group that didn't come back to class. Can't account for a few hundred yet, but a couple of dozen already, and calls are still coming in."

Mitchell groaned. "God. Right. What about thermal imaging?"

"Equipment's being brought in, ma'am," Logan told her. "Shouldn't be long."

"And ARU?"

"In position," Logan said. They were still hidden from the centre's cameras by the fire engines, but he was careful not to look up at any of the nearby rooftops, in case he gave any of the armed units' locations away. "Snow's making visibility a nightmare, though. We're trying to get eyes on the roof of the centre and the upper windows, but not having much luck so far."

"Great. That's not what I wanted to hear, Jack."

"I know, ma'am. I'm no' exactly singing and dancing about it, either."

Mitchell shoved her hands deeper into the pockets of her jacket. It was a heavy thing with a thick lining, but the cold never tired of finding ways inside.

"They're sending up a negotiator," she said. "From Glasgow."

"Who is it? Do we know?"

Mitchell glanced upwards for a moment, like she was

retrieving the name from some mental Filofax. "Simon something. Barton? Can't say I'm familiar with him."

Logan's jaw bones moved beneath his skin, grinding together.

"Barron. Simon Barron."

"You know him?"

"Aye."

"What's he like?"

Logan's nostrils flared. "Insufferable."

"Oh. Well, that's something to look forward to then. Although, he's also hours away," Mitchell said. "So, with a bit of luck, we'll have this handled before he arrives. I'll talk to them."

Outwardly, Logan didn't react. Inwardly, though, he winced.

"They, eh, they expressly requested not to speak to you, ma'am," he said.

He felt her turning towards him, but kept staring ahead. He'd been holding the coffee that Grover had brought him and using it to warm his hands. Now, though, he risked taking a sip, if only to delay answering the question he knew she was about to ask.

"And why did they ask that?"

"I don't know, ma'am," Logan lied. "Just... I get the impression they want to speak to a man."

"Well, tough shit," Mitchell said. "They can talk to me, and they can bloody well like it."

Before Logan could try and persuade her that this might not be the best idea, DS Khaled came running up holding a phone in front of him like it was a magical amulet with which to ward off evil.

"Sir! Sir," he panted, each bounding footstep throwing up a clump of fresh snow. "It's base. There's been a call."

"A call? From whom?" Detective Superintendent Mitchell demanded before Logan could utter a word.

Hamza stumbled to a stop in front of them. "It's, eh, it's from Hoon, ma'am," the DS said. "It's Bob Hoon. Asking for you, sir."

"For God's sake, that's all I bloody need," Logan muttered. "Tell him it isn't a good time. I'll call him back tomorrow."

Hamza shook his head, and all but thrust the mobile into the Detective Chief Inspector's hands.

"Trust me, sir," he said. "You're *really* going to want to take this call."

Logan narrowed his eyes. He looked from Hamza to Mitchell, then finally down at the phone he was now holding.

"What now?" he muttered, then he brought the phone to his ear. "Bob? I'm right in the middle of something here. I'm going to have to..."

His voice trailed away into silence. He listened, his eyes widening, his jaw slowly dropping until his mouth hung open in a silent scream.

"Hold on, hold on, wait a minute," Logan said. He turned and looked past the fire engines in the direction of the shopping centre. "You're *where?*"

CHAPTER TWENTY-FOUR

HOON SAT on the desk in the security room, the bank of monitors at his back, the gagged security guard tied to the chair in front of him.

There had been plenty of things in the room with which to silence his prisoner—not least of all the big roll of masking tape with which he'd been tied to the chair. Hoon had opted for the same approach he'd used with the Frenchman downstairs, though, and had force-fed the bastard his own socks. Why fix something that wasn't broken?

He sat watching the guard, one foot resting on the chair, right between his captive's legs. With a tilt of his ankle, he'd be able to slow-motion annihilate the other man's testicles—something both of them were only too aware of.

The security room's phone—the only working fixed line in and out of the centre—was pressed to one ear. The shotgun sat along the desk from him, within easy grabbing reach.

"Fuck's sake, are you deaf?" he asked, before shifting the phone from one ear to the other. "I said I'm in the Eastgate."

"What do you mean *you're in the Eastgate?*" cried Logan, so loudly that Hoon had to pull away from the earpiece for a moment. "How are you in the Eastgate? *Why* are you in the Eastgate?"

"I was away for a shite when it all kicked off," Hoon explained.

Logan said nothing. Not right away. Not for a while.

When he was finally able to speak again, there was an accusatory tone to his words.

"Hang on a minute. Is this you? Are you doing this?"

"Am I doing what?" Hoon tutted. "Am I holding up a fucking shopping centre? Is that what you're asking? Jesus. What do you think, Jack?"

"I honestly don't know," Logan replied.

"Well, thank you very fucking much. After everything I've done for you? That is fucking charming," said Hoon. "That's a fucking outrageous remark. It's fucking slanderous. Believe me, if I wanted to clean this place out, I'd be long gone before any of you clueless clogsniffing fuckwits even noticed. If I wanted to rob this place, I'd be in Monte fucking Carlo before the alarms went off."

Logan let out a non-committal sort of grunt. "And is that what's happening, is it? They're robbing the place?"

"More or less," Hoon said. He moved his foot, steering the man in the chair from side to side. "So my new pal here keeps telling me, anyway."

He heard Logan's confusion all the way from the other end of the line.

"New pal? What new pal? What are you on about?"

"One of the snidey wee fucks running around in here dressed as fucking Santa Claus."

He could practically hear Logan's confusion down the line. "Santa Claus?"

"Aye. Well, no. This one isn't, but most of his wee gang of no-hoper shitesticks are."

"They're dressed as *Santa Claus*?"

"Aye! Fuck's sake, Jack, keep up," Hoon said. "I feel like I'm talking to a fucking five-year-old here. There's a shower of pricks all dressed as Santa. Tooled up to the fucking nines, too. Serious kit. They've got signal jammers blocking all the other phones, an impressively eclectic array of weaponry, and at least one of the fuckers can explode on command."

"What do you mean, *one of them can explode on command*?"

"Aye," Hoon confirmed. "Well, not *can*, I suppose. *Could*. He *could* explode on command. It's sort of a one-and-done kind of trick. The encore's just you running down the walls and dripping from the fucking ceiling."

"Jesus," Logan muttered.

"Aye. It's been quite a fucking day, right enough."

"You're telling me," Logan muttered. "How many of them are there?"

"Dunno. Hang on," Hoon said. He removed the phone from his ear and looked down at the man in the chair. "How many of you pricks are knocking about in here?"

There was no response from the other man. Not until Hoon jerked his foot forwards and twisted, grinding the prisoner's bollocks into the chair.

"How many of you pricks are there?" he asked again, and this time he got a strangled series of grunts and whimpers in reply. "Forty-five? Is that what you're saying? Sorry, Jack, it's hard to make out. He's got his own socks stuffed down his throat."

"Of course he has," Logan muttered, like he expected nothing less.

Bradley shook his head and made a variation on the last sound again.

"Fifty-five? Fuck off!" Hoon pressed down harder with his foot. "There's no way there's fifty-five of you fuckers wandering about. So cut your shite, and..."

The prisoner tried again, sobbing as he worked hard to push the air out through the choking gag.

"Oh. Thirty-five? Is that what you're saying?" Hoon asked, which earned some frantic nodding. He eased his foot back, then returned the phone to his ear. "You hear that?"

"Aye. I heard," Logan confirmed. "Do I want to know what you're doing to him?"

"More or less fuck all, disappointingly. Sang like a fucking canary before I'd even asked him a question. Told me everything."

Logan allowed a grace period of almost five seconds before pressing for more.

"Well, don't keep us in bloody suspense here, Bob. What did he tell you?"

"He said they're after a ransom," Hoon said. "Ten million."

"Fucking hell!" Logan ejected. "They're not setting their sights low, then?"

Hoon shrugged. "No, they're trying to play with the big boys. Which is ironic, because from what I've seen of them, they've all just barely spat out their maw's tits."

He turned to face the screens. Several of them showed the huddled masses of the hostages. Leaning in closer to one of the monitors, Hoon squinted, trying to make out the details on the pixelated image while he continued to talk.

"It's hard to say for sure, but this fanny-fingered shitequake reckons they've got something like..."

The words tumbled off into silence as he stared at the camera feed. The footage was a little blurry, but there, sitting together near a door... Was that...? Could it be...?

"They reckon they've got what?" Logan asked.

"What? Oh. Shite. Aye." Hoon shook his head and looked back at the man in the chair. "They reckon they've got about four hundred people in here. Hostages, I mean. From what I can see, it's a pretty decent estimate. So, four hundred folk, ten million quid, what's that work out at?"

Hoon began to whisper as he calculated below his breath.

"Ten million divided by four hundred is... Hang on, so..."

"Twenty-five grand a head," Logan said.

"Fucking hell, how did you figure that out so fast?" Hoon asked. "I didn't think numbers were your strong point. Mind you, I wasn't aware you even had a fucking strong point, so maybe I misjudged you."

"Maybe you did," Logan said, before honesty got the better of him. "Actually, DS Khaled worked it out. He's still here listening."

"Good. He's a fucking computer whizz, isn't he?"

There was a pause. Some movement. The next voice on the line was Hamza's.

"Well, I mean, I wouldn't go that far."

"I've no' got time for false fucking modesty, son," Hoon told him. "Do you know your way around a computer, or don't you?"

"Uh, yeah. I mean, pretty much, aye," Hamza said.

"Right. Good." Even though the DS had no way of seeing what he was doing, Hoon gestured to the racks of equipment that lined the walls of the security room. "Is there a way of locking them out of all this shite?"

"What shite?" Hamza asked. "What do you mean?"

Hoon tutted. "This. All this. All these wee fucking blinking lights and buttons. I can't hang around here, and I don't think we really want them getting control of this stuff again."

"What stuff?" Hamza asked. "Where are you?"

"Oh, did I no' mention? I'm in the security room," Hoon said. "Where all the cameras are."

Logan's voice returned. "You're in the security room? So, you've got a view of the whole centre?"

Hoon turned his attention back to the screens. "Aye. More or less. All the bits with cameras, anyway."

"So, they can't see them? They can't see what we're doing?"

"Only this fucker. Hang on."

Hoon raised a foot. Bradley's eyes went wide, and he began to whimper, then the sole of Hoon's trainer connected with the side of the other man's face.

Bradley's chair toppled backwards. His head hit the floor with a *thwack*. He breathed out a groan, then lay there, eyes half shut, looking up at the ceiling.

"Right, we're clear," Hoon said. "Only eyes on these screens are mine. There's no saying the fuckers aren't watching you from the roof or something, mind you."

"Can you no' see the roof on one of the screens and check?" Logan asked.

Hoon looked across the monitors. Most of them had been turned to watch the areas around the hostages, as well as the building's obvious entry points.

"No, can I fuck," Hoon replied.

"You should be able to switch the image," Hamza said. "Change which cameras are showing up on-screen."

"And how the fuck am I meant to do that?" Hoon asked.

Logan cut in. "Can you no' ask your man you've got there with you?"

"Eh, no," Hoon said, looking back over his shoulder to where Bradley lay in semi-conscious silence. "He's having a wee doss at the minute. Someone'll need to talk me through it."

Hamza came back to the phone. "I mean, I've never actually used the system before, so I'm not quite sure what you're looking at."

"I thought you said you were a fucking whizz?" Hoon spat. "Don't blow your own trumpet if you can't carry a fucking tune, son! Can you talk me through it or not?"

"I can try," Hamza said. "It should be quite obvious. They won't hide it away. Look around the desk, see if there's anything with buttons on it that might control the inputs."

"Everything's got fucking buttons on it!" Hoon shot back. He swept his gaze across the desktop, taking in all the many complicated-looking controls. "It's nothing but fucking buttons. There's buttons *on* the fucking buttons!"

He could almost hear Hamza scratching his head. "Um, well, I don't know. It should be pretty obvious. Like, on a pad on its own, or something? Just big buttons."

Hoon shook his head. "Well, some fucking help you are, son! There's nothing like that anywhere on..."

His gaze fell on a long rectangular box connected to a cable that ran out of sight behind the bank of monitors. There were twenty or so buttons on it, about half a dozen of which were currently lit up.

"Hang on," he said, then he jabbed at a button and one of the screens changed. A shot of an empty corridor became a shot of the same empty corridor, but from a different angle. "I've got it. No fucking thanks to you, I should add."

"Can you see the roof?" Logan asked.

"Hold your horses," Hoon replied.

He prodded at another of the darkened buttons again. This time, one of the larger screens, which had been showing the empty food court, changed to show the corridor where he'd seen the two men guarding the door to the roof.

Getting warmer.

He pressed another couple of buttons. Two more screens changed. One showed the broken vending machine downstairs, the other gave a view of the centre's roof, blanketed in snow.

"Got it," Hoon announced. "I can see the roof. Well, some of it, anyway."

He leaned in closer to the screen, watching as a man in a Santa suit cleared snow off the top of a metal box the size of a treasure chest.

"What the fuck's he up to?" Hoon wondered.

"What's who up to?" Logan asked.

"This spotty-arsed wee bastard," Hoon said, nodding to the screen. "Some guy's up there pissing about with something."

There was a pause before Logan spoke again.

"That doesn't give me much to go on, Bob."

Hoon tutted. "Well, sorry my narration's no' more insightful, Jack, but I don't know what the fucker's up to, so..."

But then, all of a sudden, he did know what the man was doing. He watched, heart rising into his throat, as the Santa on-screen stepped back, revealing a tangled mass of cables, and the LED glow of what was unmistakably a countdown.

"Oh, shite. I think they've got a bomb," he said.

Logan's voice was clipped. Urgent. "A bomb? You sure?"

"Well, I've no' got the fucking blueprints handy, but it sure looks like a bomb from where I'm standing. Big bastard, too. Timer's counting down."

"Counting down? Why's it counting down?"

"Why the fuck do you think it's counting down, Jack?" Hoon shot back. "I doubt it's going to shout 'surprise' and shoot a stripper out of a fucking cake."

"No, but it doesn't make sense," Logan said. "If they want a ransom, why set a countdown? These things take time to negotiate. Why plant a bomb when you're still inside?"

"Because it isn't a ransom," Hoon said. "They're too well armed. They're too fucking organised. Anyone who can do something like this can get their hands on ten mill easy. They don't need to do something as high profile as—"

He didn't hear the approach of the man behind him. He didn't spot his reflection in the screens.

The first Hoon knew of the intruder's arrival was when a hand caught him by the head and fingers dug up his nostrils like he was being used as a bowling ball. The world lurched. The phone clattered to the floor. Hoon stumbled backwards, desperately trying to stay upright.

He might've managed, too, had a fist like a wrecking ball not hit him with a right cross, hastening his fall to the floor.

"Well, well, well," growled Ded Moroz. "And who do we have here?"

CHAPTER TWENTY-FIVE

"HELLO? BOB? YOU STILL THERE?"

Logan pressed the phone to his ear, and jammed a finger into the other one, trying to block out the surrounding noise.

He heard some rustling, then a thud, and then a long, solemn tone to indicate that the line had gone dead.

"Shite," he ejected, handing the phone back to Hamza.

"What's happening?" Detective Superintendent Mitchell demanded. "You said *bomb*. Tell me I imagined that."

"Afraid not, ma'am," Logan said.

"Dear God," Mitchell whispered. She ran a hand down her face, composing herself, then stabbed a finger towards the shopping centre. "He's in there? Hoon? He's actually inside?"

"Seems to be, ma'am, aye."

"*Bob Hoon?*" Mitchell said, stress fractures cracking her voice around the edges. "Bob Hoon is running around in there? Bob Hoon is running around in there right now?"

"Yes, ma'am," Logan confirmed. He glanced at the phone in Hamza's hand. "At least, he was. Call dropped suddenly. Don't know what happened."

This time, Mitchell buried her face in both hands. She made

a sound that was somewhere between a scream and a sob, then ran her fingers upwards through her short-cropped hair and hung on tightly, like she was worried her head was about to pop off.

"How...? I mean, *why* is...? I mean, how can...?"

She shook her head, her brow furrowing as she tried to find a question that conveyed sufficient levels of shock, anger, outrage, and dismay.

In the end, she settled for the sort of thing her predecessor might've asked under similar circumstances.

"What the *fuck*?"

"Beats me, ma'am," Logan said.

"Why is he in there? *How* is he in there? How is *Bob bloody Hoon* in there? What was he doing?" Mitchell demanded.

"I don't know, ma'am. Just the wrong guy in the wrong place at the wrong time, by the sounds of things," Logan said.

"No. No. Bollocks. I'm not buying it. I mean... come on, Jack. Does that not seem like a hell of a coincidence to you? A terrorist takeover of the Eastgate Centre, and *Bob Hoon* is right in the centre of it? Does that not seem unlikely?" the Detective Superintendent asked.

Logan considered this for a few moments, then shook his head. "Sadly, ma'am, no," he told her.

Mitchell was still clinging to her hair as if it was the only thing tethering her to reality. "But, I mean, if they've rounded up everyone else, why not him? How come he's running around in there scot-free? Why wasn't he rounded up with the others?"

Logan hesitated. "He's always been a bit of a jammy bastard," he reasoned, leaving out the gastrointestinal details of Hoon's explanation. "Although, I don't know if he's still running around now. I don't like how that call ended."

Mitchell seemed to realise all of a sudden that she was not maintaining the same largely impassive air as the other officers around her. Quite the opposite, in fact.

Forcing her fingers to relax their grip on her hair, she smoothed it down, and let her arms fall crisply back to her sides.

"I wouldn't worry about him. The man seems to have all the survival skills of a bloody cockroach. I'm sure he'll call back," she said, the hysteria that had been growing in her voice now levelling off. "Until then, if he's right about everything happening in there, then we've got much bigger things to be concerned about than the welfare of Robert Hoon..."

Hoon brought up a foot and fired it at one of the Russian's knees, but the kick was short of the target, and struck weakly. While it didn't hurt the man in the Santa suit, it enraged him. He bent at the waist, grabbed Hoon's ankle with both hands, then pulled and twisted with all his strength.

The polished wooden floor kept friction low, and Hoon slid smoothly across it as he was dragged into a fast spin. He grabbed at a leg of the desk, trying to catch hold, to stop his momentum, but his hands rattled off the metal, drawing a hiss of pain through his teeth.

And then, for a moment, he was flying.

And then, all too quickly, his flight ended with a *crunch* as he was slammed, shoulder-first, into one of the racks of computer servers.

A mug had been sat on top of the rack at some point. As Hoon gulped down a breath, he saw it tumbling towards him, but was too late to get out of the way.

It *clonked* him on the forehead. Cold coffee spilled across his face and down his neck.

"Ow! Fuck!" he spat, then he brought his arms up to protect himself as the big Russian dropped onto him, knees first, the fat sausages of his fingers curling into fists.

"You are our sneaky little rat," Ded Moroz proclaimed.

A right cross walloped against Hoon's raised arms, breaking his block and catching him a glancing blow across his left cheek. The punch might not have made full contact, but there was enough power behind it that it hurt, all the same.

"You are one who killed Pére Noel, yes?" the Russian asked. His voice was light, like laughter wasn't far away. "I recognise you from photograph on driver licence."

A fist came down like a hammer-blow on Hoon's face, bursting a lip and filling his mouth with blood.

The man in the Santa suit reached for something beyond Hoon's field of view and pulled hard. His hand returned holding a length of wire.

"You look tougher in picture," he said, wrapping the wire first around one hand, then the other. "Here, you are nothing but old man lying helpless on floor. Old man who is about to die at hands of Ded Moroz! Old man about to have life strangled from body by—"

The mug smashed twice against the side of his head. The first time hurt. The second, after the porcelain had shattered and left a couple of long shards sticking out from the handle, did damage.

Ded Moroz roared and grabbed at his face, blood gushing between his fingers.

Hoon ripped the improvised garrotte from his attacker's grasp, then started to swing for a third time with what was left of the mug. The Russian saw it coming, knocked his arm away, then reared up and brought his head sharply down.

Hoon barely had time to react. He tucked his chin to his chest, and the headbutt connected with his forehead. He felt some part of his skull or his brain make a troubling creaking noise, and pain exploded behind his eye sockets, filling the room with a flash of white light.

Still, better his forehead than his nose. At least this way he wasn't choking or blinded. Not fully blinded, anyway. Not once the white faded away again to reveal the blood soaked face of the Russian all knotted up in anger.

Ded Moroz grasped at his belt, searching for a gun that was no longer there. Hoon saw it first, lying on the floor off on his right, just beyond his reach. He lunged for it, but the weight of the man on top of him held him in place, pinned him down, made it impossible for him to reach the weapon.

He saw a fist closing in from the corner of his eye, and threw an arm up by his head to shield himself. The punch connected through his defences, but the Russian was losing strength, and the damage was minimal.

Hoon threw a hook with the mug again, this time targeting the other man's neck. There was a satisfyingly meaty sound as the last remaining shard found its target, and Hoon was left holding nothing but a porcelain handle.

The Russian's head jerked to one side, his cheek tucking in against his shoulder. Blood and spit bubbled from his lips. His eyes somehow simultaneously glazed over and came alive with pain like he was fully alert, but elsewhere, not there in that room.

Again, Hoon tried to grab for the gun. Ded Moroz was still a dead weight, but he was no longer actively trying to stop him reaching the weapon.

Hoon's fingers brushed against the gun's barrel, then a flailing foot kicked it away, sending it spinning across the wooden floor.

The once more fully conscious Bradley gave a savage, if somewhat sock-muffled roar as he lashed out with a foot, slamming it against Hoon's shoulder, against his ribs, against his head.

"Fucking... fuck off!" Hoon spat.

He caught the third or fourth kick, and saw the panic in Bradley's wide, watery eyes just before he twisted. Something—a knee, a hip, he couldn't really tell from that position—gave an almighty *pop*, and Bradley's furious cries became a plain, regular sort of crying that put an end to his involvement in the fight.

Ded Moroz seemed to be losing interest in it, too. Through a mist of blood, snot, and tears, he spotted his gun. It was a few feet away now—no way he could reach it while keeping Hoon pinned.

But then, keeping Hoon pinned hadn't exactly worked out well for him so far, so it was probably worth the risk.

Throwing one more half-hearted punch at the man beneath him, the Russian launched himself towards the weapon. Hoon caught him by the belt of his Santa suit, holding him back until an elbow caught him a sharp blow across an eye socket, and pain bloomed like a rash up the side of his face.

Hoon kept hold of the black leather belt, but it slipped through the loops in the jacket, and the Russian fell forwards, no longer restrained.

The blood *burbled* in his throat as he crawled, half-blinded, towards the gun. Three feet away.

Two.

One.

He lunged, diving for the weapon.

His belt looped around his neck and jerked him to a stop. The leather *creaked* as it was twisted, the edges of it digging into his flesh. His eyes bulged as he stretched for the weapon, lying tantalisingly out of reach on the floor.

Despite the pain, despite the lack of air, he forced himself onwards. His fingers found the grip of the weapon, but they were too slippery and blood-slicked for him to get purchase on it.

The Russian's face became an ominous bruise of dark purple. Behind him, Hoon gritted his teeth, tightened his grip, and pulled, and pulled, and *pulled*.

There was some wheezing.

There was some spluttering.

There was something not unlike a cough.

And then, Ded Moroz bucked and thrashed on the floor as his brain protested this sudden and unexpected lack of oxygen.

Hoon held on until all the fuss had stopped.

Then, he held on a little longer.

Finally, he released his grip on the belt, and the Russian fell to the floor. One of his arms twisted beneath him, so as he fell, he rolled sideways onto his back. His eyes were open, the whites now mostly coloured in with shades of red and pink.

Hoon threw the belt to the floor and took a moment to get his breath back before spitting, "Watch who the fuck you're calling old, you big arsehole," at the motionless body of the Russian.

He looked over to where Bradley was still sobbing in his upturned chair, and winced when he saw the shape of the younger man's leg.

"Oh, Jesus. That is fucking... That's turning my stomach," he said. "That's completely fucked. They'll have to cut that off."

Bradley's sock-blocked sobs rose in both volume and desperation.

"Don't fucking blame me!" Hoon told him. "It wasn't my fucking fault. You brought that on yourself."

Hoon frowned then, though he wasn't quite sure why. Something had bothered him, though. Something he'd seen, but not yet fully noticed, was niggling away at him, trying to get his attention.

Slowly, he turned his attention back to the lifeless Santa on the floor. There were deep red welts on his throat where the belt had cut in, though the blood pumping from the wounds in his face and neck was doing its best to conceal them.

Had the Russian moved? Was that it? It seemed unlikely, given his current condition, but Hoon felt it wise to check.

"Oi!" he barked. "Arsehole!"

He gave the man a solid kick for good measure. The body did move then, but no more so than might be reasonably expected.

"Ded by name..." Hoon said, but whatever it was that was niggling at him continued to do so. It wasn't the Russian, there was nothing happening there.

So, if not that, then what?

And then, he saw it. In hindsight, he couldn't understand how he'd missed it.

Without the belt holding it tied shut, the big red Santa jacket had fallen open. Not all the way, but enough to reveal something strapped to the Russian's chest.

A device. Quite a serious-looking device, with a lot of wires, and a small, stubby aerial protruding from the top.

Hoon didn't panic. What would be the point? Instead, he put his hands on his hips, and let out a long, weary-sounding sigh.

"Aye, I suppose that makes more sense than spontaneous human combustion, right enough," he muttered. He turned back to Bradley, and pointed to the suicide vest. "Did you fucking know about this? Have you got one of them on?"

Bradley frantically shook his head.

"Which one are you saying no to? The first one or the second one?" Hoon asked, then he tutted and leaned over his prisoner. "Doesn't matter. Stay still."

He pushed up the other man's polo shirt, revealing only a bare, hairless chest with a no-man's-land of acne filling the gap between the nipples.

"Well, thank fuck for that," Hoon said. "But Jesus Christ, son, do you wax, or have your balls just no' got around to dropping yet? I've seen fucking fish that are hairier than that. Man up, for fuck's sake."

He left Bradley lying there with his nipples exposed, then returned to the Russian. He'd seen more than his fair share of suicide vests over the years, but this one was unlike any he'd seen before.

Sure, he knew what it was. He got the gist of it. But where

he would expect to have seen bags of ball bearings, or random metal shrapnel, there was only armour plating.

He couldn't see what the aerial was connected to inside the vest, but its purpose was clear. Hoon very carefully patted at the dead man's pockets until he found something solid.

Parting the top of the pocket like a surgeon lifting a skin flap from an incision, he peered into the dark red folds within.

"Gotcha," he whispered, then he slowly reached inside and drew out a palm-sized detonator.

This was more familiar. It wasn't an exact match for any he'd seen before, but it seemed to work the same. There was a trigger on the front and a thumb-activated button on top. Pressing either one on their own would do nothing. Press both together, though, and things would very quickly get interesting.

"Right. Fuck. OK. This could be a problem," Hoon said.

While he'd seen plenty of IEDs back in the day, he'd tended to stay as far away from them as possible. He'd left the disarming to people who knew what they were doing. Or, more commonly, he'd stood well back while he or someone else on his squad had opened fire, triggering the explosive from a safe distance.

He knew two men who might know what to do, though. One of them was currently being held hostage downstairs, so he was out.

The other one, though, was only a phone call away.

DI Ben Forde's military career only barely overlapped with Hoon's, and they hadn't exactly swapped a lot of stories over the years.

But Ben had been trained to disarm explosives, Hoon knew. Ben had dealt with vests like these plenty of times. He'd know what to do about them. The bomb on the roof, too.

And, if the DI didn't know what to do, Hoon supposed he could always talk to the shower of arrogant bastards that currently made up the bomb squad. That was the last resort, though. Ben Forde first.

He carefully set the detonator down on the desk and kept watching it, like he was worried it might press itself, as he reached for the phone and hit the button to redial the number he'd called a few minutes earlier.

Nothing happened. He glanced at the handset, then down at the big, complicated-looking base. There were a lot of buttons on it, and at least a few of them had been lit up when he'd last looked. He was sure of it.

Now, though, the whole thing was dark. The rectangular LCD screen above the numbers showed nothing but three short horizontal lines.

He jabbed his thumb against the cradle a few times, trying to kick the thing back into life, but to no avail.

It was then that he saw the cable on the floor that Ded Moroz had been about to throttle him with. Hoon picked up the phone and, sure enough, saw that the socket where the cable connected had been torn free of the cracked plastic housing.

"Fuck!" he ejected.

So much for that plan. Ben wouldn't be able to talk him through disarming anything. Hamza wouldn't be able to explain how to disable the security systems and prevent them falling back into the wrong hands.

He had no support. No backup. He was on his own.

Still, that suited him just fine.

Hoon regarded the banks of security monitors for a few moments, rubbing his chin in thought.

Then, he picked up the shotgun from the desk, jammed it into the rack of computer equipment, and pulled the trigger.

The gun kicked and roared in his hands. Down on the floor, Bradley gave another muffled yelp.

Hoon turned to the bank of monitors just as the images on all of them blipped to black.

"Aye, that seemed to do the fucking trick," he said, admiring the smoking crater in the middle of the server. He rested the shotgun on his shoulder, and shot a disparaging look at the phone. "Who's the fucking tech whizz now?"

He smiled, quite pleased with himself. It hadn't been a particularly elegant solution, but it was certainly an effective one. Even if the terrorists had a dedicated IT specialist on the payroll, no amount of turning it off and back on again was going to get the security system up and running.

That was one problem taken care of, then. He didn't have enough fingers to count how many that left. The bomb on the roof was a biggie. The thirty-odd armed bastards ranked highly, too, as did the whole hostage situation.

And then, there was the fact that this whole thing smelled fishier than a trawlerman's wife's undercarriage.

Hoon looked down at the dead Russian with the explosive vest.

"Ransom my arse," he muttered.

He knew he probably didn't have much time. There was a good chance that someone had heard the gunshot. He picked up Ded Moroz's SMG, flicked the safety catch, then slung the weapon's strap over his shoulder.

That done, he turned to Bradley, who was still lying on the floor, gazing in horror at his disjointed leg.

"Sorry, son. Nothing personal," Hoon told him, then he brought the butt of the shotgun down between the younger man's eyes.

Bradley screamed as blood gushed from his nose. He ejected a frantic string of syllables, but they mostly remained trapped behind the sock in his mouth.

With some imagination, though, it might be interpreted as, "Ow! What the fuck?!"

"Shite. Sorry, pal. That was meant to knock you out. I thought you'd be out like a fucking light," Hoon said. He raised the weapon again. "Hang on. Hold still, I'll try again."

Bradley shook his head quite emphatically. His eyes bulged. He whimpered out another salvo of muffled nothing.

"Look, I know it's no' fucking ideal, but it's this or I shoot you," Hoon told him. "Your choice."

The man on the floor grimaced and groaned, wrestling with the decision before giving a single, solemn nod. Hoon took aim with the back end of the shotgun, squaring it up to the target.

His muscles tensed like he was about to start the swing, but he didn't yet bring the weapon down.

"Don't give me the big fucking sad eyes. It's harder when I know you're expecting it," he said. "You're making me feel fucking guilty about this now. This isn't my fucking doing, son. This is on you!"

Bradley made a pleading sound at the back of his throat. A tear rolled from one eye and down his cheek.

Hoon brought the gun down with a *crack*. This time, Bradley's head fell back to the floor, and his eyes rolled closed.

"That's what you get for fucking milking it," Hoon said. He sniffed, thought for a moment, then shrugged. "And turns out I don't actually feel too bad about it, after all."

He tucked the shotgun under an arm, rubbed his hands together, then turned to the dead Russian on the floor.

"Right, then, you big dollop of shite," he said. "Let's get you taken care of."

Bending, he caught Ded Moroz under the arms, and dragged him towards the door, complaining about the bastard's weight every inch of the way.

Manhandling him through the doorway and out into the corridor wasn't easy, and the proximity of Hoon's face to the explosive device on the Russian's chest made it something of a *squeaky-bum-time* journey.

Finally, though, Hoon reached the door to the office he'd peeked into earlier, opened it, and dragged the body inside.

He abandoned it just inside the room and straightened,

letting out a big sigh of relief. Nobody had come running yet, which meant that maybe no one had heard.

And that meant that maybe, just maybe, he had time.

He picked his way between the limbs of the other corpses in the room until he reached the desk. Grabbing a pen and a notebook, he started to work on a plan.

"Right. One. Bomb."

The pen scribbled across the page.

"Two."

He chewed the end of the pen thoughtfully for a moment, then started to write.

"Kill Santa. Three."

He waggled the pen between his fingers for a while, then tapped it on the page.

"Fuck it, that'll do," he announced. "Hardly seems worth writing it down."

He tossed the pad back on the desk, then looked up at the ceiling of the office. The bomb was up there somewhere, counting down. He had no idea how long was left on the timer.

And, more importantly, even if he could somehow get to it, he had no idea how to disarm it.

Fortunately, he knew a man who did.

CHAPTER TWENTY-SIX

LOGAN STOOD motionless while one of the CID detectives relayed the news. He didn't think they were being watched, but it was impossible to say for sure, so everyone was strictly controlling their body language and facial expressions, so as not to give anything away.

Not that they currently had much to give away.

"Sniper up on the car park reckons he can see the bomb, sir. It's on the roof above the older part of the centre. Where the thermal cams tell us the hostages are being held."

"Shite," Logan muttered, impassively.

"There's a guy dressed as Santa pissing about with it. Do we take him out?"

Logan shot a sideways glance at Detective Superintendent Mitchell, who stood beside them, saying nothing. Her face, like those of the other polis around her, gave nothing away.

The decision was his, then. Great.

"Not yet," he said. "We don't want to escalate. But get angles on him, if you can. I want to know what that timer's saying. I want to know how long we've got."

"I'll see what can be done, sir," the CID man confirmed, then he turned and marched off, and was quickly swallowed by the swirling snow.

Falcon Square was in near silence now. Barricades had been set up on the main road and all the pedestrian areas, keeping Joe Public out of sight around the corner. Messages had been broadcast on the radio, warning people not to come to the city centre. With all that, plus the cold, Logan felt like he was standing in a ghost town.

At least, he would've done, were it not for the army of polis standing around. They'd been drafted in from as far away as Fort William, and pulled in off annual leave. And now, they were all just standing there, waiting for orders.

At the moment, though, 'Wait,' was about the only order he could give them.

And then, through the silence, came the tolling of a bell.

"Boss! Phone!" DC Neish announced. He pointed to the handset ringing loudly for all to hear. "Phone, boss."

Logan just nodded. Now wasn't the time to fire a withering put-down at the lad. This was all too big, too important, the situation too grave.

Besides, knowing Tyler, there'd be no shortage of opportunities for that in the future.

Logan waited for the nod from Hamza to say the recording was running, and one from Detective Superintendent Mitchell, too, authorising him to take the call.

He allowed himself a moment—just one moment in the day —to breathe. To actively inhale, then exhale again. To be aware.

And then, when the moment passed, he pressed the speakerphone button, silencing the ringing.

"Detective Chief Inspector Logan," he said.

There was a slight delay as the signal bounced off the satellite, then found its target just a few hundred yards away.

A fraction of a second later, the reply crackled from the speaker.

"Your time's up, Mr Logan," the American declared. "I sure hope you've either found me someone to talk to, or have grown the balls to start making big boy decisions on your own."

"It's sorted. You can talk to me," Logan told him. "You can tell me what you need."

Santa Prime laughed. "Need? I don't need for nothing, Mr Logan. I got everything I need already. What I *want* is money. A whole bunch of money."

"They've got money in there," Logan said. "You could've taken that. You could grab that now and go."

"Empty the cash registers? Is that what you think of me, Mr Logan? Come on, now. When I say a whole bunch of money, I mean a *whole bunch* of money."

They heard him pause for what was clearly dramatic effect.

"I want you to bring me ten *million* dollars."

Logan frowned. "Dollars?"

There was another momentary hesitation, though this one was less deliberate.

"Pounds," he corrected. "Ten million pounds."

"Aye. That *is* a bunch of money," Logan confirmed.

"See?" Santa Prime said, and his smirk travelled all the way down the line. "I told you."

"That's going to take time to sort out," Logan told him.

"I don't much care. We ain't going nowhere. Nobody in here is," the American replied. He lowered his voice into a conspiratorial whisper. "Although, I have to tell you, some of my guys in here, they're getting kinda antsy. Nervous, like. I'm hoping it don't get messy, but, well, scared folks do scary things, and there ain't a whole lot can be done about it."

"We'll work as fast as we can," Logan assured him. "But, anyone dies, and that changes the conversation. Hostages? Aye, we'll pay for them. Dead hostages? Well, that's a different matter. I'll get you your money. I'll hand it over myself as a big comedy cheque, if you like, and then get you a helicopter to fly you out of here, and we can all have a lovely Christmas."

"I sure do like the sound of that, Mr Logan."

"Good. I'm glad to hear it. Because none of that happens if anyone dies. Anyone dies, and my hands are tied. The whole deal is off," Logan said. "Anyone dies, and this ends badly. Anyone dies, and I come in there. But, I won't be bringing you money. That money'll be forever out of your reach. Is that understood?"

He took a breath. Held it. Waited for the response, not daring to look at the faces of the others around him, in case he saw their doubt. Their disbelief.

He was supposed to go along with what the other man said. Keep him chatting. Get him onside and talk him down.

Making threats was nowhere in the guidelines.

There was no reply from the other end. Logan felt his stomach turn over and his skin go tight. He did risk a glance at the others then. Mitchell's face was like thunder. Tyler's eyes were wide, while Hamza and Ben were both staring at the phone, their body language suggesting that every single part of them was currently clenched.

Logan ran a hand down his face, his fingers kneading his cheeks and his jaw.

He'd arsed this. He could feel it. One minute into the call, and he'd completely and totally—

"I like your style, Mr Logan," Santa Prime replied. "You don't mess around. In different circumstances, I think you and me might even get along."

Logan breathed out. All around him, the other detectives unclenched.

"Maybe, aye," Logan said. "If you like, we can go get a drink and just talk all this out? My round."

The American laughed. "You know, I'm almost tempted.

Maybe I can fly you to my private island someday. I'll send the jet to collect you, and we can drink margaritas on the beach."

"I'm more of a back room in a dingy pub man myself, but aye, sounds like a plan. Let's just make sure we get you there, eh? And that means everyone has to stay safe."

"Sure thing, Mr Logan," Santa Prime said. "I think we got a good thing going on here between us. We got an open and honest relationship. That's a rare thing these days. Don't know about you, but I value that."

"Aye. Open and honest. That works for me," Logan confirmed.

"Good. In that case, you can answer me one question. Who is Robert Hoon?"

Aware that someone might be watching him, Logan tried very hard not to flinch. He almost succeeded, too.

"Who?" he asked.

"Open and honest, Mr Logan. That's what we said. Don't you fucking let me down now," the American shot back, his anger building. "Who is Robert Hoon? He one of your guys?"

"No," Logan said, which *technically* wasn't a lie. "No, he's not one of ours."

"Then who the fuck is he, and what's he doing sneaking around in here causing trouble?"

"I don't know," Logan said. "Honestly, I don't know."

The delay before the reply came seemed to take forever.

"Are you lying to me, Mr Logan?" Santa Prime asked.

"No. No, I'm not lying," Logan insisted. "I'm telling you the truth. I don't know who that is."

"Then I suggest you find out. Because I was calm, Mr Logan. I honestly was. I had no intention of hurting a living soul. But then this guy starts John Mc-fucking-Claneing around in here, and suddenly, I find that I ain't so calm no more. Suddenly, I got me a case of the fucking jitters."

There was a pause, just for a moment. When the American spoke again, his voice was low and menacing.

"You ever seen what happens to four hundred hostages when a guy with an assault rifle gets a case of the jitters, Mr Logan? You ever seen the mess that can make? That's sure going to spoil a whole bunch of Christmases."

"I don't know who he is," Logan insisted. There was no backing out now. He couldn't exactly admit he'd lied. He had to double down. "I don't know who he is, but I'll get someone on it right away, and we'll find out all we can."

"You do that. I want to know everything about this guy. And, hell, you're going to be interested, too. He's killed someone, you know that? One of my guys. Blew the poor bastard to pieces. So, he's a murderer, Mr Logan. And I'm going to do you a favour, and take care of him for you. Free of charge. You find me everything you can about him, and then you leave the rest to me."

"If he's broken the law, we'll deal with him," Logan said.

Santa Prime laughed again. It was a low, sickly sounding snigger that made Logan's skin crawl.

"I don't give a shit what law he's broken. He killed one of my guys. This is personal. Whoever he is, whatever he thinks he's doing, I'm going to tear him apart, strip by strip, piece by piece."

Logan almost wished the bastard luck. He'd need it.

"We'll see what we can find out. And we'll get working on that money," he said. "But we'd like a show of faith."

"Oh, I'm sure you would, Mr Logan. I'm sure you would. What sort of thing are you thinking?"

Logan glanced around at the others. Their grim expressions mirrored his own.

"You've got kids in there. How about you send them out? That'll show you're willing to negotiate. It'll help us get you your money faster."

"Huh. That's an interesting suggestion, but how about I make you a counteroffer?"

"I want those kids out," Logan insisted.

"Oh, come on now, Mr Logan. You ain't even heard what I'm about to say here. I think you'll prefer my offer, I really do. You should at least listen to what I got to say."

Logan's nostrils flared as he took a breath. Something about the tone of the other man's voice was worrying him. There was an arrogance to it that suggested the bastard knew something Logan didn't.

"OK. You're right. Let's hear it," he said.

"How about, as a show of faith, we don't put a bullet through the head of that fucking mongrel bitch who's standing beside you?"

Logan's head snapped up, his eyes scanning the windows of the shopping centre, then up to the roof above. Around him, Ben, Hamza, and Tyler all did the same, searching for any sign of a sniper.

Detective Superintendent Mitchell was the only one not to move. She just stared at the phone, her arms crossed over her chest, her face fixed in a mask of stoic fury.

"You won't see us. There ain't no point in looking, Mr Logan." The American sniggered. "But we see you."

"In there," Logan barked, catching Mitchell by the arm and steering her towards the closest fire engine. "In there and stay down!"

"That's right! You tell that fucking slut! You tell her how it's gonna be!" Santa Prime hissed. "You put her in her fucking place!"

Mitchell pulled free of Logan's grip, glared at him for a moment, then leaned in to the phone to talk.

"She opens her fucking mouth, she says one fucking word to me, and I kill everyone in this place," Santa Prime announced. "That ain't a threat. It's a promise. I ain't Dr fucking Doolittle. I don't lower myself to talk to no animals. And while I'm on the subject, the same goes for the fucking Muslim, or Apache, or whatever the hell it is that you got down there. They're turning my stomach. I want them gone. I want them out of my fucking sight."

Logan met the eyes of Mitchell and Hamza. They both looked angry, but worse than that, they looked embarrassed. Ashamed, even.

Logan shook his head and started to reply, but Mitchell put a hand on his arm. She straightened to her full height, steeled herself, then nodded, just once.

Hamza sighed, almost imperceptibly, but then gave Logan a reluctant thumbs up. Mitchell beckoned for him to follow, and after accepting a touch on the shoulder from Tyler, he fell into step behind her and they both hurried across Falcon Square towards the barricades around the corner.

"Good boy, Mr Logan. Consider that a show of faith from both sides," Santa Prime drawled. "Now, we both got a lot to be getting on with. I'll be in touch."

"Wait—" Logan began, but the line went dead before he could go any further, and he hissed, "Fuck," below his breath, while fighting to keep his face as immobile as possible.

"So, they can see us, Jack," Ben muttered. His head was level, but his eyes were still searching the windows for any sign of movement.

"Aye, so it seems," Logan confirmed. "Get a message to the ARU boys. I want them searching every window, and every inch of that roof."

"Will do, Jack," Ben said. Painfully aware that he might be in a sniper's crosshairs every step of the way, DI Forde allowed himself a single steadying breath before setting off across the square.

"I really don't think I like this guy, boss," Tyler muttered, shooting daggers at the phone.

"No. I'm no' his biggest fan, either," Logan agreed.

"We're going to get him, though, aren't we, boss? We're going to nail the bastard."

Logan nodded, but it wasn't entirely convincing. "I hope so, son," he said. "I really bloody hope so."

CHAPTER TWENTY-SEVEN

BERTA HOON HAD HAD QUITE ENOUGH of this shite.

She'd sat patiently for what felt like a ridiculous amount of time.

She'd sat fuming while various men in Santa outfits had walked past, snarling from under their hats and behind their beards, trying to scare everyone into silence.

Berta had snarled right back, and while a couple of them had stopped and considered throwing their weight in her direction, they'd all soon thought better of it. She had that sort of look about her—a look that said dealing with her was going to be far more trouble than it was worth. It was a look that ran in the family.

Now, Berta sat with Iris and the music teacher, who she was still choosing to refer to as 'Beardy McTwat,' the three of them shielding the children who sat, cross-legged and all-cried-out, behind them.

"Look at them. They're acting like bloody panto villains," Mr McTwat whispered, as another passing Santa fired a scowl at the crowd.

"Still, better a panto villain than a dame," Berta said. Her expression darkened, and she shook her head. There was a story there, but whatever it was, she wasn't telling it. "Don't get me fucking started on panto dames."

"I've never been to a panto," Iris said. "Are they any good?"

"God, no," Berta told him. "They're tedious shite."

She was still glaring at the passing Santa. She recognised him as the lad she'd spoken to earlier. *Shaggy Goat*, or whatever he was calling himself. He wasn't putting quite the same venom into the whole scowling thing as some of his colleagues. The lad seemed to be completely out of his depth.

Had she not been a Hoon, she might've seen him as someone to almost be pitied. Instead, she saw him as what he was.

The weakest link.

"We could have that wee bastard," she muttered, leaning closer to Iris. "We could put him on his arse and get his gun."

Iris cocked his head to look at the lad. His glass eye didn't share his interest, though, and kept checking out the ceiling.

"We could! I bet we could!" Iris agreed. His enthusiasm quickly waned. "What then, though?"

"What do you mean?" Berta asked.

"I mean, we'll have one gun between us. Maybe you haven't noticed, like, but there's quite a lot of other guys around. I reckon we might just kind of make things, you know, like, worse."

"Worse?" Berta spat, turning to look over her shoulder at him. "We're being held hostage by a gang of spotty teenagers dressed as Father fucking Christmas. How could it get worse?!"

"Well..." Iris nodded around at their fellow captives. "All these people, plus us, could be machine-gunned to death. I'm pretty sure that'd be worse."

Mr McTwat leaned closer to offer his contribution. "That would be worse," he confirmed.

"See? And he's a teacher, so..."

Berta scowled. "Oh, come on! He's a fucking music teacher. He knows fuck all about fuck all."

"I mean—" Beardy began to protest, but Berta quickly cut him off.

"Look, don't get me wrong, I fully respect what you do," she told him. "And, in the unlikely set of circumstances that I ever need someone to wrestle a tune out of a fucking trumpet, you'll be the first to know. Until then, though, how about you just keep your pointless wee opinions to yourself, and leave this up to us?"

She kept staring at him until she was certain he wasn't going to interrupt again, then sniffed loudly and turned back to Iris.

"I reckon we can take these fuckers," she told him. "You and me. Start with him, grab another one, and just wing it from there."

"Sounds a bit risky, Berta," Iris fretted.

"A *bit*?" the music teacher squeaked.

"I'm fucking warning you..." Berta growled.

"He's right, though. It's dead risky," Iris said. "And, believe me, coming from me, that's really saying something, because, like, crippling paranoia aside, I'm usually the first one up for this sort of stuff. But, I mean, there's a lot of people here, and we don't know if..."

It was then that he spotted a pair of jolly red trousers standing beside him.

Right beside him.

"Oh, for Christ's sake, are you a man or a fucking mouse, Iris?" Berta demanded.

Iris swallowed. "Um, Berta."

"We can't sit around waiting for these fuckers to make their minds up. If we're going to do something, we need to get our fingers out of our arses and do it now, before—"

Iris reached over and gripped her forearm. His eyes opened so wide that one of them fell out. Fortunately, it wasn't the functioning one.

"Berta!" he hissed, then he tilted his head to the right.

Following his cue, Berta turned until she found the legs.

"Shite," she muttered. "Why didn't you fucking say something?"

"I'm pretty sure I did," Iris countered weakly.

Berta's gaze crept up, past the legs, to the big red Santa coat, and the black leather belt tied around the waist. Up past the shiny buttons and the white fur trim.

It lingered for a moment on the bloodstain on the Santa's collar, then continued on until it found a face that made her eject a "Fucking Nora!" in surprise.

"Shut up," Hoon hissed from behind a wisp of white beard. "Keep your voice down."

"What the fuck are you wearing?" Berta asked.

"What does it look like I'm wearing?" Hoon kept his head down, but his eyes were scanning the crowd for signs of trouble. "Anyway, if you think this is bad, you should've seen the last getup I was in."

"Why, what were you then? The fucking Easter Bunny?" Berta asked.

"Boggle?" Iris practically cried out in surprise. "Is that you?"

"Fuck me. Well done on waking up, Iris. But maybe don't fucking announce it," Hoon whispered.

Iris nodded, reinserted the eye that had fallen out, then wrinkled his nose as he looked Hoon up and down. "What are you dressed like that for?"

"Is this a rescue?" Berta asked. "Because, if so, you can forget it. I don't need rescuing. I've already got a plan."

"Aye. I heard. It's shite. It'll get everyone killed."

"Oh, ye of little faith, Bobby," Berta said.

She dusted herself down, then started to get to her feet.

She stopped when the muzzle of a machine gun came into view.

"Sit. On. Your. Arse," Hoon said, practically spelling the sentence out for her. "I'm handling this. Just you hold your fucking horses, alright?"

Berta glowered at the gun like she could melt it just by staring at it. Then, when she didn't, she flicked her gaze in her brother's direction.

"I could scream," she said. "I could scream blue bloody murder and give the whole game away."

It was the music teacher who jumped in then. He'd been as surprised as anyone to see the Santa appearing beside them, but seemed to have got the gist of what was going on.

"What? Why would you do that?" he squeaked.

"Because she's a fucking cow," Hoon said. He shook his head. "But she won't say a word. Will you, Berta?"

"Of course I fucking won't," his sister replied. "But you'd better have something good up your sleeve."

"I do, aye." He pointed to Iris. "But I need him."

"Me? What do you need me for?" Iris asked.

"Long story. I'll explain on the way," Hoon said.

He glanced back over his shoulder at the door he'd come through. It led to a corridor that ran behind the shops on this level. A flight of stairs, and they'd be back by the security room. From there, it was just a quick dash to one of the doors leading to the roof. And then...

Well, that was as far as his plan currently went. Everything after that was up in the air.

Still, over the past few months, he'd developed a real knack for improvisation.

Right now, the problem was getting Iris up and out without any of the terrorists noticing. It was one thing to come striding through the doors himself, but quite another to take one of the hostages with him.

"We're going to need a distraction," he concluded.

"No problem. Give me that gun and I'll shoot one of the fuckers," Berta said.

"A distraction I said, no' a fucking bloodbath," Hoon countered.

Berta sighed dramatically, rolled her eyes, then placed both hands on the floor beside her, palms down.

"Fine," she said, pushing up and turning on the spot.

The music teacher was forced to dodge to avoid being K.O.'d by Berta's swinging backside as she got herself onto her knees.

Leaning on Iris' shoulder for support, she made it all the way to her feet, stretched her back, then rolled her head around, working the kinks from her neck.

"Right, you two fuck off as soon as you can," she whispered, setting her sights on Shaggy Goat, or whatever he was called.

"What are you going to do?" Hoon asked, and there was a note of worry to his words, and a glint of it there in his eyes. "Don't do anything stupid."

"Just do as you're fucking told, Bobby," Berta said.

Then, with her head held high, she marched through the crowd, forcing the other hostages to part and clear a path for her. They soon got a sense of where she was going, and the young, nervous-looking Santa seemed surprised to find a line of empty floor suddenly stretching away from him.

His heart visibly sank when he saw who was striding towards him.

"Right, young man! I think we've all had quite enough of this fucking nonsense for one day!"

An increasing number of paces behind her, Hoon stared in dawning horror.

"The fuck's she doing?" he muttered. "She's going to get herself killed."

The Santa she was approaching didn't look like he was ready to put a bullet through her brain, though. In fact, he didn't look like he was capable, or that he even wanted to be holding the gun he clutched awkwardly in both hands.

The sight of Berta approaching had drained most of the colour from the lad's face, leaving only a dot-to-dot puzzle of angry red plooks. His head turned sharply left and right, like he was searching for backup. One of the two closest Santas, and a couple of men in security uniforms, seemed to have noticed what was happening, but they seemed content, for the moment, to leave him to deal with it.

"We're all sick to the back fucking teeth of this, I can tell you," Berta boomed, as she closed in on the lad, and her raised voice drew the interest of not only the other terrorists standing along the concourse, but all the hostages sitting on it, too. All eyes turned in her direction.

Except one, which stubbornly remained pointed at the ceiling.

"I reckon that's our cue, Boggle," Iris whispered.

When he got no answer, he turned to look back at Hoon, who hadn't moved a muscle, and was still staring at the back of his sister's head like he could drag her back to safety through just the power of thought.

"Boggle!" Iris hissed. "We doing this, or what?"

"What?" Hoon mumbled, like he was coming out of a trance. He looked down at his friend on the floor, blinking slowly. "Eh, aye. Aye. Wait for my move."

The stubby heels of Berta's sensible shoes *clacked* on the hard floor as she stopped in front of Shaggy Goat, blocking his view of her brother and Iris. There wasn't a person within earshot who wasn't watching her now. And, given the volume of Berta's voice, earshot extended quite a long way.

"Um, sit down, please," the lad in the Santa suit said. The words themselves were clearly meant to be an instruction, but the tone made it sound like a question. Earshot for him didn't extend very far at all, given that his voice was a wobbling whimper of worry. "You, uh, you shouldn't be out of your seat."

"Seat? We should be so fucking lucky!" Berta bellowed. "If I had a seat, both my arse cheeks might not be fast asleep right now! You ever had piles, son?"

Shaggy Goat swallowed. "What?"

"Piles, boy! Piles! Like a great big bunch of seedless grapes hanging out of your back alley? Have you had them?"

The lad frantically shook his head, his face contorting in panic and horror.

"Jesus. No! No, I haven't. But, look, could you sit back down and just—"

"Well, aren't you the fucking fortunate one?" Berta shot back. "Because, believe me, sitting on a cold hard floor with the bloody things is no fucking picnic. I'll tell you that much for free!" She lowered her voice, so that only the lad in the Santa suit and those sitting in immediate earshot could hear. "So, no, *Mark*. I will not sit down."

His whole body tensed at the mention of his name. His expression became gaunt and haunted, like someone who knew too much. Specifically, like someone who knew too much about what would happen to him if it was found that he'd accidentally shared his real name with one of the hostages.

Berta smirked, rocked on her heels, then tucked both hands behind her back. Out of sight of the lad in the Santa suit, she raised a middle finger to her brother.

"Right. That's definitely our cue now, Boggle," Iris whispered. "We going or what?"

Hoon was still glowering at his sister, though not with his usual contempt. Or, not *only* with his usual contempt, at least. There were other things mixed in there, too. Concern mostly, but also—God help him—admiration.

"For fuck's..." he began, but then he gritted his teeth, shook his head, and back towards the door. "Aye. Right. Slide this way."

The music teacher and others around him watched as Iris slid himself backwards towards Hoon and the door. A couple of them started to move to follow, but a low, menacing, "Where the fuck do you think you're going?" from Hoon stopped them again.

"You can't just leave us here," whispered the music teacher. "Take the kids, at least."

"Everyone's safer here," Hoon replied, his voice low and clipped. "Just keep your fucking heads down and your drawers clean. Everything's under control."

Berta's voice rang out across the concourse. "Well, I don't give a flying fuck how much trouble I'll be in, sunshine, I'm not planting my arse back down until someone gets me a cushion!"

And on that note, Hoon edged the door open, grabbed Iris by the scruff of the neck, and hauled him through into the darkness of the corridor beyond.

CHAPTER TWENTY-EIGHT

MILES PACED BACK and forth along the length of the room, anxiously chewing on a thumbnail. As the room was barely five paces long, he was in danger of getting dizzy.

"You, um, you're going to wear a hole in the carpet, sir."

Miles shot a questioning look at his assistant, Kevin, like the lad had lost his mind, then pulled a crisp about-turn and headed back in Suranne's direction.

She sat at the desk, watching him with a sort of idle, detached curiosity, like he was a moth battering itself senseless against a light bulb, or a spider trying to climb out of a bath.

Something creepy and crawly, anyway. Something she'd very much like to squish.

A knock at the door brought his pacing to a sudden, jolting halt. It was a proper knock. A *serious* knock. It was the sort of knock that could not, would not, be ignored.

"Get that, will you, Kevin?" Miles asked, shuffling around to face the door. It was the only way in and out of the room, and since their police escort had upped and left them, it had remained firmly shut.

Kevin rose from his chair, but otherwise didn't move. Not

yet. Instead, he just stared at the door for a while, like he was considering his options.

Finally concluding that the only other one open to him was 'resign,' he took a breath, steeling himself, and crept over to the door.

"Hello?" he said. It came out as a squeak, so he cleared his throat and tried again, but deeper and with slightly more authority. "Hello? Is there someone there?"

"Of course there's someone there," Miles whispered to him. "It didn't knock itself."

"Mr Crabtree?" came a voice from the other side. It sounded as serious as the knock had, and Miles flinched at the sound of his name.

Kevin, on the other hand, quickly retreated from the door, his body practically glowing with relief.

"Um, yes?" Miles said, not yet moving to take his assistant's place.

"It's Colin."

Miles ran a hand through his thinning hair, his fingers moving like they were flicking through a rack of index cards in his head.

"Ah. Colin!" he said. It sounded quite confident, but the puzzled look and shrug of his shoulders he threw in Kevin's direction were anything but.

Kevin puffed himself up so he looked as big as possible, used his hands to mime a beard, then pulled his hair back so that, at first glance, he appeared to be receding.

"Oh, *bald* Colin!" Miles cried, then he winced and slapped a hand over his mouth.

At the back of the room, Suranne let out a snort.

"Sorry, yes. Sorry," Miles said to the door.

He took a moment to pull himself together, then opened it to reveal a bearded MI5 man with a monk's haircut dressed all in black in the corridor. He did not look particularly impressed, but had either the professionalism or good grace not to let on.

"Colin. Officer Walton. Hello," Miles said. "Is there... Is there a problem?"

"Afraid so. Just had word about the flight. Snow's grounded everything. No planes getting in or out of the airport."

Over Miles' shoulder, Kevin let out a little *cheep* of distress. "Oh, great! They were meant to be picking us up. What happens now?"

Officer Walton peered at the younger man, let his glare linger uncomfortably for a while, then directed the reply to Miles.

"We reckon we can get a chopper in. It'll fly us to Aberdeen. Plane's being diverted there. You happy with that?"

Miles frowned. He wasn't delighted with it. There had been a plan in place, and this wasn't it. It was close to it, perhaps, but it wasn't it.

"Do we have other options?" he asked.

The MI5 man in the doorway shrugged. "Sure. We can sit out the weather. Forecast to stop just after eight."

Miles perked up at that. "That's not too bad," he said, checking his watch. "That's just a couple of hours."

"Tomorrow morning," Colin clarified. "It's due to stop just after eight tomorrow morning."

"Oh." Miles squeezed the bridge of his nose, looked back at Kevin and Suranne, then sighed. "Christ. Alright. We'll do the helicopter plan. How long until it's ready?"

"Can have us in the air for around seven," Colin replied.

"Oh, thank God for that!" said Kevin, bending over with his hands on his thighs like he was trying to get his breath back after a marathon. "That's roughly the same timeline, then. I was starting to think I was going to have to redo a *lot* of paperwork."

Colin barely bothered to look the assistant's way, and what little attention he did show him was not complimentary.

"So?" he asked, his steely grey eyes demanding an answer from Miles. "Is it a go?"

"It looks like it," Miles confirmed, though he still didn't seem best pleased about it. "It looks like a go."

The other MI5 officer didn't waste any time. With a curt nod, he turned and started to stride off, only stopping when Miles called him back.

"And, uh, sorry to chase you up, and all that, I know you're busy, but... Those guards I asked for. Any sign?"

"I'm working on it," Colin told him. "But I can't conjure guys out of thin air. The police were supposed to be here. That was the arrangement."

It was Suranne who answered, smirking as she spoke. "Guess someone changed the arrangement."

Colin studied her face, analysing her expression. She continued to smile back at him, unfazed by his scrutiny.

"I guess so," he eventually grunted.

And with that, he was gone.

CHAPTER TWENTY-NINE

IRIS HAD SEEN enough death up close to know a corpse when he saw one. Still, even he would admit that his grip on reality perhaps wasn't quite what it once was, so he felt compelled to ask the obvious question.

"They're dead, aye?"

Hoon closed the office door behind them, peeked through a crack in the blinds, then shut them all the way.

"*Obviously* they're fucking dead," Hoon replied. "They're no' all sleeping with their eyes open."

Iris nodded slowly as he surveyed the human wreckage piled up before him. "What happened to them?"

"Them three were hee-haw to do with me," Hoon said, pointing to the two dead centre staff members and the unlucky shoplifter. "This jolly looking big fucker was, though."

"You strangled him?" Iris asked, bending so he could study the body a little more closely.

"Aye. He had it coming, though. Didn't leave me with a lot of choice in the matter."

Iris held his hands up like he was warding off the explanation. "None of my business, Boggle. If you want to strangle a guy, you go ahead and strangle a guy. You're your own man, like. I trust your judgement."

"Aye, well, thanks for the vote of confidence," Hoon said. "But that's no' why I brought you here. What the fuck do you make of this?"

He rolled the dead Russian over to reveal the contraption strapped across his chest.

Iris' face lit up like he was a kid in a sweet shop. "Ooh, nice! That is very cool," he declared, getting down onto his knees beside the body.

He whistled quietly through his teeth as he examined the device from all angles, gently poking and prodding here and there at those bits he'd hopefully concluded were safe to touch.

"Well?" Hoon pressed. "What are you thinking?"

"Well, I mean, it's a bomb, innit?" Iris concluded. "I mean, it's obviously a bomb. It might as well have B-O-M written down the front of it in big red letters."

Hoon waited.

"B," he said, when it was clear that Iris wasn't going to.

Iris nodded. "O-M," he concluded.

Hoon waited again.

And again, nothing.

"B," he stressed. "B-O-M-B."

Iris looked up, frowning. "You what?"

"Bomb. B-O-M-B."

Hoon watched the other man's lips moving silently, like he was trying out this new spelling for himself.

"Nah, Boggle," Iris said at last. "I don't know where you've got that from. That's *bomb-uh*."

"Is it fuck! It's bomb! B-O-M-B, bomb!" Hoon snapped. "How could you be a fucking explosives expert in the EOD and no' know how to spell bomb?"

Iris fired a look at Hoon like he thought he might be on the wind-up, then turned his attention back to the explosive vest.

"It's an odd one," he remarked. He gave the aerial a flick. "Remote detonation, by the looks of it."

"Aye. Here."

Hoon fished the detonator from the pocket of the Santa suit and held it out. Just like he'd done with the vest, Iris examined it from a range of angles, but didn't make any move to take it.

"Here," Hoon said again, pushing it closer.

Iris shook his head. "Best not, Boggle. You know what I'm like with buttons. I'll just get tempted to push it and see what happens."

The man had a point. It was exactly that sort of thing that had earned him his nickname in the first place. Hoon drew back with the remote switch a little, and tightened his grip on it, but allowed Iris to continue his examination.

"Hmm." The Liverpudlian sat back on his haunches.

"What's that meant to mean?" Hoon asked.

"Not sure yet. Doesn't matter." He pointed to the late Ded Moroz. "You haven't got another one of these somewhere, have you?"

"What, a naked human corpse? No, Iris, funnily enough, I don't."

Iris tutted. "Damn. Shame. What about a vest? You got another one of these kicking about?"

Hoon shook his head. "No. I think I saw one in action, mind you. Lucky it didn't take my fucking head off. Turned the poor bastard wearing it into mush."

"Yeah, well, it would, wouldn't it?" Iris said. He pointed to the armoured plating on the chest—the same plating that had confused Hoon earlier. "Set up like that. Bound to make a mess of him. It's a suicide vest."

"Aye, well, obviously."

Iris looked up. "No, I mean *exclusively*. It's just a suicide vest, I mean."

"The fuck do you mean? What are you saying?" Hoon asked, leaning in closer.

"Well, I mean, all this here, like... This whole front section, see it?"

Hoon nodded to confirm that he did.

"That's containment. You want to do damage, that should be packed with shrapnel. It isn't. It's solid plating. Dense, too. Which means, the blast's basically aimed in the way. That's why you didn't get caught in it. The explosives in this vest aren't meant for the people on the outside, Boggle."

He rapped his knuckles hard on the plating.

"They're meant for the guys on the inside."

Hoon stared at the vest, then at the detonator in his hand. "What's the fucking point in that?" he wondered.

"Beats me, Boggle," Iris said.

"Could they just...? No." Hoon shook his head. The idea was almost too ridiculous to say out loud. "They're no' just wearing the fucking things inside out, are they?"

Iris considered this possibility, then shrugged. "I mean, it's not impossible, like. These straps are just clipped on, so you could reverse it if you really wanted to." He gave the contraption another once-over. "It's decent kit, this. Well made. Whoever put it together seemed to know what they were doing."

"Well, given that it's back to fucking front, obviously they didn't know what they were doing all that well," Hoon pointed out.

"Obviously," Iris agreed. "Unless, you know, they did."

He gave the vest a couple of slaps, then sprung to his feet. The sudden movement sent his glass eye lurching downwards in the socket, so it was looking at the bodies piled up on the floor.

"I want to see another one."

"Another vest? What for?" Hoon asked.

Iris extended a finger and tapped him on the nose. "Boop.

Never you mind. Might be nothing. I just want to see another one."

"Aye, well," Hoon said. His gaze went to the ceiling above them. "There's something else I need your thoughts on first."

"Is it that light fitting?" Iris asked, also looking up. "Because I don't really have an opinion either way."

"What? No. Of course it's no' the fucking light fitting," Hoon snapped. "Why the fuck would I be asking your opinion on a light fitting at a time like this?"

"I did think it was a bit strange, like," Iris admitted. "It's just... you looked up at it, so..."

"The roof. The thing I want to show you is on the fucking roof!" Hoon explained.

"Ah, right. Gotcha, Boggle. Lead the way, then."

"Aye, well..." Hoon clenched his jaw, grinding his back teeth together. "I don't think it's going to be quite that fucking straight-forward."

CHAPTER THIRTY

BERTA HOON PRIDED herself on her ability to be a pain in the arse. It was something she had worked hard at over the years. A skill she had spent time and effort cultivating. Anyone could be annoying—most folk, in her experience—but to be as utterly infuriating as Berta took real dedication.

The Santa calling himself Shaggy Goat was in the process of discovering just how deep that dedication went. He'd asked her to sit down half a dozen times now. Ordered her to do it half a dozen more.

And yet, still, she stood in front of him, ranting away about her long list of medical complaints, refusing to budge an inch.

Part of him had been hoping that help might arrive. That one of the other Santas might intervene and get her told. And yet, another part of him didn't want that. He was trying to de-escalate the situation, but there was no saying any of the others would.

Annoying as she was, he didn't know if he could stand by and watch an old woman be beaten and kicked.

Or worse.

"Look, please," he urged. "I'm trying to help you here. Just sit down, alright? Just go back to your bit there, and sit down. It'll be... Everything'll be alright. OK?"

Berta scoffed. "Oh, stop for a minute to sniff your own shite, son! You don't believe that any more than I do." She gestured around them with a crooked finger. "There's something going on here. Something more than you gaggle of dog cocks are saying."

Shaggy Goat's eyes darted to the other Santas, and to the security men all watching on. Those who had their weapons on show were adjusting their grips, like they were getting ready to put them to use.

"Please. I don't know what they'll do if you don't sit down," the lad whispered. "I don't know what'll happen. I can't protect you."

"Protect me?" Berta snorted. "A wee streak of piss like you? I'll thank you to know that I don't need your fucking protection, sunshine."

"*Please*," Shaggy Goat whispered. "You don't know what they're like."

Berta searched his face. There was no malice there, only worry, and a suggestion that tears might be about to come. He didn't want to be here. The silly bugger was floundering, miles from shore.

Her nostrils flared as she inhaled the deepest of breaths, puffing herself up to her full height and girth.

"Well, then," she said. "Maybe I should find out."

It wasn't the lad in the Santa suit who replied to her, but a soft, shaky voice from down at floor level.

"Please, just sit down."

Berta peered down her long nose at a young woman sitting cross-legged on the concourse, a toddler held close to her chest, his eyes puffy and red, his top lip raw with snot.

"We don't want trouble," the woman whispered. "We just want to get home."

There were some rumblings of agreement from the others

around her. Berta swept her gaze across the crowd. Men, women, children, all terrified—not just of the terrorists, but of her, and of what she might bring down upon them all.

"Just take a seat, um, *lady*," Shaggy Goat said. "Please, just take a seat before it's too late."

The eyes of all those watching her were in clear agreement on the matter. Berta interlocked her fingers and flexed them outwards until the knuckles went *crack*.

Then, with a sigh that shrunk her back to normal size, she rolled her eyes and turned away.

"Fine. But someone had better find me a fucking cushion, or this won't be the last you hear about my arse troubles."

She set off back towards the music teacher and his choir, and got three whole steps before another voice rang out behind her.

"Wait!"

Berta's sensible shoes *clopped* to a stop on the hard floor. It had only been a single word, but she recognised the accent. She recognised the look of fear on the faces of those around her, too.

"We got ourselves some kinda problem here?" drawled Santa Prime, putting his hands on the hips of his jolly red coat.

"Uh, no. No, sir," Shaggy Goat replied, and his tongue clicked against what was suddenly the dry desert of his mouth. "No problem. This, uh, this woman was just going to sit back down."

"Well, OK then." The American nodded.

Berta, who hadn't yet turned, moved to walk on.

"Except..."

She stopped again, and this time she knew that she was going nowhere.

"Don't cattle fucking lie down when a storm's coming? Big old heifer like this, seems to me like she oughtn't to be standing up in the first place."

Berta still didn't turn. She didn't have to. The hostages sitting nearby frantically shuffled aside as Santa Prime paced around to stand in front of her, a big, rotten-toothed grin lighting up the scarring of his face.

"Seems to me you should be sitting on your ass like you were told," he said. "So, in answer to my earlier question about if we have a problem here, I'm gonna have to say that, *yes...*"

He took a sudden step towards her, so they were nose to nose. Berta, who had the height advantage, didn't blink.

"We have ourselves a problem here," he whispered. There was something manic in his eyes. Some spark that might ignite and bring the whole place down around their ears. "So, what do you have to say about that?"

Berta gave her answer some thought.

But not much.

"I'd have to say your breath is fucking honking," she told him, not flinching. "What've you been doing, gargling dog shit? I've got a packet of *Polos* in my bag. How about you do us all a favour and neck the lot of them?"

There was silence from the crowd—a heavy, oppressive sort of silence that even a pin wouldn't have the nerve to drop in.

"The hell did you just say to me?" Santa Prime asked.

His tone was light and inquisitive, like he was sure he'd simply misheard, that this was all just some funny misunderstanding they'd laugh about later.

"I said your breath stinks," Berta reiterated. She winced. "And the fucking body odour? I mean, for God's sake, son, have you been living under a bridge?" She tilted her head to the left, still not breaking eye contact. "There's a *Boots* just along the way there. Go treat yourself to a can of deodorant and some mouthwash. And maybe a fucking overdose of paracetamol while you're at it."

He frowned. He blinked. She saw the uncertainty in his eyes, like he didn't know what to say, like he had suddenly realised that the train he was on was rapidly running out of track.

"Who do you think you are?" he asked, but with much less of his usual bombast.

And there, in that moment, she saw him not as some big scary terrorist leader, but as the pathetic, mewling excuse for a man that he truly was.

Berta leaned in closer still, so the tip of her nose was practically touching his. When she spoke, her voice was like the surface of a calm ocean, with all the same danger lurking just below.

"I'm just an old woman who's sick of your shite," she told him.

Behind her, Shaggy Goat cleared his throat. "Uh, maybe we should just let her go and—"

Santa Prime held up a hand. "Ah-ah, hold on now,"

"Aye, you stay out of this," said Berta.

"No, but, I just think that it would be best for everyone if—"

Berta practically snarled at the lad. "I told you to stay out of this, Mark!"

She realised, right away, her mistake. Her mind raced, searching for a cover story, for an explanation, but finding nothing remotely convincing.

Santa Prime took a slow half-step back. He shifted his gaze to the younger Santa, then back to Berta.

"The fuck did you just say?"

"I told him to stay out of it," Berta said. She smoothed down her coat and hooked her handbag higher on her arm. "But he's right, I should go sit down. Sorry to have caused..."

She tried to step past, but a hand on her chest blocked her. Santa Prime held her there, his attention now fully diverting to the sweating Shaggy Goat.

"What did she call you?" he asked. "You know this bitch?"

"What? N-no. No, sir. No, never seen her before today."

"But you told her your name?"

There was a swallow. A shake of the head. Shaggy Goat's face turned the same shade of red as his jacket.

"No. No, I mean, I didn't—"

There was no real finesse to the way Santa Prime drew the gun from his belt. No great rush, either.

And yet, it seemed to happen so fast that Berta could only stand there, frozen in time, watching as the silenced pistol was raised, listening to the throaty, desperate cry of the young man behind her.

Even with the silencer, the gunshot was deafening. It roared along the concourse, drawing screams from the hostages, and ending the one that had been in the process of rolling from Shaggy Goat's throat.

She turned her head in time to see him falling. He wasn't launched backwards or anything as dramatic as that. Instead, as the bullet passed through his skull and pulled his brain along behind it, his body just sort of gave up. His legs folded like he was trying to sit down on something that wasn't there, and what had been a man hit the floor as nothing but fresh meat and old memories.

The screaming and sobbing continued around her, rising in volume, growing in urgency, like it was a bubble on the build-up to bursting.

Slowly, like she was fighting to keep all her muscles under control, Berta turned back to Santa Prime. He was admiring a curl of smoke rising from the barrel of his gun, and as her eyes met his, he blew the smoke away, then twirled the gun around his finger like a cowboy in a Hollywood Western.

"I ain't a bad man," he told her.

That's fucking bold, she thought, given all the evidence to the contrary.

"I'm generally pretty patient. Folks say that about me. I've tolerated a lot of shit in my life. Hell, I'm even tolerating you. But what I don't tolerate—what I will not stand for—is dissent in the ranks. What I will not accept is disobedience from men who should know better." He shook his head. "Nuh-uh. No, ma'am. That shit don't fly here."

The racket from the hostages was dying down now. Not because they weren't still crying, but because they were working hard to muffle their sobs, their sense of self-preservation over-powering their fear.

"You didn't have to kill him," Berta said through her teeth.

"You're right. In here, I don't *have* to do anything," Santa Prime said. He stepped back in close again, and his voice was a low, aroused-sounding murmur. "But I get to do all the things I want. Like, maybe I'll get you to pick out five folks, and watch real close as I put bullets through their heads, too. You like that idea?"

Berta stood her ground. Held her nerve. Hung on to her dignity.

He'd won. She'd lost. He was in charge here, and her self-respect was the only thing she had left to cling to.

"No," she said.

"Then say, 'Please.' Say, 'Please don't do that. Please don't make me watch that.'"

She pursed her lips, but then did as she was told. "Please don't do that," she mumbled. "Please don't make me watch that."

The smirk on his face almost made her take it back, but she bit down on her tongue before it could get anyone else into trouble.

"Well, look at you! And they say you can't teach an old dog new tricks!" Santa Prime laughed, then held a hand out to her. "Bag."

Berta tightened her grip on the strap. "What?"

"You heard me. Give me your bag."

She wanted to argue. Of course she did. In almost any situation, arguing was her go-to response.

But not now. She couldn't now. Not after what had just happened.

Not after what she'd just caused.

Instead, she slipped the strap of her tartan handbag off her shoulder, and tried not to resist as he took it from her.

He rooted around in it for a few moments, humming below his breath, before finally letting out a loud, "Aha!" and producing her thick, sturdy purse.

The bag fell to the floor, spilling its contents around their feet. Santa Prime unfastened the clasp of her purse, and then fished out her bus pass, which was tucked in there for safe-keeping.

He held it up, checking the photo against her face.

"Roberta..." He stopped short when he saw the surname. His eyebrows raised halfway up his forehead, stretching the burned skin on the side of his face. "Well now," he said, a little breathlessly. "Ain't that just one hell of a coincidence?"

CHAPTER THIRTY-ONE

IRIS JOGGED UP THE STEPS, shoved his hands deep into his pockets, then went striding along the corridor towards the door that led up onto the roof, whistling cheerfully right up until he saw the two men standing at the other end, all decked out in Santa attire.

They had already seen him, but clearly hadn't yet made up their mind on who he was, or what he was up to, as they hadn't yet made any move to either intercept him, or shoot him repeatedly in the chest and head.

Instead, they both just stood leaning against the wall, staring at him in silence. One of them chewed slowly on a piece of gum, his expression suggesting that the task was a laborious one that he took no pleasure from.

Both men had guns. Neither one, thankfully, looked ready to open fire.

The gum-chewing Santa was the first to step away from the wall that had been supporting him. From behind his fluffy white beard, he regarded Iris with cold curiosity.

"Who the hell are you?" he asked. "And what are you doing up here?"

"You're not supposed to be up here," the other said. He, too, broke away from the wall.

Both men began advancing along the corridor. They reached for their weapons, and Iris realised that his likelihood of getting shot was increasing with every step they took.

He backed up, hands raising in surrender, both eyes wide but only one really paying attention.

"Sorry, lads. Don't mind me, like. Wrong turn," he told them. Then, still walking backwards, he retreated out of the corridor, back into the stairwell, and beyond their line of sight.

The Santas exchanged looks, then broke into a run, giving chase. Their boots clattered on the concrete floor, then skidded as they tried to stop at the corner Iris had vanished around.

The spray from a fire extinguisher hit them both the moment they rounded the bend, blinding them with a blast of fast-expanding white foam. It clogged up their noses and took root in their open mouths.

Coughing, spluttering, and still stumbling forwards, neither of them noticed the man in the other Santa suit step into their paths, an iron bar raised like a baseball bat.

One of them very much did notice, however, when the bar connected with him at head height, busting his nose, shattering several teeth, and forcing him to swallow his gum. The momentum of his lower half sent his legs bicycling into the air for a moment. He went horizontal in the air, then he went down. Hard.

Within his rapidly-growing suit of foam, the other man was fiddling with the safety catch of his SMG. The contents of the fire extinguisher was burning his eyes and slicking his fingers, though, and he couldn't move nearly fast enough.

Before he could even try for the trigger, the metal pole swung down, *clonking* him on the top of the head, and ushering him swiftly and neatly into unconsciousness.

Hoon twisted his wrist in a circle, *whumming* the metal bar through the air like it was a lightsaber. Beside him, Iris looked down at the two fallen men, gave them another quick blast with the fire extinguisher, then returned it to its spot on the wall.

"On second thoughts," Hoon remarked. "That was an absolute piece of piss."

Iris knelt in the foam and checked the men. Their eyes were closed, but judging by their pained little whimpers and groans, both were still alive.

"What are you doing?" Hoon asked. "We need to get to the roof."

"Hang on, hang on," Iris said. "I want to check something."

He pulled open the red coat of one of the men, revealing another explosive vest identical to the one on Ded Moroz.

"That one backwards, too?" Hoon asked, looking over his shoulder.

"Dunno. Depends what you're aiming at," Iris reasoned. He held a hand up. "Let me see that detonator again, Boggle."

Hoon took the device from his pocket, but stopped short of handing it over. "You're no' going to press the buttons, are you?"

Iris looked up at him. "Would I?" he asked, then he waved that question away. "No, you're right, of course I would. But I won't. Promise. I just want to check something."

Hoon still didn't exactly look happy about it, but he handed Iris the detonator, then took a step back, ready to duck into cover around the corner should the urge to blow something up prove too tempting for the Scouser to resist.

Instead of triggering the bomb, though, Iris fumbled around in the Santa's foam-soaked pockets until he found the other detonator, and immediately set about comparing the two.

Hoon glanced back over his shoulder, checking the stairway behind them. The fire extinguisher hadn't exactly been quiet, and nor had the series of bone-crunching impacts that followed.

If anyone had heard them, though, they didn't seem to be making a move.

He looked along the corridor to the door with the camera above it. The room with all the monitors in it had been secured— or, more accurately, completely fucked up—which meant there was now nothing between him and the roof.

"Hurry the fuck up with that," he instructed. He stepped around Iris and the two unconscious men, his feet squelching in the foam. "Grab a gun and follow me when you're done."

When he got no reply, he looked back at the crouching Liverpudlian.

"Iris!"

Iris tore his attention from the detonators. "Hmm?"

"I said be quick. Tool up and follow me when you're ready."

"Will do," Iris said. He pushed the top of one of the detonators with a thumb, and Hoon practically ducked when the mechanism suddenly sprang open. "Be right with you, Boggle. This'll only take me a minute."

Hoon had left the shotgun back in the security room, preferring the range and rapid-fire of Ded Moroz's submachine gun to the wide-angle spray of the shotgun's single remaining cartridge.

The SMG was a Russian-made PP-2000. It was a relatively modern weapon, and not something Hoon was familiar with. Still, he'd handled similar enough firearms that a cursory glance had told him more or less everything he needed to know about how this one operated.

What it fired like, he had no idea.

He expected that to change, soon enough.

The door to the roof opened outwards, which wasn't ideal as it increased the chances of anyone out there spotting him making his entrance. He took his time, inching the door open just enough for him to let the gun lead the way, before squeezing himself through behind it as quickly and as quietly as he could.

He snapped up the PP-2000, scanning the rooftop around him for any signs of movement that wasn't the diagonal bluster of falling snow.

The door swung closed behind him, his feet crunched on the thick carpet of frosty white, and as the cold wrapped itself around him, he suddenly felt like he'd stepped out of one world and into another.

Up here, everything was muted and muffled by the snow. Up here, hemmed in by falling flakes and a dome of pale grey sky, everything going on in the centre felt like it was happening long ago and far away.

Up here, the problems down below didn't feel so pressing.

He plodded on, boots scrunching, furry hood raised, one hand held above his eyes to help him see through the glare and the blizzard. The roof was a vast expanse of mostly flat space, large enough for an experienced pilot to land a helicopter on, though probably not in this weather.

A number of blocky concrete constructions stood spaced around—maintenance rooms for the elevator mechanisms, heating controls, ventilation ducts, or for any one of a dozen or more other purposes vital to the safe running of the centre.

When Hoon had stood up here in the past, it had allowed him to see what a Frankenstein's Monster of a place the shopping centre was. Usually, you could see all the joins between the new areas and the old, and marvel at the metal and concrete stitching that held them together.

Now, though, the snow had unified everything. For once, it all looked like one big building. Like it all actually belonged together.

Nice as that was, it made it difficult for him to figure out exactly where he was standing in relation to the rest of the building below.

The few landmarks he could remember from the last time he was up here—the glass roof above the old concourse being the main one—were fully concealed by the snow. Were he able to see more than a few feet through the blizzard, he might be able to pick out some Inverness landmarks to help him get his bearings.

Instead, he pressed on through the eerie silence, painfully aware of the sound of his footsteps, which were sure to act like a Siren's call to anyone else lurking up here.

Still, he was dressed like one of them, and carrying one of their guns, too. Someone would have to get close to get suspicious. Close would be a very big mistake on their part. Close, he could work with.

He stopped then, spying footprints in the snow. They crossed his path, headed left to right, so fresh that he wondered if he'd left them himself and wandered around in a circle.

But, no. The prints were smaller than his. Lighter, too. The falling snow had done little to cover them, which meant that whoever had made them was almost certainly still up here with him.

He raised the gun, taking aim in the direction the footsteps led. But then he thought better of it. Guys dressed as Santa were ten a penny round here at the moment. There could be plenty of reasons one of the bastards would be knocking around on the roof.

Go in waving the SMG around, though, and suspicions would surely be aroused.

"Fuck," he whispered, and his breath bloomed as a cloud of white mist as he swung the strap of the weapon over his shoulder.

He set off, following the prints through the snow, still shielding his eyes from the falling flakes. To aid in the charade that he was meant to be here, he picked a random Christmas carol and hummed it quietly—but not too quietly—as he walked.

The footprints continued straight on for a dozen yards, then hung a left between two big ventilation pipes that rose like pillars from the roof. His instincts told him to stop. Think. Survey the scene.

But if he was meant to be there—if he was just another of the spotty-arsed Santas checking in—then he'd do none of those things. He'd stride on through like he fucking owned the place. Like he had as much right to be there as anyone.

And so, ignoring the screams of, '*What the fuck are you doing?!*' echoing around inside his head, he turned and side-stepped between the metal chimneys, and briefly enjoyed the envelope of their warmth.

When he emerged on the other side, the owner of the foot-prints was still nowhere to be seen. What he could see, though— what immediately drew his eye—was the bomb.

It looked bigger *in the flesh* than it had on camera. It was about the size of a kitchen table—the sort meant for four, but which you could squeeze six around in a pinch—and most of it was now covered in dark blue canvas.

A pile of snow on top of it was glowing a supernatural shade of blue. Hoon used the back of his hand to brush the soft powder away, revealing a screen.

Revealing a countdown.

A countdown, he was dismayed to note, that didn't have a huge number of digits left on it. There were enough minutes left that he didn't have to immediately throw himself off the roof and hope that the snow was significantly thicker down at ground level, but not enough that he would have time to do anything useful, like evacuate the building, or write a will.

Hoon pushed back his fur-lined hood, scratched at his scalp with both hands, then spat a short but creative string of swear words into the falling snow. If this thing was as packed as it looked—if even half of the bulk beneath the canvas was explo-sive material—then it wouldn't just blow the roof off the centre, it would bring half the place down.

If detonated, something this size would compromise the

integrity of this entire section of the building. Everything from the ground floor upwards would eventually settle in the lower level of the car park as red hot rubble and melting glass.

And anyone inside the building, not to put too fine a point on it, would be utterly, wholly, and comprehensively fucked.

"For fuck's sake, Iris, hurry up," he muttered, turning back in what he hoped was the direction of the door.

He didn't get a chance to see if he was right, however, as he found himself nose-to-barrel with a handgun. It was too close for him to focus on, so he couldn't identify the make or model, but he got the gist of the weapon, all the same, and concluded that he probably shouldn't make any sudden movements.

The man holding it was the same one he'd seen messing with the bomb on-screen earlier, he thought, though it was hard to be sure, since they all looked more or less the same. He was tall and gangly, and seemed young behind his fake beard. Not much more than a teenager, Hoon reckoned.

And yet, there was a cold, steely sort of look in his eyes. A howling emptiness that suggested there was a gaping void filling the spot where this man's soul was meant to be.

Oh, marvellous, Hoon thought. A soulless twenty-something holding a gun to his face while a dirty great bomb ticked down behind him. *What a fucking day*.

"Who are you?"

There was no wobble to the younger man's voice. No uncertainty. Nothing that gave Hoon the sense that he'd hesitate to pull the trigger.

Only one way to play it, then.

"I was about to ask you the same fucking thing," Hoon said, looking him up and down in a way that made clear he wasn't impressed by what he was seeing. "So, get that fucking gun out of my face, and start talking, son."

The handgun didn't budge. The man's thumb did, though, shifting just enough to click off the weapon's safety catch.

"You're not one of us," he said in a dull, lifeless monotone.

His accent was practically non-existent, making it impossible to place. If human beings came with a default voice setting, it would be this one.

"The fuck I'm not," Hoon continued to protest. "I was sent up here to—"

"I'm going to shoot you," the younger man told him. "I'm going to shoot you in your mouth. I'm going to shoot you in your mouth and then I'm going to watch you die."

"My mouth?" Hoon frowned. "That's a bit fucking weird. I mean, the head, aye. Between the eyes? Classic. Even just the face in general. But the *mouth*? Why the fucking mouth?"

Under his hood, the man with the gun half-smirked. Quarter-smirked, maybe. Perhaps even less. But there was a definite turning up at one corner of his mouth.

"Because it's funny."

Hoon scowled. "I bet you're one of those creepy bastards that tore wings off flies, and put fireworks up cats' arseholes, aren't you?"

"Yes."

"Oh," Hoon raised his eyebrows, somewhat deflated. "Didn't think you'd own up to that quite so fucking quickly."

The snow gave a soft *crunch* as the terrorist shuffled closer. "Like I said, I'm going to shoot you in the mouth. It's only a matter of when. Either I do it now—which is my preference—or you put down that gun, I take you downstairs to the others, and I do it then."

Hoon rubbed his chin like he was considering his options. "Can you run that first one by me again?" he asked. "Got a memory like a fucking sieve these days."

The other man moved his finger inside the trigger guard of his weapon, and Hoon raised his hands in surrender. The bastard was still too far away to make a grab for. Hoon just had to hope that Iris popped up and took the gunman by surprise.

There was no sign of that happening anytime soon, though, so best to play along.

"Fine, fine! I'm just trying to have a bit of fucking banter," Hoon said. He very slowly and deliberately slipped the PP-2000 from his shoulder and held it out by the strap.

"Throw it over there," the terrorist instructed, jerking his head to indicate a direction. "Well out of reach."

Reluctantly, with all his instincts quietly muttering, 'I fucking told you so,' as he did it, Hoon tossed the SMG several feet to his left. It plopped down into the snow, and he watched as it sunk out of sight.

"So, what do they call you, then?" Hoon asked. "I've had Pére Noel and... another one. Fuck knows. Can't remember. A Russian Santa, I'm guessing. Dead... something. Which is quite appropriate, actually." He looked the man with the gun up and down and sniffed. "So, what about you? What shite wee nickname have you gone and given yourself? Father Pissmas?"

"I'm the Ash Man," the lad said.

He did so in a way that suggested Hoon should either be scared or impressed, and preferably both at the same time. Despite the gun still pointed at his face, though—and at his mouth, in particular—Bob was neither.

"The Ash Man? Who the fuck's he when he's at home? Is he the poor bastard who stands in the fireplace looking up while the big man comes down the chimney?"

The man with the gun started to reply, but Hoon interjected.

"And by *comes*, I mean ejaculates," he clarified. "Just, you know, I didn't want there to be any confusion there."

The Ash Man didn't bite. "It's German," he said, in his usual flat drone.

"What, ejaculating down chimneys? Should've guessed. Dirty bastards."

"The name," the Ash Man said, and there was a touch of

weariness about him now, like he was already growing tired of Hoon's shit. "The name is German."

"Oh. Right. Aye. Fair enough," Hoon said. "Anyway, you were saying something about... *Get him, lads!*"

He bellowed those last two words past the gunman, over his shoulder and into the swirling snow behind him.

The Ash Man didn't flinch. The gun remained trained on the lower half of Hoon's face. The ruse had failed.

"Ah, shite." Hoon sighed, then shrugged his shoulders. "Still, worth a try though, eh?"

"I'm not an idiot," the Ash Man told him. "You'll have to try harder than that."

"Fair enough, aye. Daft, really," Hoon said.

He fixed his gaze firmly on the younger man, his eyes shuddering in their sockets as he fought to resist looking past him a second time.

"So, are you no' going to tell me your plan in detail?" Hoon asked, raising his voice to drown out any other sounds the Ash Man might otherwise hear. The crunching of footsteps, for example. "Isn't that what you pricks usually do?"

The man in the Santa suit narrowed his eyes, watching Hoon closely. Hoon tried to keep staring straight, tried not to look behind the gunman, but there was a fleeting moment—barely a fraction of a second—when his gaze was drawn away before he forced himself to look at the gunman again.

Ash Man spotted the glance. He turned his head sharply, checking behind him. Like the look Hoon had fired over his shoulder, it lasted almost no time at all, but long enough for Hoon to make a grab for the gun that was pointed in his face.

The younger man reacted quickly, firing a jab into the side of Hoon's head while they both wrestled for the pistol. There wasn't a lot of force behind the punch, but Hoon hadn't been ready for it, and the sudden burst of pain in his ear almost made him lose his grip on the other man's wrist.

The fist came at him again. Hoon drew back, avoiding it, then kicked out at a knee. Ash Man dodged, then the same knee slammed into the ribcage that Hoon had left wide open.

Christ, he was fast.

Fingers clawed at Hoon's face, nails digging into his cheek, probing for his eyes. He couldn't get clear without letting go of the bastard's wrist, and if he did that, he was dead.

Getting further away wasn't an option, so he took the other option and threw himself in closer, slamming the rounded hump of his shoulder into the Ash Man's chest.

They staggered. Slipped. With a whirl of white dancing around them, they went down, the cold cushion of the snow making the impact with the roof less jarring.

They rolled, both still battling for the gun, the fingernails still gouging at Hoon's face. Over and over they tumbled through the snow, headed away from the ticking time bomb.

There were no opportunities to just wallop the bastard. Every time Hoon thought he might be able to get a hit in, they tumbled on again, the cold biting at their backs, the blizzard blinding them.

And then, out of nowhere came a drop. The roof beneath them suddenly ceased to be.

There was no moment of weightlessness. No *Wile-E-Coyote* style half-second of hanging there in mid-air. Gravity got to them immediately, and with the cold wind whipping around them, Hoon and the Ash Man began their fall.

CHAPTER THIRTY-TWO

DOWN ON THE CONCOURSE, the hostages and terrorists all heard the *thump*. Along with everyone else, Berta's eyes were drawn up to the snow-covered glass far overhead.

A red shape now lay on it, pressed flat against the glass. It wasn't hard to see that it was the outline of a man dressed as Father Christmas. He jerked around, and the knees of another bright red suit appeared on either side of him, like another Santa was straddling him.

"What the fuck?" Santa Prime mumbled, staring up at what was clearly a fight taking place on the skylight.

Or at least, he hoped it was a fight.

He lowered his head and looked around. All the other Santas and security men were just standing there, looking up, doing nothing.

"Well, come on then!" he screeched, making at least a hundred people jump in fright. "Do something!"

One of the Santas raised his gun and took aim, drawing terrified screams from hostages and terrorists alike.

"Don't shoot it, for fuck's sake!" Santa Prime cried. "You'll bring the whole thing down on us!"

"Oh. Yeah. Right," said the man who had been about to open fire. "Sorry."

"Get up there!" Prime ordered. "Get up there and find out what the fuck is happening!"

Half of his men sprang into action. They stormed through the crowds, kicking people aside and sending them scrambling for safety.

Santa Prime scowled at them as they hurried through the doors. He raised his head to look up again, but not before he caught a glimpse of Berta's face. He didn't think much of the look that was on it, but had he known her better, he would have. Had he known her at all, that look would have churned his guts and chilled him to his core.

Berta Hoon was smiling.

The fall had not been as bad as Hoon had braced for.

At first, he'd thought they'd rolled right over the edge of the building, and were falling to their deaths. But then, half a second later, they hit a lowered section of roof—one of those *Frankensteined* on new bits, no doubt—and the snow wasn't enough of a cushion to stop Hoon's breath being slammed out of him.

On the upside, the impact also knocked the Ash Man's gun from his hand. They both watched as it sailed a few feet, then plopped into the snow. Unfortunately, this left the fucker with both hands free, and he immediately put them to use.

One hand, and most of the Ash Man's weight, pressed down on Hoon's throat. With the other, the teenage terrorist swept mounds of snow over Bob's face, covering him in it, smothering him with it, filling his airways with raw, biting cold.

Blinded and choking, Hoon grasped desperately for the Ash Man's face. If he could find that, he could find his eyes. A couple of thumbs pressed into those should loosen the bastard's grip.

But the Ash Man was too tall, his arms too long, and Hoon could barely reach the top of his chest.

He could taste the snow on his lips, on his tongue, in his throat. Could feel its cold creeping down into his lungs, squeezing out what little air was left in there.

The pressure on his windpipe doubled as the Ash Man pressed both hands down on it, and leaned all his weight on them.

Lights danced behind Hoon's eyes—a spectrum of colour bursting across his snow-blinded field of view. His lungs burned and his head went light as his body screamed for air.

A thought struck him—a single, crystal clear idea that rose above the racket of panic that was reverberating the inside of his skull.

He was going to die here. Now. Like this. He was going to end his days on the roof of the Eastgate Centre, being strangled to death by a lanky bastard dressed as Santa.

A second thought followed the first, this one even clearer than its predecessor.

Fuck that.

The eyes were not the only weak spot, just the most obvious one. There was another one, much closer to hand. One that the bastard had left completely unprotected.

With the last of his strength, Hoon shoved a hand down the back of the Ash Man's trousers, and jammed a middle finger right up his arse.

The effect was instantaneous. The grip on Hoon's neck was released. The weight pressing him down began to writhe and convulse, as a high-pitched wail of shock pierced the freezing air.

Coughing and gasping, Hoon raised his head enough to get it clear of the snow, his finger still rammed up the other man's hoop. No longer blinded, he took aim and slammed the heel of a hand against his attacker's jaw, snapping his head back.

The Ash Man twisted and fell back. Hoon felt a *crunch*, and an excruciating burst of pain as his finger dislocated, yanking his hand free before any more damage could be done.

The other guy was still convulsing in pain, or shock, or both. The strike to the jaw had hurt him, too, and he seemed to have momentarily forgotten that Hoon even existed.

Pushing with his injured hand, Hoon dragged himself backwards. As he did, light appeared in the clearing where his body had been. He looked down and saw hundreds of frightened faces gazing back up.

Glass. He was lying on glass. That wasn't good, especially given the enormous drop on the other side of it.

He rolled sideways until the floor beneath him was no longer transparent, and flailed in the snow with his good hand, searching for the dropped pistol. He was still too weak and too breathless to fight the Ash Man one on one. He needed the gun. He needed an advantage. He needed—

"Don't."

Hoon froze at the sound of *clacking* metal. He managed a thin, exhausted exhale, and the mist it made encircled his head like a wreath.

The Ash Man loomed over him, the Russian-made SMG in his hands. He was standing oddly upright, most likely because of the force with which he was clenching his buttocks together.

He was too far away. No way Hoon could get to him. No way he could stop him opening fire.

"You sick weirdo freak!" the Ash Man hissed.

"Ah come on, son," Hoon said. "Don't try and tell me you didn't enjoy it."

The gun raised, took aim. A finger pressed on the trigger.

"Wait, wait! Not yet!" Hoon cried. "You're going to miss your big chance. You're throwing it away."

The Ash Man hesitated. "What?" he demanded gruffly.

"This is your big moment," Hoon told him. "You've got me dead to fucking rights. I'm done for. You've won. Now's when you get to do your big villain monologue. Rub my face in it. Tell me what your real plan is, and gloat about how I can't do fuck all about it."

The gun remained trained on him. The finger, though, didn't budge any further.

"It would be funny watching the penny drop," the gunman admitted. "Seeing the moment that you realise how fucked everyone down there really is." He shrugged. "Fine. You want to know what's going on? You want to know what's really happening here? Then brace yourself, because it is going to blow your tiny fucking—"

Hoon didn't hear the shot. Not really. Not right then.

Instead, he just saw the spray of red exiting through the side of the Ash Man's skull, pinkening the snow around him.

Both men held eye contact—although, for obvious reasons, not for long—then Hoon watched as the Ash Man's legs lost the signal from his brain, and took it upon themselves to collapse beneath him.

"The fuck...?"

Hoon continued to stare at the dead man, holding his breath, keeping his head down. A sniper. It had to be. Impressive shot, given the near-total lack of visibility.

But still, talk about bad timing.

He slowly raised both hands, then poked his head up and peered in the direction the shot must have come from. There was a multi-storey car park out there somewhere in the snow, he knew, though right now, it was almost impossible to see it.

Hoon gave a shaky, cautious thumbs-up in the car park's direction, being careful not to make any sudden movements. His hood was still down, and he pointed very deliberately at his head, turning it this way and that, presenting it to anyone currently squinting at it through a scope.

The ARU boys knew him. They'd recognise him.

Of course, whether that would make them more or less likely to shoot him was open to debate.

No bullet came whistling through the air, though. No brain matter exited his skull in a bloom of high-speed colour.

He rose fully to his feet, gave the shooter a thumbs up, then ran to the edge of the roof that overlooked Falcon Square. Even through the snowstorm, he could make out the small army of polis assembled down there. People, cars, motorbikes—and, most importantly, a great big lumbering bastard standing slap bang in the middle of it all.

"Jack!" Hoon bellowed, cupping his hands around his mouth. "Jack, listen to me! There's something you need to fucking know!"

Down at ground level, Logan, Tyler, a couple of CID officers, and an assortment of Uniforms, all looked up to the rooftop where the shouting was coming from. The blades of the chopper were *whumming* away high overhead, cutting the sound into chunks, which the whistling wind then stitched back together again in completely the wrong order.

They all craned their necks, struggling to make out what Hoon was shouting down to them.

He finished with a loud, clear, "Alright?!" and then he retreated, out of sight, further back along the roof.

Logan looked at the other officers around him.

"Did anyone catch a word of that?"

"Just the last one, boss," Tyler said.

"Yeah, I got that, too," one of the CID guys said.

"Right. But apart from that one?" Logan asked. "Did anyone hear what else he said?"

There was some shaking of heads. Some puffing out of cheeks.

"Your guess is as good as mine, boss," Tyler told him. "But, whatever it was, it sounded pretty damn important..."

Safe in the knowledge that he'd passed on his warning, Hoon allowed himself a moment to catch his breath.

Then, looking up into the falling snow to distract himself, he jerked his dislocated finger back into place with a grunt and a hiss of pain. Even once back in position, it hurt, and—he brought it to his nose and gave it an experimental sniff—it smelled, too.

He 'rinsed' it off in the snow, then pressed a clump of the cold stuff against the swollen knuckle, numbing the discomfort.

By the time he made it back to the bomb, Iris was there, peering down at it, looking concerned.

"Alright, Boggle?" the one-eyed man asked.

"Where the fuck have you been?" Hoon demanded.

Iris blinked in confusion, then pointed in the direction of the door. "In there. Do you not remember?"

"Course I fucking..." Hoon pinched the bridge of his nose. "Doesn't matter. What have we got?"

"Eh, a big bomb," Iris said. "Haven't had a chance to look any closer yet. Countdown's ticking down to..."

"Half-six. Aye. I know," Hoon said. "Can you stop it?"

"Don't know yet," Iris said. "Fingers crossed though, eh? Because, if this goes off..."

"We're in big fucking trouble," Hoon concluded.

Iris shook his head. "Oh, no. We're dead. We're totally dead."

Hoon sighed. "No, I know, I was just—"

"Everyone downstairs, too. They'll all be dead. Police outside, maybe. Basically, a lot of us will be dead."

"Aye. I get it. Just fucking shut it off, will you?"

Iris tapped a finger to his forehead in salute, then turned back to the bomb.

His focus lasted barely a second before he turned back.

"Oh! Nearly forgot," he said, fishing in his pockets. "I've got a present for you, and I think it's going to come in pretty handy..."

CHAPTER THIRTY-THREE

A MINUTE LATER, WITH IRIS' present tucked in the pocket of his jolly red coat, Hoon inched open the door that led from the rooftop into the building below, and peeked his head inside.

The corridor was empty. Or, at least it was if you ignored the two men still lying on their backs at the far end, in a puddle of fire extinguisher foam and blood.

Fuck.

Empty wasn't good. Empty meant they were being smart. Or being cowards. There was no way they didn't know where he was. He'd been hoping he'd open the door to find them running towards him in a big group, so he could machine-gun the lot of them in one fell swoop.

But the corridor was deserted. They were waiting for him. Biding their time.

"You sure about this, Boggle?" Iris whispered. "Isn't this, like, certain death?"

"Nothing's certain in this fucking world, Iris," Hoon told him. "Just block this door behind me and stop that fucking bomb. I'll keep the bastards busy."

Iris smiled, but it was a grim, hopeless sort of thing. "Just like the old days, Boggle."

"Aye," Hoon said, stepping through the doorway and into the corridor. "Just like the old days, pal."

Iris put a hand on Hoon's shoulder. They locked eyes, and for once both of Iris' were looking in the same direction.

"Listen, Boggle. If we survive this. Like, if you don't get shot and everything doesn't get blown to bits..." Iris swallowed, clearly building up to something. "Could I come for Christmas dinner? At yours, like?"

Hoon frowned. "Christmas dinner?"

"Just, you know, if there's space, like. No problem if there's not," Iris said, already backtracking.

Hoon was scowling at him now. "Christmas fucking dinner? What sort of fucking question is that?"

Iris withdrew his hand. "No. No, you're right, I know. Not the right time to—"

"Course you can come for fucking Christmas dinner."

Iris leaned back a little, his eyebrows rising. "What, seriously?"

"I'm annoyed you felt you had to fucking ask," Hoon told him. "You stop that bomb, and I'll cut your turkey up into bite-sized fucking pieces myself. So, block the door, and get to work."

Iris saluted again, and this time it was a much crisper, more official affair.

"On it, Boggle. You can count on me."

He retreated onto the roof. The door closed, and Hoon watched through the frosted window as Iris lashed the handle to the frame with a leather Santa belt. They both raised a hand, each waving to the other, then Iris turned back towards the bomb, and was swallowed by the snow.

Hoon looked ahead along the corridor. It was long and narrow, with nowhere to hide, nowhere to take cover. From here to the other end, he was a sitting duck, and the bastards knew it.

He thought about the present that Iris had given him, but it was too risky to use. Riskier, even, than marching straight down that corridor towards whoever was lurking around the corner at the other end.

They'd be gathered there in the stairwell, he knew, either waiting to hear him approaching, or holding fire until he turned the corner and walked right into their line of sight. Either way, it wouldn't end well for him.

But what other option did he have? He could wait here and guard the door. That was a possibility. Surely someone would poke a head around the corner eventually?

Or maybe he could reason with the bastards. Explain to them that what they thought was going on wasn't what was *actually* going on at all. Reveal that their role in all this wasn't what they thought it was.

But then, it would be tricky to break that news with hot lead ripping through his internal organs.

He could've just stayed on the roof, of course. He could've hung back and waited.

But they had guns. And they had hostages.

And, God help them, they had his sister.

Staying put wasn't an option.

Which left him just one viable one. Although, 'viable' was being generous. The chances of it working were tiny. The chances of it going wrong were huge.

It was a long shot. In every sense of the word.

Hoon raised the SMG, closed one eye, and took aim. It wasn't a weapon designed for accuracy, but for indiscriminately spraying death at relatively close quarters. If that was what you were after, it was ideal. For his purposes, he'd have given anything for a rifle with a scope on top.

But, he had what he had, and if nothing else, the military taught you to do the best you could with the tools available.

Hoon took a breath. Braced his feet. Steadied himself. One

burst of fire. That was all he had. The men waiting at the other end would panic at the sound. They'd rush in, shooting wildly. He might get a couple of them, but that would be his lot. That would be his end.

It was this or nothing. It was this, or it was all over.

He lined the shot up. It looked right, but he waited a second longer until it *felt* right, too. Then, as tenderly as he could, he coaxed the trigger back, and a three-round burst of gunfire roared along the corridor.

Like Pére Noel had before him, one of the fallen Santas erupted. Blood, bone, brain, and assorted other body parts flew in all directions like sparkles from a firework, coating the wall, and the ceiling, and all the unfortunate bastards hiding around the corner at the top of the stairs.

The muffled *whumf* of the explosion disguised his running footsteps. Hoon was two-thirds of the way along the corridor when he heard the first screeched, "What the fuck?!"

He locked his legs at the last moment, using the blood and the foam to slide the final few feet, the SMG raised in front of him at head height.

This time, he was less gentle with the trigger. He held it down, drawing a straight line across the opening. The sharp *brrraaap* of gunfire drowned out the screams of the blood-splattered Santas, and the bullets cut them short.

By the time he finished his slide, all but one of the terrorists lay slumped in a heap on the floor. The one who remained had only survived because he was shorter than the others. A hole had been punched through the pompom of his now fully red hat, the white trim having absorbed quite a lot of the blood spray from the explosion.

He was holding a shotgun, not unlike the one Hoon had used earlier. It was pointed down, though, and as Hoon took aim with the SMG, the diminutive hostage-taker let his weapon clatter to the floor.

"Please. Please, don't!" the tiny Santa whimpered. "Please, I didn't mean it. I didn't mean to do anything. I just... I got carried away."

"Aye, well," Hoon grinned at him down the barrel of the Russian-made weapon. "You and me both, pal."

The Santa screwed his eyes shut and squealed. Hoon swung with the butt of the gun, slamming it against the side of the smaller man's head and dropping him to the floor, unconscious.

"Don't say I'm not fucking good to you," he spat.

He turned towards the staircase, then stopped and looked back at the man he'd just knocked out.

He looked around at the bodily fluids on the floor, and on the ceiling, and on the walls.

And standing there, with blood dripping on him like rain, Bob Hoon had a terrible, wonderful idea.

Iris finished peeling back the canvas covering of the bomb, then just knelt there in the snow for a while, giving it all some thought.

Part of him had been hoping that there'd be nothing under there. That the whole thing was just a joke to be laughed about over Christmas dinner at Boggle's.

Another part of him, though, had wondered where the fun would be in that.

It was the first part that found itself disappointed.

The bomb was clearly civilian-made, since no arms manufacturer in the world would go this overboard. It would be a waste of money, if nothing else.

There was enough C-4 plastic explosive here to flatten a building several times higher than the shopping centre. It was densely and clumsily packed onto what looked, from the little gaps in the putty Iris could see through, to be a metal box with inexpertly welded edges.

It was probably too much to hope that the box would be empty. Anyone who'd gone to this trouble had probably packed it with something unpleasant. More explosives, maybe, but something radioactive wasn't out of the question, either.

"Well, that's great news," he remarked, and the idea of roast turkey with all the trimmings suddenly felt like a very unlikely one.

He could run, he realised. He was a wiry bugger, and there was bound to be some way off the roof. He could even warn the ring of police around the building. Maybe save a few lives. He'd be a hero!

And, more importantly, he'd be alive.

But, again, where was the fun in that?

He had no tools. No blueprints. No real idea what he was dealing with.

Iris straightened his wonky eye.

He rubbed his hands together, warming them against the cold.

This was going to be interesting.

As he made a plan, a hundred yards away on the other side of the roof, a door swung silently open.

CHAPTER THIRTY-FOUR

THERE WAS nobody waiting for him on the stairs. Nobody lurking at the bottom. Hoon had almost managed to convince himself that he'd killed everyone when a screech of feedback rang out over the centre's PA system, and a now-familiar American drawl addressed him directly.

"Oh, Robert! Yoo-hoo! I think you're going to want to come out here," Santa Prime said, and he sounded like he was stifling a giggle. "I got something of yours."

Hoon guessed what he meant, but his heart didn't sink all the way down into his stomach until he heard his sister's voice crackling from the speakers.

"Don't listen to this scabby-eyed fuckwit, Bobby! Don't you worry about me."

"Fuck!" Hoon spat the word at the empty hallway around him. "Fuck, fuck, fucking, *fuck-fuck* fucking fuck!" He roared the last one so hard that the effort of it doubled him over. "*Fuuuuck!*"

"I'm going to kill her, Robert. I am. And it's going to be a beautiful death. It's going to be something nobody's ever seen before. Something glorious. Something so fucking awesome, that every time any of these folks here close their eyes, they'll see it playing out, over and over and over again."

"God, this bastard loves the sound of his own fucking voice, doesn't he?" Hoon heard Berta say, and he couldn't really argue.

"And she'll just be the first, Robert. Next will be the men. Then the women. And then, once they've watched it all, once they've heard every fucking last scream of everyone else dying around them, I'll kill the children, too."

Hoon ejected a few more 'fucks,' but they didn't have the same energy behind them as the last lot. They were less of a furious outburst, and more of a grim acceptance of his fate.

The choice the bastard was offering was clear. It was Hoon, or it was everyone else.

And, much as he might like to pretend to the contrary— much like he might try to fool people into believing otherwise— that left him with no choice at all.

He unhooked the strap of the SMG from over his shoulder, ran a hand along the length of the weapon like he was saying farewell to a faithful old dog, then he set it on the floor at his feet.

Santa Prime kept talking, kept making threats, as Hoon walked along the corridor towards the door that would lead him out onto the concourse. Hoon was no longer listening, though. He'd heard quite enough from that fucker for one day.

He stopped at the door. Through the glass he saw Berta, an arm across her throat, a gun pressed against the side of her ribcage. She looked thoroughly disappointed to see him, and genuinely annoyed when he pushed open the door and stepped through with his hands up.

"Oh, for Christ's sake, Bobby," Berta said with a sigh. "Is there *nothing* you can't make a complete arse of?"

"Alright, alright, I can fucking turn around again if you like?"

"Suits me down to the bloody ground," Berta replied, rolling her eyes in contempt. Try as she might, though, she couldn't hide the fact that she was scared.

"Aye, well." Hoon sighed and let the door swing closed behind him. "Tough shit."

Santa Prime laughed loudly and forcefully in Berta's ear. "God, you two really are alike, ain't you? Both royal pains in the ass."

Hoon began to walk slowly, and the hostages slid aside to let him pass. He could feel all their eyes on him. He could hear the rasp of their breathing as they fought their urges to scream, or beg, or weep.

Three Santas moved to flank him, keeping their distance and their weapons trained on him. Even if he hadn't ditched the machine gun, he'd have been hard-pressed to get a clean shot in before they took him down.

There were others around the edges of the crowd, watching on. More Father Christmases. Several security guards, too. A dozen in total, maybe, it was hard to tell.

"So. The guys I sent upstairs...?" Santa Prime asked. He gave a jerk of his pistol, indicating for Hoon to stop where he was.

"What guys?" Hoon asked. He came to a halt a couple of paces beyond where the terrorist had ordered, deliberately testing his authority. "Oh. The dead guys?" He shrugged. "Aye, what about them?"

Santa Prime didn't look surprised. Given that Hoon was here and the rest of them weren't, their fate wasn't exactly a shock. He didn't look much of anything else either, in fact. Not sad. Not angry. And not in the least bit remorseful for sending all those men to their deaths.

He might be dressed in a Santa suit—and almost certainly a virgin, Hoon reckoned—but this man was dangerous.

"Sorry if that news upsets you," Hoon said, although clearly, it didn't. "It was them or me. And, you know, I wanted to see you face to face. There's some stuff I reckon you need to know."

Santa Prime sniffed. "I reckon I know about as much as I need to."

"Aye, well, that's where you're wrong, son," Hoon said. "I've got some big fucking news for you. Some intel that's going to blow your ugly fucking head wide open."

He glanced down into the puffy, upturned faces of the hostages on the floor around him, and tried very hard to look like he knew what he was doing.

"Fine. Let's hear it, Robert. Hit me with it. Blow me away!"

"Ha. If only," Hoon said. He jabbed a thumb back over his shoulder. "Left my gun out there somewhere."

He sniffed, wiped his nose on the red fabric of his sleeve, then lowered both arms to his sides. Santa Prime watched the movements with a detached, lazy sort of interest. Around them, the Santas who had been training their weapons on him all sharpened their focus.

"I'm still waiting, Robert. You gonna share this big news of yours or not?"

"Let her go first," Hoon said, nodding to Berta. "Then I'll tell you everything."

"Now what good would that do anyone?" Santa Prime asked. "Letting this sow here go? What good would that do you, me, or her?"

"Did he just call me a fucking sow?" Berta demanded. "Cheeky bastard! I'd be careful throwing insults around if I was you, sunshine, given you look like the Phantom of the Opera's come down with fucking shingles."

"Berta, shut up," Hoon told her. And, to his surprise, she did, allowing him to turn his attention back to the man holding her. "Look, I've not got any weapons. I couldn't shoot you if I wanted to. But I want to show you something."

He brought both hands slowly to the bloodied white trim of his Father Christmas coat and pulled it open. Santa Prime's eyes went to the device strapped to Hoon's chest and lingered there for a moment.

"I know about these," Hoon said. And then, from his sleeve, he produced a detonator and held it up so that all the other Santas and security men could see it. "And I've got this, too."

Santa Prime snorted out a laugh, but his scarred features arranged themselves into a confused sort of frown.

"So... what? You're going to blow yourself up?"

"If I have to," Hoon said.

"Uh... sure. Fine. Go for your life," the terrorist told him. "You want to save me the effort of killing you? You go right ahead, buddy."

"Aye, but that's no' the plan, is it?" Hoon asked. "I detonate this, there's a big *boom*, and the polis come running. And it isn't time for that yet, is it? It's too early. It fucks up your schedule." He shrugged, watching the other man closely. "Or *their* schedule."

Santa Prime's reaction didn't tell Hoon everything, but it told him enough. And, more importantly, it told him he was right. About the vests. About the plan. And about the fucking idiocy of the man he was talking to.

"Because, see, I've realised something. Something about you," he said, passing the detonator from one hand to the other. "You're no' the bad guy."

The terrorist sneered, trying to laugh it off. "Oh, I assure you, I'm the bad guy, Robert."

Hoon shook his head. "No. You're not. Maybe you're that fucking deluded, though. Maybe you genuinely believe that you are the bad guy. But, no. I mean, aye, I'll give you that you're probably *a* bad guy. I see you as a sort of creepy stalker type who hurls abuse at women on the internet all day long because they wouldn't touch your cock if it was made of solid gold and jizzed big fucking diamonds. I'm wholly positive that you're *that* sort of bad guy," Hoon conceded. "But believe me, son, you're a million fucking miles away from being *the* bad guy. And you know what that makes you?"

Santa Prime was still trying to hold his smirk in place, but it was desperately in need of some scaffolding. "Enlighten me, Robert. What does that make me?"

Hoon's smile was sharp and shark-like. "Just another arse-hole standing in my way."

Iris had run the numbers now. He'd examined the bomb mechanism from all available angles, mapped the build in his mind, and gone through all the possible outcomes.

All this had led him to come to a somewhat unexpected conclusion.

"This is a piece of piss," he remarked.

That, in itself, shouldn't have been entirely surprising. Most IEDs he'd come across back in the army were basic bodge jobs, often with cheap digital watches for timers, and a couple of Double-A batteries as a power source.

To be on the safe side, they'd generally detonate them from a distance, but disarming them was usually as simple as pulling out a wire or even flicking a switch.

The reason he was surprised on this occasion, though, was because this set-up didn't match the sophistication of the explosive vests. Those were made by someone who knew exactly what they were doing, inside-out or not.

This, though? This was amateur hour.

Beneath the fancy iPad screen counter, and the sheer volume of explosive material, this one wasn't much more complicated than the cobbled-together roadside bombs he'd worked on back in the Gulf.

The iPad was connected by a single USB cable to a small

detonator, which was designed to deliver an electrical charge to the C-4.

Two wires ran between the detonator and the explosive putty. Once the timer hit zero, the circuit would be completed, and the reaction would trigger the blast.

Iris wasted a couple of seconds *Eenie Meenieing* between the two wires, then decided to just go ahead and pull them both.

Before he could touch them, though, he heard footsteps crunching closer behind him. He turned, and through the falling snow saw four Santa Clauses closing in, all armed, all pointing their weapons his way.

"Ah, bollocks," he muttered, reaching for the wires that would disarm the bomb.

Out of nowhere, the butt of a rifle connected hard with his head. Iris fell, grabbing for the detonator, but catching only snowflakes.

He saw his eye plopping into a pile of pinkening white. He felt blood pouring from his nose, tasted it as it surged back into his mouth and down his throat.

When his vision cleared enough, he looked up. He could see six of them now, all dressed in red, all pointing their guns down at him.

One of them—the tallest, in the middle, with the biggest gun —spoke in a voice so deep and low that it made Iris' stomach vibrate on some sympathetic frequency.

"Who the hell are you? And what the fuck are you doing to our bomb?"

And, behind him, the timer ticked down.

CHAPTER THIRTY-FIVE

NOBODY DOWNSTAIRS on the concourse had moved. Santa Prime still had his arm around Berta's neck and the gun jammed against her ribs. Hoon stood a dozen feet away from them, idly tossing the explosive vest detonator from hand to hand.

All eyes in the room followed it on its journey back and forth, back and forth.

"See, this whole story about all this being for money, that's no' true, is it?" he said. "I'm no' buying that."

Santa Prime fell momentarily silent, like he was deciding how much he should reveal. Then, with a nonchalant shrug, he answered honestly.

"No. You're right. It ain't about the money. We don't give a shit about money."

"Aye, I thought not," Hoon said. "I mean, all this, this whole thing, the investment it must've taken... The planning. I knew there had to be more to it than cash. So, what then? What's the fucking point? From your perspective, I mean. I know the real answer, but I'm looking forward to hearing your take on it."

"We're making a statement. All of us. We're making a big, bold statement that the whole world will see."

Hoon snorted. "In Inverness? Fucking hell, son. Could you have picked anywhere less high profile? Was Outer Mongolia too cold at this time of year? Was the dark side of the moon too fucking jam-packed? And what's the statement, anyway? 'Lassies won't shag us'? Is that it?"

"You can laugh, Robert. You can mock us. You won't be the first," Santa Prime said. His voice became a cold, unyielding rasp. "But I reckon you'll be about the last. When folks out there see what happened here—see what we accomplished—then maybe they'll think twice about disrespecting us in the future."

"Considering your future will largely involve you being a gristly fucking paste with bits of red fluff in it, why do you give a shite?"

"Because we ain't doing this for us. We're doing this for all our brothers out there. All them downtrodden, put-upon, straight, white, God-fearing young men, all cowed and broken by a World Order that hates us. That wants to rid itself of us."

"Oh, for fuck's sake," Hoon muttered. He twirled the detonator around on a finger, and everyone sitting within thirty feet held their breath. "So, just to be clear here, you think the plan is to blow this place up in order to make a statement?"

"Bingo."

"The statement being, as far as I can tell, that you're a bunch of sad, bitter, unshaggable cunts."

"Bobby!" Berta barked, her whole body bristling with fury. "What have I told you about using that word?"

Hoon sighed. "I thought, given the fucking circumstances..."

"No! That word hates women. And there are plenty of other words you could use for this lot. *Plenty* of other words," Berta told him. "Pricks. Arseholes. Wankers. Bastards. Knobs. Pissfucks. Dildos."

Hoon frowned. "Pissfucks?" That was a new one on him.

"Cocks. Shitestains. Arse munchers. Pavement fuckers. Bellends. Bawbags."

Berta fell silent then, apparently having run out of suggestions.

Hoon blew out his cheeks. "Right, well—"

"Quims," Berta added.

Her brother watched her for a moment. "You done?"

"Aye," Berta confirmed with a nod. "Aye, that's me."

"Good." Hoon sniffed and shuffled on the spot for a moment. "I've forgotten where I was now. What the fuck was I saying?" His eyes widened and he let out a sharp, "Aha! Your plan. Blow everything up. Send a message. Blah-blah-blah."

"You may mock us, Robert—"

Hoon waved the detonator and quickly cut the other man off. "I'm no' the one mocking you, son. Someone's been laughing at your expense from the minute you fucking got here."

He leaned in a little closer, like he was sharing a secret. Santa Prime didn't move, but some of the other terrorists took a few shuffled steps nearer, not wanting to miss what Hoon was going to say next.

"See, that might be *your* plan, but it's no' *the* plan. *The* plan is way above your pay grade and higher still above your fucking IQ. *The* plan is for your wee fucking virgin collective here to keep the polis busy, while a dodgy bastard at the airport is either kidnapped or killed, so she can't testify against some other equally dodgy bastards."

Santa Prime said nothing, but Hoon could see the uncertainty filling in the lines in his scarring.

"You didn't think it was a bit weird someone kitting you out with all this stuff? All these guns, and state-of-the-fucking art explosive vests? It didn't strike you as odd that someone with the connections and power to let you take over an entire fucking shopping centre would have even the *slightest* bit of interest in how lassies aren't being nice to you? You really think they fucking care about how you're no' getting your end away?"

"It ain't about that. It's bigger than that!" As he spoke, specks of foam flew from Santa Prime's mouth. "They're making it a crime to be a patriotic American male. They're making it illegal to be a goddamn red-blooded Englishman!"

He made the mistake of gesturing at Hoon as he said that last word.

Silence fell.

Even the background murmuring of muffled sobs that had been the concourse's soundtrack for the past few hours fell away.

"The fuck did you just call me?" Hoon asked.

"Oh, Christ," Berta muttered. "Now you've fucking done it."

"Did you just call me English?"

Santa Prime looked confused. "Well, ain't you?"

"No, I am fucking not!" Hoon replied, his voice rising in pitch and volume. He wore the face of a man who'd just been mortally offended. "I mean, don't get me wrong, I've got nothing against the English. But then, I've got nothing against goldfish either, doesn't meant I'd want to fucking be one!" He shook his head, and reconsidered his response. "Actually, no, I can't fucking stand goldfish. Arrogant wee pricks."

Santa Prime still looked utterly lost. Hoon spelled it out for him.

"I'm Scottish, son. You're in fucking Scotland. No' England."

"Ain't it the same thing?"

"Fucking hell!" Hoon cried. He pointed around to the crowd of hostages. "You'd better be fucking careful what you're saying there, son, or this lot here'll tear you a new arsehole. A third one, to go next to the one on your face that you're fucking talking out of. No, it's not the same thing. It's very much not the same fucking thing."

"Fine. OK. Jesus. They're trying to make being a red-blooded *Scottish man* illegal, then. Happy?"

"Scotsman, but fine, go on."

Santa Prime looked a little lost standing there now, like he couldn't quite remember what he was supposed to be saying.

Then, all of a sudden, it clicked back into place, and he launched back into his rant, albeit with a little less conviction.

"That's what this is about. It ain't about sex, or a lack of it. It's about power. They have it, and they want to take what little we have left from us. From folks like me and you. That's why we're here. That's why we're doing this. We're standing up. Standing up to the New World Order. Standing up to all the fucking queers, and the blacks, and the sluts who think they can—"

"Oh, away and bile yer fucking heid, son," Hoon told him. "If you..." He decided to try it out. "...*pissfucks* really represent young white Christian men like you say you do, then I hope you're right. I hope they make the whole fucking lot of you extinct. I hope they round you all up at the rim of a big fucking volcano, and push you in one by one. I'll be there waving flags and selling the fucking popcorn. Just tell me who I have to vote for to make that a fucking reality."

Santa Prime's jaw was clenched tightly now. From Hoon's distance, it looked like the terrorist's eyes were shaking in their sockets.

"Jesus Christ. Are you greeting, you fucking wretched-toothed mollusc?"

"What? I don't... What the hell does that mean?"

"Greeting. *Crying.* Are you fucking crying?"

"What?! No! Of course I'm not... Fuck!"

He shoved Berta aside, sending her stumbling into the crowd. A dozen faces looked up in horror as she *timbered* towards them, her shadow growing. She was flailing her arms, and yet her face had a strangely impassive quality about it, like she wasn't going to let anyone think this fall was anything but deliberate.

Hoon winced as she landed heavily on top of a couple of

unfortunate younger lads, but quickly turned his attention back to Santa Prime. His gun was now pointing at Hoon. It rattled slightly in his hand, all his earlier confidence and bravado being overwritten by the doubts that Hoon had hammered into him.

"You're a fucking liar. This was *my* plan! This whole thing, this was all my idea! Nobody else's!"

"My arse. Aye, they let you think it was, but if you were really making some big point, sending your sad wee fucking message out into the world, why piss about pretending to be after a ransom?" Hoon asked. "Because you were stalling. Because they told you to bide your fucking time until they'd got what they wanted. Because they've got you on a fucking leash. Because, no matter what deluded bullshit you might think, you're no' some big fucking folk hero to a race of snidey wee goblin-men wanking themselves dry in their mother's fucking basement. You're nothing, son. You're a fucking joke."

The gun shook. What was left of Santa Prime's awful teeth ground together.

"I ain't a joke! You're the joke!"

Hoon snorted. "Is that the best fucking comeback you've got? Jesus Christ, son, you need to start working on some decent material."

"They didn't do everything," Santa Prime said. A suggestion of his old smile returned. "Sure, they gave us the guns. They gave us these sweet-ass vests. Laid out the plan, and gave us everything we needed to take this place."

The smile broadened. Hoon didn't like that. Not one little bit.

"But we brought a little surprise of our own," Santa Prime said. "A cherry on top. Something to make sure all this really went with a bang!"

"The bomb," Hoon said. "On the roof. The bomb. You guys made that?"

The terrorist's grin was fully formed now. Glee lit up his eyes like fireworks.

"You bet your ass we did!"

Hoon stood there in silence for a while, then let out a breath in one big gasp.

"Oh, thank *fuck!*" he cried. "Jesus. *Phew!* To think I was fucking worried about it, too. I thought it might actually go off. But if you bum-fluffed fucks built it..." He put a hand to his chest and exhaled again. "Oh! Thank Christ. I mean, clearly you lot don't have the first fucking clue what you're doing, so it'll be disarmed by now. I've got a guy up there who knows all this stuff, but now I know that you titflumps built it, I reckon I could've probably just yanked the fucking wires out myself."

"No! It's good! It's a good bomb!" Santa Prime hollered, his smile vanishing again.

"A '*good bomb*'? Shite, maybe I've misjudged you, because clearly you know all the proper fucking lingo, eh?" Hoon said, taunting him. "Still, that makes sense, you building it. See, I couldn't figure it out. These vests, and then that bomb. It didn't fit. It didn't make sense. Now it does. So, cheers for that."

He pointed with the detonator at Santa Prime's gun, then around at the other men with their weapons.

"But I'm in a bit of a fucking rush here, lads. See, the polis are already on the way to the airport, and I want to be there when they nick the bastards who arranged all this. You know, so I can rub their fucking faces in it. So, I'm going to give you one chance to do the right thing. Put down your guns. Give yourselves up. Let all these people go."

Santa Prime hissed out a high-pitched laugh of disbelief. "Are you kidding me? We're about to go down in history."

Hoon scratched his nose with the detonator, drawing a collective gasp from the people sitting around him.

"Right. I said one chance, but lucky for you, I'm in a generous mood. Must be that fucking Christmas spirit you hear so much about," Hoon said. "So, last chance. Final fucking offer. Are you going to give yourselves up? Yes or no?"

Santa Prime drew back the hammer on his silenced pistol. "What do you think?"

Hoon looked around at the other Santas and security men. Those with weapons all still had him in their sights. None of them looked like they were about to back down.

"I need you to say it," Hoon stressed. "Just for my own fucking peace of mind. Are you going to surrender peacefully?"

"No. No, we are not."

Hoon nodded. "Right. Aye. And, do you intend to kill these people?"

The smile returned, just at one corner of the terrorist's scarred mouth. "Yes. Yes, we do."

A ripple of panic started to go through the crowd, but Hoon raised his voice above it.

"Right. Fine. Everyone here heard me give you a chance to give yourself up. Two chances, in fact. Loud and fucking clear. I'm no' happy about it, but you've left me with no choice here."

He held the detonator up in front of him, turned it so his finger and thumb were resting on the buttons.

Santa Prime sneered. "Oh, is that your big finale? Is that how you're going to end this? By blowing yourself up?"

Hoon shook his head. "No. Like I said, I've got a friend who knows all about this stuff, so there's two reasons why that won't happen," he said. "Firstly, I'm no' fucking daft enough to be wearing my vest the wrong way round, just because some shady bastards told me that's how they go on. And secondly..."

He pressed a thumb down on the top button, priming the trigger.

"This switch isn't for my vest," he said. "It's for all yours."

He waited, just a moment, just long enough to see the shock registering on the face of the terrorist leader.

And then, he placed his finger on the trigger, closed his eyes, and squeezed.

Iris stood frozen to the spot, blinking away the aftermath of a tidal wave of blood that had just washed over him in one sudden, overwhelming gush.

He had no explanation for why the six men who'd assembled around him had become quite so *disassembled* in such a short space of time. Their stinking, quivering innards lay piled up on the roof, steam rising from them as they sizzled away in the snow.

The only thing he could think of was that he'd been hoping something like this would happen to them. They'd been about to shoot him, and he'd been thinking how nice it would be if something untoward had befallen them all before they had a chance.

Had he done this? Had he killed them with his mind? Was that what had happened?

It had to be. There was no other explanation. It was the only—

"Oh. No. Wait. The bombs," Iris said out loud, suddenly remembering the detonator he'd given Hoon.

Tying it into the frequencies of the other explosive vests hadn't been difficult. One press of the trigger, and every vest in range went *kaboom*.

Or, in reality, *kasplat*.

Iris ran a hand down his face, trying to wipe away the blood. It didn't really help. If anything, because quite a lot of intestinal matter had splattered against his forehead, it just made things worse.

He looked down at what was left of the terrorists. Mostly, this just amounted to legs. Legs, guts, and a pervasive red haze in the air that turned the snow pink before it even landed.

They'd certainly think twice about pointing a gun at him again.

It was at this point that Iris heard the screaming coming from below. This was quite impressive, given how badly his ears were ringing, and a real testament to the level of panic going on downstairs.

He used a foot to clear some of the soggy red snow off the skylight, and peered through the glass at the concourse below. A lot of Santas seemed to have exploded down there, too, plastering the hostages in their smouldering remains.

It was the hostages who were screaming. Hoon was doing his best to calm them, but they mostly seemed to be ignoring him.

"Looks like someone needs a hand," Iris said, chuckling.

He fished around in the snow until he found his eye, then popped it into the empty socket and immediately clutched at his head.

"Brain freeze!" he hissed.

Shaking off the pain, he picked his way through the mess of body bits, and headed for the door.

He had just finished untying the belt from around the handle when a thought occurred to him.

"Shit! The bomb!"

Quickly backtracking, Iris found the detonator had been coated in human innards, which wasn't ideal. He scooped them aside as best he could, then took hold of a wire in each hand and pulled.

They popped out of the C-4 with the lightest of tugs. Iris waited a moment to make sure he wasn't dead, then he lifted out the detonator, turned it over, and flicked the big square *Duracell* battery out of the back.

To be on the safe side, he unplugged the blood-soaked iPad from its cable, turned it over in his hands a couple of times, and then—for reasons he wouldn't be able to explain even if asked—buried it in the snow.

That done, he got to his feet, blowing on his hands to warm them. The blizzard danced and swirled around him, the dots of white like shooting stars against the darkening night sky.

"Well," he announced to the world at large. "That was certainly eventful."

Everything was dripping. Everything and everyone.

Iris hadn't been kidding around with the detonator. The moment Hoon touched the trigger, almost every vest in the place had gone off, turning Santa Prime and the other terrorists into what was essentially a flying soup.

Only his own vest hadn't detonated, thanks to him unplugging the connection between the receiver and the detonator on his way down the stairs.

There had been a few moments of blissful silence after the bombs had all triggered. It was shock, mostly. All the hostages had been working hard at staying quiet so as not to get on the wrong side of the gunmen.

When those same gunmen had been spontaneously liquidised before their very eyes, they hadn't known how to react. They'd just sat there and stared as a literal shitstorm of blood and innards had battered them.

Those closest to the terrorists had it worse, of course. They took the brunt of it, the gore plastering them from head to toe, and larger body parts like hands, and noses, and the occasional genital, landing in their laps.

It was these people, perhaps unsurprisingly, who started screaming first. Their terror at being shot was suddenly replaced by a primal, overwhelming urge to *get this shit off* and they erupted to their feet like a crowd at a football match, before several of them slipped in the blood pools and immediately fell back down again.

Hoon raised his hands and shouted for calm, but that ship had already sailed. With no one around to tell them otherwise, the hostages surged for the stairs and the escalators, pushing and shoving, every man for themselves, along the concourse.

"Well, thanks a fucking lot, Bobby."

Hoon barely heard his sister over the screams of the fleeing crowd. When he turned in the direction of her voice, it took him a moment to recognise her.

She looked like she'd been painted red, then pebble-dashed with hundreds of squishy purple bits. There was something draped across one of her shoulders like a sash. Part of a trachea, Hoon thought, though he chose not to look too closely.

"A bit of warning would've been nice."

Hoon indicated his own front half. It wasn't in the same league as Berta, but it hadn't completely escaped the spray.

"Join the fucking club," he told her.

He indicated the thinning crowd around them. The music teacher and his choir were still huddled together, but were being shoved around by all the other people fleeing past them.

"Sort this lot out, will you?" he told her. "Make sure they don't fucking stampede over each other."

"And how the fuck am I meant to do that?" Berta asked.

"Don't know, don't care. Shout at them. Boss them around. Be your usual fucking self," Hoon said.

He was already setting off towards one of the doors leading through to the back corridors of the centre. No way he was getting through the crowds in a hurry, but they were all headed for the main doors. There was another exit through the loading bays that would take him around the side of the building and into Falcon Square.

"Where are you going?" Berta demanded.

"To fucking finish this," Hoon told her. He pushed open the door. "Once and for all."

"Wait!"

Berta's cry was sharp and urgent. It was enough to stop him in his tracks.

"What's the matter?"

Berta stood there, gazing at him, blood and bits oozing down her front.

"Just... be careful, Bobby," she told him, and there was a softness there that was completely out of character. "Please be careful."

Hoon opened his mouth like he was about to say something. But then, he just tipped her a nod, carried on through the door, and was gone.

CHAPTER THIRTY-SIX

THE CROWD HAD FORCED its way out through the front doors by the time Hoon got there. Police and paramedics were already racing in, ushering the hostages clear of the building, dragging those whose legs had given out on them the moment they'd reached fresh air.

When Hoon appeared through a side door, caked in blood and dressed like Santa, he suddenly became aware of a couple laser targeting dots sweeping across him, and quickly raised his hands in surrender.

"You! Stay right where you bloody are!"

Hoon could barely see the person speaking to him through the snow, but even if he hadn't recognised the voice, the size of the silhouette would've been a dead giveaway.

"Jack? *Jack?*" he spat, hurrying forward.

"Bob? For fuck's... Bob, is that you?"

Hoon ran an arm across his face, trying to clear some of the blood and gristle away.

"Aye! Aye, it's me!"

Logan looked him up and down. "Jesus, what happened to you? And why are you dressed like Father Christmas?"

"Never fucking mind that! What the fuck are you still doing here?"

Logan spotted the red targeting dots and waved up to the snipers, giving the all-clear. "What do you mean?" he asked, turning back to Hoon. "Where the hell else would I be?"

"The airport!"

Logan frowned. "The airport?"

"Aye, the airport! For fuck's sake, Jack! I told you to go to the fucking airport!"

Logan pointed up in the direction of the roof. "Is that what you were shouting from up there?"

"Yes!"

"Oh." Logan put his hands on his hips. "We couldn't hear you."

"Jesus Christ! So nobody's at the airport?!"

"No. Why? What's happening? What's wrong?"

"I'll tell you what's fucking wrong, Jack. This—all this—is all just a fucking distraction," Hoon barked. He jabbed a thumb back over his shoulder at all the fleeing hostages. "Oh, and you're fucking welcome, by the way. Everyone's safe, no thanks to you lot."

"Aye, well, we'll see. Some of them look a bit worse for wear," Logan said. "What about the hostage-takers? Where are they?"

Hoon gestured vaguely at the bloodied front of his Santa jacket.

Logan stared at the coat in disbelief. "Fuck. All of them?"

"Well, clearly that's no' all of them," Hoon shot back, indicating the blood stains. "Who the fuck do you think they were, the shoemaker's elves?"

"I meant are they all dead?"

"Aye. But I've got several hundred fucking witnesses who'll tell you I gave them every possible opportunity no' to be." He held out a hand. "Now, shut the fuck up and give me your car keys!"

Logan almost argued, but someone needed to take charge of the chaos, and he didn't have time to debate Bob Hoon.

"Here," he said, handing the keys over.

"Where's your car?"

"Back at the office," Logan said.

"For fu—" Hoon threw the keys back at him and spun around to search the surrounding area.

"What's happening, Bob? What's the problem?"

"They're coming for her, Jack! That bitch, Suranne, or whatever her fucking name is. This was a false flag. They're coming to get her. I don't know if they're going to rescue her or take her out, but they're coming."

Logan groaned. It was a long, low, pained-sounding thing. "Christ," he muttered, then he turned and searched the crowd. "Tyler's car's here somewhere. Or we can take a squad car, blue light it. I can redirect the chopper, send it to the airport ahead of us. We'll call in and get the airspace shut down."

He turned back, expecting to find Hoon still standing there.

Instead, there was only an empty space where he'd just been, and some bloody footsteps heading towards the centre of Falcon Square.

"Bob?"

No answer came through the storm, but Logan was forced to raise a hand in front of his face, shielding his eyes from the blinding glow of a single headlight that burst into life just a few feet away.

An engine roared. A siren wailed.

And Logan was forced to stagger out of the way as a Police Scotland motorbike sped past him, its two fat tyres chewing hungrily through the snow.

"Christ, it's cold."

Miles blew on his hands, rubbed them together, then wrapped his arms around himself to try to trap in some heat.

They stood under what was essentially a bus shelter at the edge of a helicopter landing pad, listening to the distant *whump-whump-whump* of approaching rotor blades.

The gang was all there—the shivering Miles and his assistant, Kevin, who was tucked away in the corner keeping out of everyone's way, plus Suranne, who was flanked by two monosyllabic MI5 officers.

Officer Walton, the most senior member of the security team, paced around in the snow outside. Miles wasn't sure if he was scouting the area for signs of trouble, or just avoiding being in the company of the others. Either way, he seemed to be keeping busy.

"Shouldn't be long now, sir," Kevin announced. It was the fourth time he'd made the same announcement, though nobody had ever asked him for an update.

"Good. Right," Miles said. He blew on his hands again, then shoved them deep in his pockets. "And the place we're going...?"

"Aberdeen, sir."

"Right. Is it warmer than this?"

"Well, it's not snowing," Kevin said. "But I don't think we'll have to worry about suntan lotion."

A phone rang, sounding shockingly loud in the confines of the shelter. Miles shot a reproachful look at his assistant, who was making no move yet to silence the ringing.

Suranne sighed heavily. "It's your phone," she said.

"What? Oh. Yes. Shit."

Miles patted his jacket until he found the vibrating lump of his mobile. He checked the screen, then grimaced slightly when he saw the name displayed there.

"I'll, uh, I'll take this outside," he said, sidling through the opening of the shelter, and immediately recoiling from the fury of the blizzard.

He trudged away from the covered waiting area as far as he dared before thumbing the green button on his screen and putting the phone to his ear.

"Hello? Bob?"

The voice on the other end was broken up, the signal poor. When Miles could hear words being said, they were partly obscured by the sound of an engine, and the roaring of the wind. A screaming siren wasn't exactly helping matters, either.

"I can't... What are you saying, Bob? It's a really bad... Hello?"

The reply was a series of squawking noises, with just a few words audible within the racket.

"—the fuck a——ou?"

Miles jammed a frozen finger in his ear and concentrated on the sounds coming out of the mobile. "Where are we? Is that what...? We're at the airport still."

There was a cacophony of sound from down the line. From somewhere, Miles could hear the angry honking of a car horn, though he wasn't sure if it was on the phone or nearby.

In amongst it all, Miles thought he heard Hoon say something about an aeroplane.

"Plane can't get in, Bob. Snow. Helicopter's coming to get us now."

"—at di——say? Can't hea——ou."

Miles raised his voice and slowed down his diction. "I said there's a helicopter coming for us. Hel-i-cop-ter." He shielded his eyes and looked up into the snow. Lights were descending cautiously through the blizzard. The sound of the blades made it even harder to hear Hoon's response.

"I didn't get that. Say again," Miles all but shouted into the mobile.

There was another crescendo of sound from the other end.

Another horn blasted, and this time Miles turned and looked along the road leading to the airport's helipad. That one had definitely been closer.

The line went dead. The sound of the wind and the engine were both cut off.

Strangely, though, the wailing of the siren continued. Miles continued to stare towards the road for a few moments, but the shifting curtain of white that was obscuring everything made it impossible for him to see much.

He considered calling Hoon back, but the poor signal and all the noise had made the call so thoroughly unpleasant that he was in no rush to put himself through it again.

Hopefully, Hoon would find somewhere less noisy and call him back. By then, with a bit of luck, Miles would be warming up inside somewhere, ideally with his fingers wrapped around a mug of steaming hot tea.

On his way back to the shelter, Miles saw Officer Walton standing alone in the snow. He wanted nothing more than to get back under the cover of the shelter's glass roof, but felt compelled to at least check in with the other man.

"Everything alright?" he asked, taking a detour Walton's way.

Walton's eyes were narrowed against the storm. It made him look like he was deeply suspicious of something. Or maybe just a bit of a shifty bastard.

"As much as it can be," Walton replied. "I've spoken to the pilot. ETA two minutes. I want us in the air in three." He shot a look at the shelter, and his top lip arched into a sneer. "The sooner we get her off our hands, the sooner I'll start to feel better about all this."

Miles glanced furtively around them, like he was sensing danger.

"You've got concerns?"

"Don't you?" Walton asked, sounding surprised. "I don't like it when plans change. And especially not when we're dealing with the Loop." He met Miles' eye and held it. "I mean, you just don't know who you can trust, do you?"

The snow fell silently around them. The thunder of the approaching helicopter was the only sound.

"Uh, no," Miles said, shifting back a pace. "No, I suppose you don't."

"You'd better get back in there. Hang fire until I tell you otherwise," Walton instructed. "And keep an eye on..."

He frowned and turned towards the road. The siren, which had sounded far off, was suddenly almost upon them. A blue light rounded the outside of one of the airport buildings, and Walton's hand went to the holster under his arm as a motorbike came speeding straight towards them.

"Wait, wait!" Miles cried, piecing it all together. "It's fine. It's fine."

The bike turned, its back wheel skidding in the snow, clearing a tarmac path behind it.

"It's fine," Miles said again, though with a touch less certainty this time.

Hoon's arrival was unexpected. The fact he'd come roaring up in what was presumably a stolen police motorcycle, even more so.

The bloodied Santa suit was just the icing on the cake.

"Bob?" Miles said, looking him up and down. "What the hell are you wearing?"

"Doesn't matter," Hoon said, dismounting the bike. He didn't bother standing it up, so it immediately fell sideways into the snow. "Where the fuck is she? She still here?"

"Who?"

"Who do you fucking think?" Hoon spat. He barged past both MI5 men and ran towards the shelter. When he saw Suranne still in there, he let out a sigh of relief. "Oh, thank fuck for that."

Suranne, on the other hand, did not seem pleased to see him.

"What's he doing here?" she demanded, looking past Hoon to where Miles and Officer Walton were both rushing up. "Why the hell is he here?"

"I'm just here to break the fucking bad news that your wee rescue mission's no' happening," Hoon told her.

Her expression didn't change. If she knew what he was talking about, she was doing a good job of masking it.

Kevin—or 'Mini Miles' as Hoon thought of him—jumped in with a question before anyone else could ask.

"Rescue mission?" he fretted, his wide eyes darting from face to face. "What do you mean?"

"Yes, what are you talking about?" demanded Walton. He put a hand on Hoon's shoulder and spun him around. "What the hell is this about?"

Hoon sized the MI5 man up. He was big. Solid. Looked capable. A lump under the left arm of his jacket suggested he was packing, and the look on his face said he wouldn't hesitate to unpack and unload should the need arise.

This was good news. Or possibly bad. It all depended on whose side the man was on.

The helicopter was visible through the snow now. Its underbelly was angled towards them, so it loomed through the blizzard like a great whale through the ocean. The sound of its blades was like approaching thunder. Searchlights on its underside dazzled against the snow as they swept their beams towards the shelter.

"Get her inside," Hoon said.

"What do you mean?" Miles asked. "Why? What's going on? We're meant to be taking the chopper."

"Aye, well, change of plan," Hoon said.

Walton shook his head. "No, no, no, no. You don't make the plans. You've got no say in this. This is nothing to do with you."

"Miles, trust me," Hoon urged, still watching the helicopter coming closer. "Don't let Captain fucking Cock-a-tronic here take charge. Get her inside. Now."

"We're getting her on that helicopter," Walton said. His hand went into his jacket again, and this time it came out clutching a Glock 19 pistol. "No games. No pissing about. She gets on that chopper, and we get her out of here."

"Jesus!" Kevin cheeped. "Can we all just calm down here?"

At the sight of Walton's weapon, the two MI5 men flanking Suranne both drew guns of their own, though they didn't appear to know who or what they should be aiming at.

"Kevin's right. Guns away. Come on, guys," Miles said, asserting as much authority as he could muster while his whole body was shaking with the cold. "If Bob has concerns, then we should take them on board. He's proven himself time and again as someone worth listening to. If he's got concerns, we listen. We listen, then we—"

Miles sputtered to a stop when a spray of warm liquid hit him in the face. He watched, stunned into silence, as Walton slumped sideways against the outer wall of the shelter, then slid down it, painting a line of blood and brain matter in a straight vertical line with the side of his head.

"What the fuck?" Miles spluttered.

"Move!" Hoon cried, grabbing him and hauling him clear just as another rifle round shattered one of the glass panels into diamond-sized chunks

The two MI5 officers stared in mute disbelief at the body of their colleague lying slumped against the shelter's side.

"Don't just fucking stand there!" Hoon barked, pointing to the helicopter. A figure was hanging out of the side, taking aim with a high-calibre rifle. "Shoot that fucker out of the sky!"

Hoon stormed inside the shelter, caught Suranne by the arm, and dragged her out. Not that she took a lot of dragging. She was surprisingly compliant, and kept her mouth shut and her head down as instructed, as Hoon ushered her, Miles, and a terror-stricken Kevin back towards the main building.

"Side to side. Zigzag. Hurry the fuck up, and don't look back!"

They'd gone a dozen feet or so when Hoon remembered Walton's gun. He shot a look back over his shoulder for it, but it must've fallen beneath him, because it was nowhere in sight.

He saw light reflecting off the lens of a telescopic sight, and shouldered Suranne sideways into a snowdrift. A short distance ahead of them, a bullet *whumffed* off the ground.

"Up. Go," Hoon cried.

From behind them came the boom of gunshots, as the MI5 men returned fire at the hovering helicopter. The snow and the blinding spotlight made it hard to get a clear shot, but after a few rounds, glass shattered and the powerful beam from the chopper's belly disintegrated into darkness.

That was good. That meant they had a chance. Somewhere, far back in the direction of the city, sirens had started to scream. The polis were coming. He just had to keep this bitch alive for a few minutes more.

"In here," Miles urged, throwing open a door that led into some sort of hangar or warehouse.

They all rushed in, and the darkened building sprang to life around them, lights illuminating on the high ceiling to reveal rows of crates and old, rusted machinery.

Hoon slammed the door behind them, but couldn't find a way to lock it in place.

"Fuck," he hissed, breathing hard. There was still gunfire popping away outside. Noticeably less than there had been just a few seconds before, though.

Hoon hoped one of the agents was just reloading.

"What about in there?" asked Kevin, stabbing a trembling finger towards a heavy-looking wooden door at the back of the warehouse. "Might be a back door, or a place to hide."

"Yes!" Miles cried. He clapped his assistant on the shoulder. "Good call, Kevin."

Kevin almost blushed. "Thank you, sir." He shot Hoon a sideways look, then tried again, this time dropping the final word. "I mean, thank you."

"Aye, very good," Hoon said. "But can you maybe save bumming one another until later?"

He shoved Kevin towards the door, then caught Suranne by the upper arm again. Like before, she made no attempt to resist. He was, after all, the only reason she was still alive. And, for all her talk, she clearly liked the idea of remaining that way.

The door Kevin had spotted didn't lead to an exit. Instead, it opened onto a small store room lined on all sides with racks of tools, bolts, filters, gaskets, and other assorted engine parts.

There were no windows. No other way out. So, no escape, then, but also no way of anyone sneaking up behind them.

Not a great position to be in, but better than being out in the open. They could hunker down here until the polis arrived. Either the chopper would get taken down, or it would clear off. Either way, the fuckers wouldn't get their hands on Suranne.

Hoon closed the door, turned the lock, and rested his head against the inside, catching his breath.

"You OK?" Miles asked. "You look like..."

"Shite?" Hoon guessed.

Miles shrugged and smiled. "Well, I was going to say 'Santa,' but I suppose yours works, too."

Hoon laughed at that. Not a lot, but enough to count.

The sound of gunfire had stopped now, but they could still hear the helicopter hanging in the air. The din of it vibrated the shelves around them, rattling their contents until it sounded like the anxious chatter of teeth.

"Do you think they're dead?" Miles asked. "The other officers, I mean? Do you think they've been shot?"

"Maybe they're out of ammo," Hoon said. He didn't believe

that, of course. Not really. But he kept lying to himself, anyway. "Might just be taking cover. Like us."

"Yeah," Miles said. He looked back at Kevin and Suranne, then bit his bottom lip. "I owe Walton an apology. Probably a bit late for that now, mind you. I was starting to think he might be dodgy. That the Loop might have gotten to him."

"No saying they hadn't," Hoon said. He shot a deliberate look at Suranne. "I mean, it's not like it's unheard of for the fuckers to kill one of their own."

"True," Miles agreed. "And someone had to be in on it."

Hoon kept his head against the cool wood of the door, but frowned.

"What?"

"How else would they know to send the helicopter?" Miles asked. "I mean, the flight's cancelled, yes, that's just bad luck. But someone knew to arrange a helicopter to come for us. Someone obviously passed that on. Had to be someone on the inside."

He grimaced and ran a hand through his hair, thinking back to his last conversation with Walton.

"He told me I shouldn't trust anyone. Right before you turned up."

Hoon straightened so he was no longer leaning against the door. "You think he was bent?"

"Who, Walton?" Miles shook his head. "No. No, I'm pretty sure he has a wife."

Hoon tutted. "I don't mean is he fucking... *Crooked*, I mean. Do you think he was working for the Loop?"

"I don't know. I mean, no. No, I doubt it," Miles said. "I mean, yes, they might kill one of their own if they're a threat, but if he was with them, he'd have been an asset, surely? He could've taken us all out there and then."

He sighed, and lowered himself onto a shelf so his backside was perched on the edge.

"But then, someone has to have talked. And if not him, then...?"

It was the look on Hoon's face that stopped Miles going any further. They stared at each other in silence for a moment, the realisation hitting the MI5 man just a moment after Hoon.

Slowly—ever so slowly—they both turned their attention to the man at the back of the room.

CHAPTER THIRTY-SEVEN

KEVIN STOOD IN AWKWARD SILENCE, eyes darting from Miles to Hoon, then back again.

"What?" he asked. He looked back over his shoulder, in case they were staring at something behind him, but there was only a shelf there. "What is it? Why are you looking at me like that?"

"He was on his phone," Miles muttered. "During everything. The whole time waiting, you were on your phone."

"We were playing games, sir!" Kevin protested, and the shrillness of his voice was like fingernails on a blackboard. "You suggested it, to pass the time! 'Let's play *Wordle*,' you said!"

"No." Miles shook his head. "All the time, though. You had your phone in your hand all the time. Not just then."

"Well, I mean, yes. Maybe," Kevin conceded. "There's always work to do, isn't there? There's always something to be done."

Suranne, who had been observing the conversation with interest, shuffled sideways away from Kevin and closer to the other two men.

"Show me, then," Hoon said, holding a hand out to the assistant. "Give me your phone. Let me see."

"What?" Kevin let out an incredulous snort. "No! I can't. You don't have clearance."

"Fuck your clearance, son. Give me the phone."

"Give him the phone, Kevin," Miles urged.

"Sir, you can't be serious! It's top secret government data, we can't just let this... this..."—He seemed to be searching for something insulting to say, but then thought better of it—"*man* have access to that."

"Fine, I'll just fucking take it," Hoon said, striding towards the assistant.

A couple of things happened then, one after the other.

From behind him, tucked into his belt beneath his jacket, Kevin whipped out a Glock 19 pistol and took aim at the centre of Hoon's chest. Hoon managed to skid to a stop just inches from the end of the weapon, but stood his ground there, shielding the other two occupants of the room.

Meanwhile, after shouting, "Oh, Christ! Oh, Christ!" in a panicky voice, Miles barked out an order with more authority than Hoon had ever heard him use before.

"Drop it, Kevin! Drop the gun, or I shoot."

Shoot?

Hoon risked a glance back over his shoulder and saw Miles standing there, his legs in a wide, bracing stance, an identical Glock clutched in two lightly trembling hands.

"Wait, you've got a gun?" Hoon asked. "You've had a gun this whole fucking time?"

"Just in case of emergencies," Miles said. He flicked his gaze in Hoon's direction for half-a-second. "I'm not very good with it."

Hoon tutted. "Well, don't tell him that, for fuck's sake!"

"Oh. Yeah. Sorry," Miles said.

"I'm so going to die," Suranne muttered.

"Yes," said Kevin. "I'm afraid it's looking that way."

His voice sounded much less shrill now, and his twitchy, nervous mannerisms had been replaced by a steely coolness.

"We wanted to get you out. Take you somewhere. Rescuing you was always our preferred choice."

"I'm honoured," Suranne replied. "And I'm still up for that, if you are."

"Too late for that now, I'm afraid. The police are coming." He glanced up, indicating the fading sound of the helicopter. "Extraction team's already leaving. You know how it works. You and me, we're both already dead."

"You don't have to be, Kevin. I can help," Miles said. "Just put down the gun, and we can talk. I can help you. We can fix this."

"Oh please. You can't even fix your own laptop. And honestly? This is a relief, actually. I don't have to pretend to like you anymore. Because I don't, *sir*. I really don't."

Miles' mouth pulled downwards. "There was no need for that," he mumbled.

Hoon shuffled a little closer to Kevin, keeping himself centred in the assistant's sights.

"So, what? You were sent in to get her out?" he asked.

"I was sent in to do whatever was necessary to prevent her—"

Suranne cut in from behind Hoon, keeping him between her and the Glock. "I wasn't going to talk! I know the score."

"Good. Then you know why they can't take any chances," Kevin replied. "You know too much. They can't risk it. They won't."

"And what?" Hoon cut in. "All that with the Eastgate. That whole fucking thing. That was you?"

"It was *us*," Kevin corrected. "I can't take full credit. But yes. We needed a distraction, and we found that group online. They were already talking about doing something," —He made air quotes with his free hand— "'epic' and so we just nudged them along a bit. Gave them what they needed."

"Very fucking generous of you."

"Really, you should be thanking us. We'd arranged it all so as to keep civilian casualties to a minimum. I mean, those vests we provided were a work of art. A unidirectional high explosive, aiming inwards. Genius, if I say so myself. And, yes, sure, of course people would be scared, and there might be a handful of casualties, but at the end of the day, all the world would lose would be a couple of dozen nasty little trolls, and I doubt anyone will be shedding any tears over them, do you?"

Hoon was giving Kevin both barrels of his boggle-eyed stare. It was a rare man who didn't flinch under such conditions, but the assistant—or assassin, maybe—had no trouble with it.

"We're not monsters," Kevin clarified. "We don't kill indiscriminately, and certainly not for pleasure. The Loop is a... corporation, that's all. Many corporations, in fact. It's a global industry, generating billions in revenue every year. Paying tax on a lot of it, too." He smirked. "Hell, we're even cutting our carbon footprint. Those people in that shopping centre, they were never in danger. Well, no more than we considered acceptable. And you don't have to be, either."

Kevin indicated Hoon and Miles with one quick flick of his head.

"Neither of you. You can both walk away from this."

Hoon shook his head. "I don't buy that, son. You'll shoot us both, first fucking chance you get."

"We know too much," Miles agreed.

This prompted a sharp guffaw of laughter from Kevin. "Oh! Oh, that's good. That's funny. Rest assured, gentlemen, you know nothing. There is no information you have that could possibly threaten my employers. None. Remember, I've seen your files, *sir*. You're obsessing over a few tiny droplets of information you've managed to get your hands on, completely blind to the reality of it."

"What reality's that?" Hoon asked.

Kevin met his gaze again and held it. "The Loop isn't a

droplet. It's the ocean." He shrugged. "So, take that information you have with my blessing. Go. Do your worst. And you get to live. You get to enjoy your Christmas."

Hoon continued to eyeball him. He planted his feet, making it clear he had no intentions of moving.

"So, if you want her dead this much, she must know a lot," he reasoned.

"Maybe." Kevin shrugged. "But you'll never get to find out."

The sound of sirens seemed to surround the building now. The shelves no longer vibrated, the helicopter having flown out of shuddering range.

"Miles," Hoon said.

"Yes?"

"Get out of here."

"What? No. No, I'm not just leaving you."

"Aye, you are," Hoon said. He jerked his head back in Suranne's direction. "And take her with you."

Kevin shook his head. "I can't let you do that."

"Go. Now," Hoon said, stepping in closer so the end of Kevin's pistol was all but jammed against his chest.

Suranne didn't share Miles' hesitation. Shielded by Hoon, she unlocked the door and ducked out.

"Go. Get after her," Hoon barked. "Go!"

Miles danced on the spot, too conflicted to make a decision. "He'll kill you. If I'm not here to shoot back, he'll—"

"She's getting away! Go fucking catch her!" Hoon bellowed. "Go catch her, or all this has been a waste of fucking time!"

This time, finally, Miles obeyed.

He backed to the door, keeping his gun trained on Kevin for as long as he could.

"He's right. I'll shoot you the moment he leaves," Kevin told Hoon. It didn't sound like a threat, just a statement of fact.

Hoon nodded. "Aye," he said. He widened his eyes and

grinned, showing off his shark-like smile. "Aye, I'm fucking counting on it, son."

Miles ran out of the room, ending the standoff.

Kevin was true to his word. He hadn't been lying earlier, either. He took no visible pleasure from pulling the trigger. No satisfaction from firing the shot.

At that distance, it was impossible to miss. The bullet crossed the three-inch gap between gun and target in a fraction of a fraction of a second.

Hoon didn't even have time to register the sound.

Didn't have time to feel the impact.

The bullet tore through the bloodied fabric of the Santa suit.

It struck the vest Hoon wore strapped across his chest.

The vest he had taken the time to turn the other way.

And the whole world erupted in a crescendo of fire and light.

CHAPTER THIRTY-EIGHT

PAIN.

That was the headline.

The breaking news.

It wasn't too pressing yet, though. It felt like it was going to be a problem soon, but not yet. Not right now. For now, he could just drift there in the dark and the deathly quiet.

It was nice. Relaxing. He'd never been in a flotation tank before—he wasn't, after all, a pretentious arsehole—but he imagined this would be what it was like.

Only maybe wetter.

He couldn't fully relax, though. Not all the way. Not with the prospect of that pain still out there.

It was coming towards him now. He could sense it. He could see it, almost, thundering towards him like a train down a tunnel, headlights blazing, burning the darkness away.

And talking of lights...

The colour behind his eyelids went from black to charcoal, and then through a rainbow of greys.

He heard noises. Muffled. Far off.

Voices. Footsteps. The steady beeping of a heart monitor that told him he was still alive.

That was a bonus.

It was then that the pain hit. It paid most attention to his chest, had a good solid go at his ribcage, and then just jabbed enthusiastically at all his other bits.

He jackknifed in the bed, his eyes popping open, his mouth and throat combining forces to produce a sound like a backward cough.

He followed this up with a cry of, "Atcha-*fuck!*" then fell back against the pillow again, blinking furiously in the glare of the overhead light.

"Bobby? Bobby!"

He was suddenly aware of his sister. There was no fucking missing her. She launched herself out of an armchair beside his bed on the first attempt, and then her arms were around his head, pulling him in tight against her chest, cradling him to her.

"Ow! Fuck! Easy!" he slurred.

Berta dropped his head again and stepped back, brushing aside her moment of elation and replacing it with something much sterner and more... Well, more *Berta*.

"About fucking time, too," she told him. "You've had us worried sick."

She stopped short of calling him a selfish bastard. She didn't need to, though. He could see it in her eyes.

"Alright, Boggle?"

Iris' head appeared at the foot of the bed. It rose up from below until his chin rested on the metal frame.

"What the fuck are you doing down there?" Hoon rasped. "You look like Humpty Dumpty."

"There's just the one seat," Iris explained, getting to his feet. He dusted himself down. "So Berta made me sit on the floor."

Pain rattled around behind Hoon's eyes as he looked at them

both in turn. Neither of them was caked in blood now, and they wore different clothes to those he'd last seen them in.

Outside, beyond the window, Hoon saw the sky was bright and crisp and blue.

"What day is it?" he asked.

Berta and Iris swapped looks. Iris nodded, deferring this one to Hoon's sister.

"Thursday," she said.

Hoon's dry, cracked lips moved as he tried to work out what that meant.

"Is that Christmas?" he eventually asked, giving up.

"Christmas? Christmas was three weeks ago, Bobby," Berta told him. "It's the twelfth of January."

Hoon's chest tightened, and pain bubbled out of him as a gasp. Christ. Had he been out that long? His injuries must have been bad.

He tried wiggling his fingers and toes. They all responded, though the little zaps of pain they sent through him said they weren't happy about it.

"You've been in a coma, Bobby," Berta said.

Hoon's head felt heavy against the pillow. "Christ," he muttered. "And you two have been here this whole time?"

"Oh, God, no," Berta said, scowling at the very thought. "Me and Iris, we've been having a lovely time, haven't we?"

Iris shot Hoon a worried look, but nodded.

"We spent Christmas Day together. Turns out, we've got a lot in common," Berta continued.

Slowly, and despite the pain, Hoon raised his head an inch off the pillow. The beeping of his heart monitor picked up speed.

"Oh?"

"Yes. And we've got an announcement."

She thrust a hand out to Iris, like a mother getting ready to guide a toddler across a busy road. Iris hesitated, but then sheepishly took it.

"We're engaged!" Berta proclaimed, beaming from ear to ear. "Iris and I are getting married!"

Iris shot the man in the bed a weak, watered-down smile. "Sorry, Boggle," he whispered.

"Married?"

Hoon put a hand on his chest, and the thick, padded dressings that were taped there. The pressure of his touch brought another wave of pain, but he barely noticed.

"You're... You two are... You and... Both of... The pair of you are..."

Try as he might, he couldn't bring himself to finish any of those sentences.

His head went light as his throat tightened and his lungs cramped.

It was only when Berta's face contorted in glee that he was able to breathe again.

"Look at his fucking face!" she cried. "I knew that would get him going! I told you. Didn't I fucking say?"

Iris quickly withdrew his hand from Berta's. "Eh, aye. Aye, that got him, right enough," he said, then he mouthed a silent, "I'm sorry," to Hoon.

"What?" Hoon wheezed. "What the fuck are you saying?"

"Of course we're not getting married!" Berta said, all but roaring with laughter. "Marry this puddle of duck's piss? I wouldn't employ him as a fucking window cleaner, never mind marry him!"

"It's Christmas Eve, Boggle. You've been out for about fourteen hours. They kept you under to recover a bit," Iris explained. "Berta thought it'd be funny to wind you up. *Berta* did," he stressed. "Berta thought that."

"And I was fucking right! The look on your face! You looked like you'd ruptured a bollock." She laughed again until she had to take a scrunched-up tissue from her sleeve and wipe away a tear. "Anyway, serves you fucking right. I hear you invited this calamity to Christmas dinner."

Hoon was still in shock from the wedding announcement, and could only mutter out a vague, "Eh, aye. Aye, that's right."

"Thanks for the bloody warning," Berta said. "You said you weren't wanting Christmas dinner, so I'd got nothing in."

Hoon waved vaguely, brushing the problem aside. There were, after all, bigger things to worry about.

"It's fine. We can get something," he told her.

"It's taken care of," Berta told him. "I got us a big turkey from Markies. *Free range*, no less."

"I take it I'm paying for that, am I?" Hoon grunted.

"No, actually," Berta said. She glanced from the door to the window, then leaned in closer. "I slipped through their food section while the police were evacuating us." She tapped the side of her nose and winked. "Got us all the trimmings, too."

Hoon didn't quite know what to say about that, so he settled for arranging his aching fingers into what was a reasonable approximation of a thumbs-up.

"Right. We'll go tell the doctors you're awake. Your big boyfriend's outside, I think, waiting to talk to you. The copper. You want him sent in?"

Hoon tried to sit up in bed. He made it about three or four inches up the pillow, then decided that was quite far enough.

"Aye," he said. "Aye, send him in."

"Right. Fine," Berta said. Then, to Hoon's surprise, she leaned over and planted a kiss on his forehead. "But don't you fucking overdo it," she warned. "Or you'll have me to answer to."

Berta headed for the door of the private room, pulled it open, then stopped.

"Oh, I nearly forgot. All them people from yesterday. The hostages. They're singing your fucking praises today. You'd think you were the second coming of Christ, the way some of them are talking. Papers and TV doing a big story about it. Crawling all over the place like fucking cockroaches, they are."

"Aye?" Hoon said, feigning interest.

"That choir. The kids from the school."

"Brass band," Iris corrected, earning himself a warning look from Berta.

"Whatever they are. They came this morning. Wanted to sing, or play for you, or whatever they do. I thought that was nice of them," Berta said, then she sniffed. "I mean, I told them all to fuck off, of course—the last thing you need is those wee bastards in here making a bloody racket—but what a lovely thought, eh?"

Hoon knew better than to disagree. "Aye," he said. "Lovely thought."

On that note, Berta went storming out into the corridor. Iris, meanwhile, hovered around at the end of the bed, wringing his hands together.

"Sorry about that, Boggle. The wedding thing, I mean. I didn't want to go along with it, but she's..."

He left the rest of the sentence hanging there. Hoon nodded in agreement.

"Aye. She is," he confirmed. "She really is."

Iris smiled. He started as if to leave, then stopped again as an idea struck him.

"Here, Boggle. You want an orange?"

Hoon blinked. "An orange?"

"Yeah. You know, like... an orange? Do you want an orange?"

Hoon looked at Iris' hands, then at his pockets. "Eh, aye. Fine. Suppose."

Iris nodded. "Right. OK," he said, and Hoon could see the uncertainty creeping over the Scouser as he glanced surreptitiously to his left and right. "I'll see what I can do."

And with that, he turned and scurried off after Berta.

Hoon watched him go, muttered a quiet, "What the fuck?"

then shuffled himself another inch up the bed when a towering figure in a big coat stooped his head through the doorway.

"You're alive, then," DCI Logan noted.

"Apparently so, aye," Hoon confirmed. "You here to arrest me?"

"Surprisingly, no," Logan said. "I mean, no saying that won't change once everything's been sorted out, but for now?" He shook his head.

"Shame," Hoon said. "Might've got me out of Berta's Christmas dinner."

Logan unhooked the medical chart from the end of Hoon's bed, and flicked through a couple of pages.

"I wouldn't worry too much about that, Bob," he said. "I reckon you'll be in here a while yet."

"Nah, fuck that," Hoon said. He threw back his covers, then grimaced when he saw the clear plastic tube running up the front of his hospital gown in the direction of his crotch. "Shite. No' again."

Logan returned the chart to the holder at the end of the bed and frowned. "What?"

"Fucking catheter," Hoon said, indicating the pipe. "Help me take it out, will you?"

"Eh, no," Logan said.

"Oh, come on! I can't just pull the fucker out, or I would. Believe me, I've tried it. It didn't end well. There's a wee bubble bit you need to burst first. You can bite it."

"Can I fuck!" Logan retorted. "You were blown up, Bob. It's a miracle you're still alive. You need to rest."

Hoon shook his head. "No' a miracle. Totally fucking planned. Unidirectional explosive vest, I'll have you know. A work of fucking art."

"Work of art or not, it shot you twenty feet through the air. Would've been further, if it wasn't for that big stack of crates you hit. You're in no fit state to be going anywhere."

"What about the other guy?" Hoon asked.

"The one I assume was standing in front of you when you went up?"

"Aye. Him."

"We've got him in custody now," Logan said. "And by 'custody,' I mean a big bucket and several plastic bags. I wouldn't hold your breath for a confession. But, in more positive news, your MI5 pal caught up with his lady friend."

He checked his watch, and did some quick calculations.

"And, as of about fifteen minutes ago, they were back in England, and so no longer my problem."

"Nice one. No more worries for you then, eh, Jack?"

Logan glowered down at the man in the bed, his nostrils flaring. "Aye, well, I wouldn't say that, exactly," he remarked. "I'm sure you'll come up with something."

Hoon snorted out something that was almost a laugh. It hurt, but then so did most things.

"Merry Christmas, Bob," Logan said, returning his hands to the depths of his coat pockets.

"Aye. You too, Jack," Hoon said. "You sure I can't tempt you to chew through my piss tube, though?"

"I'm a hundred percent positive," Logan said. He turned for the door, then stopped. "Oh. One more thing."

From a pocket, he produced a gold-coloured Christmas cracker and sat it on the table beside Hoon's bed. It was slightly misshapen, like it had been partially crushed in Logan's pocket.

Either that, or someone had taken it apart and put it back together again.

"From your MI5 pal," Logan announced. "Asked me to pass it on when you were awake."

"Cheers," Hoon said. "Shut the door on your way out, will you? Should try and get some sleep."

"Sounds like a plan," Logan said. He hovered at the door like he had something more to say, but then decided it could wait.

With a final nod, he stepped out into the corridor and closed the door at his back.

Hoon waited until the sound of the policeman's plodding footsteps had faded, then turned his attention to the Christmas cracker.

He wasted no time in grabbing both ends and jerking his arms outwards. On the third attempt, the shiny golden card tore open, and the snapper inside gave a *crack*.

A paper crown flew out, curved by the cracker's cardboard inner tube. He ignored that, like he ignored the slip containing the undoubtedly awful joke.

Instead, he focused exclusively on the toy that had tumbled out of the cracker and landed on the blanket that lay across his stomach. It was red and white, with a little winder key sticking out of the back.

A smile spread across Hoon's face. "Miles Crabtree, I take back every fucking negative thing I've ever said about you," he muttered.

He took the plastic tube of his catheter in one hand.

With the other, he picked up the set of chattering false teeth that had fallen from the cracker.

And then, with the light from a bright, crisp, Christmas Eve sky shining in through the window, Hoon set to work.

JOIN THE JD KIRK VIP CLUB

Want access to an exclusive image gallery showing locations from the books? Join the free JD Kirk VIP Club today, and as well as the photo gallery you'll get regular emails containing free short stories, members-only video content, and all the latest news about the world of DCI Jack Logan.

JDKirk.com/VIP

(Did we mention that it's free...?)